# SONS, DAUGHTERS

*a novel*

W0008268

## IVANA BODROŽIĆ

TRANSLATED BY
## ELLEN ELIAS-BURSAĆ

SEVEN STORIES PRESS
New York • Oakland

This book was published with the financial support of the Ministry of Culture and Media of the Republic of Croatia.

Seven Stories Press
140 Watts Street
New York, NY 10013
www.sevenstories.com

Library of Congress Cataloging-in-Publication Data

Names: Simić Bodrožić, Ivana, 1982- author. | Elias-Bursać, Ellen, translator.
Title: Sons, daughters : a novel / Ivana Bodrožić ; [translated by Ellen Elias-Bursać].
Other titles: Sinovi, kćeri. English
Description: New York : Seven Stories Press, 2024.
Identifiers: LCCN 2023043067 | ISBN 9781644213353 (trade paperback) | ISBN 9781644213360 (ebook)
Subjects: LCGFT: Psychological fiction. | Novels.
Classification: LCC PG1620.29.I44 S5613 2024 | DDC 891.8/336--dc23/eng/20231201
LC record available at https://lccn.loc.gov/2023043067

College professors and high school and middle school teachers may order free examination copies of Seven Stories Press titles. Visit https://www.sevenstories.com/pg/resources-academics or email academic@sevenstories.com.

Printed in the United States of America

9  8  7  6  5  4  3  2  1

# Part One

# 1.

My darling mother. Most of all I'd love to snuggle up with her and tell her everything. Now I can't anymore. Most of the day my eyes are trained on the ceiling. Covered in tiny imperfections, it is spacious, shadow retreats across it in the morning and then the sunlight lets loose a whiteness as if a thick, dark curtain has been drawn back to reveal a stage on which another endless day will play out. Around noon, before the blaze of midday begins, the ceiling is hard and impermeable. Something is dripping warmly across my face from the corners of my eyes. The doctors say it is not tears, just the bodily fluid that moistens the cornea. Then I have to squint some because the whiteness starts to fragment and scatter before me, piercing and drilling holes in my irises until I can no longer see. There are times when I doze off. My cycles of waking and sleeping are there just as they are for normal people. And though I know nothing will have changed, when I wake, I run my dry gaze across the ceiling, gradually and steadily ingesting meter by square meter. I start above the head of the bed and then swim slowly toward the other side as far as I'm allowed. Sometimes there is a fly, plump, frisky, and loud, with rapid, silken wings, and nuzzling, tacky legs. It's poised up there and stares down at all thousand of me. Not one of me moves and I start worrying that my immobility will be replaced by the rot that houseflies are happiest gorging on, even when there is something else to eat. I'm what's here and that's why the fly will first explore me with the shiny tip of its proboscis, perhaps starting with the thin skin of my translucent forearms, and then whatever it can't chew it will dissolve with its potent saliva. Once while I was jogging down a road by a wooded area, I happened across the putrid remains of a cat. Early summer, morning. The plant world was insufferable with the burgeoning of life, midges rammed themselves mindlessly, frantically into my eyes and mouth, huge rabbits came all the way down to the road, the smells in the air were so honeyed that they dizzied the mind and stoked aggression, but from beneath the splendor of abundance came the reek of decay. First, I smelled it, and only then did I spot the carcass lying in a greasy stain on the washed-out pavement. All its fur was gone, there were two shallow holes where its eyes had been, and the entire, still clearly feline, shape looked as if it had been drenched in gasoline. A swarm of flies had bathed it liberally with slobber, sucking from it the last crumbs of nourishment as if they'd live forever, instead of surviving scarcely more than two weeks. But that is the way we feed too. The putrid smell rankled my nostrils, lungs, and brain. I needed to run at least two more kilometers for the smog to override it and release me. Sometimes I feel, while I'm lying in the dark, that I can sniff out the edge of rot, almost cloying and certainly mortal, so much so that it makes me retch. This is a life-saving reflex, a reflex given by nature to aid in steering us away from the rotten and the diseased. But how do we get away from our own selves? I draw the vapors in deep, but still I can't be sure whether this really is the smell or just my yearning for the feline form which there, by the side of the road, couldn't have cared less while other creatures were guzzling it. The fly abruptly buzzes off, circles around the dead neon light, swings even closer, hawks spit into its tiny hands, rubs them together, shoots a glance at me and gauges that the time has not yet come. It drops back, gives a buzz, and soon it's gone. Back to the white. The central point on the ceiling is occupied by a neon light fixture, made of four elongated, ribbed bulbs, one of which is flickering. When I close my eyes, instead of seeing it I see a chandelier that used to hang in a room long ago. I know its every curving surface, every stretch of shadow, which, spider-like, circles the black hole in the center. Four downward-facing cup shades made of milky white glass, and in each—a little narrow bulb. Each shade was threaded onto the end of a stylized rounded wooden arm; along the side of each of the arms ran a groove and in the groove was dust. A skinny, gray, splendid stripe of dust she never touched. A site of defiance in the room, a veiled rebellion, a hope into which I send my thoughts, with every ounce of my strength, when I stare so long behind my lids. I moisten my eyes, open them, and count the neon ribs. It's not that there will be more this time, but giving meaning to brief stretches of time during the endless day is the most I can do. Though the result is easily predictable, I'm tickled when the effort I'm making briefly blurs my vision so that instead of twenty-four I count twenty-three. The agreeable joy of those little self-delusions.

When a day is cloudy, the ceiling softens by twilight, it descends tenderly toward my motionless face and then I let myself lower my eyes, I'm no longer confrontational, I'm not drilling into it with my gaze, it offers no resistance, so I float. We merge, my sky and I, and for those several moments of twilight I feel a mild breeze caress my face, I rise, pull out the feeding tubes without a thought, peel the rubber band off my wrist and fix my hair back in a high ponytail, slip on my shoes, get up off the bed, and carefully smooth the bedding. I square my shoulders, take the three steps to the door, drop a hand onto the doorknob, overcome the resistance of the brass, turn it, and out I go.

When I return the sky is black. Barbed with protruding shadows, it descends in toothed jags to right above the surface of my body whose borders nobody acknowledges, a body melded by the desires and assessments of others, a body neglected and squandered. The light no longer shines in through the window but gleams from across the room through a slender gap at the half-closed door, the bluish light of a television set, the yellow light of someone's cough, the oily light of antiseptics. The touch of her smooth hand to the cheek shuts them off one by one. The ceiling drops off to sleep. She pushes me gently over the edge and until morning I fall.

## 2.

I can picture her so easily. When they let her know I was in the hospital, I'll bet she was polishing dinner glasses. The odor of vinegar stung her eyes though she'd opened all the windows to keep the air moving through the room. She always trusted most the solutions that required she suffer. Sterilizing cloth diapers by boiling them on the stovetop instead of in a washing machine, she'd hold forth with a passion about their whiteness and the absence of bacteria, swiftly pivoting to the challenges of childrearing. She always repeated, with the same rhythm of unquestioned prophecy: the littler children drink your milk, the bigger ones drink your blood. The home phone rang, this may have rattled her, she was hardly ever called except by a random telephone operator or someone conducting a survey, and then she'd vent her bitterness. She'd purse her wrinkled upper lip and with disgust she'd snap, "Not interested." She'd mumble into her chin, "Whatever inspired them to call me? Fuck their survey." Maybe she was hoping the caller was her son: "Just called to see what you're up to, Ma, sending a fond word your way." At the sound of the phone she cringed. Her small, tense frame tensed even more, and then she quickly straightened her aching knee. She set the polished glass on the cupboard shelf, grumpily registering out of the corner of her eye that there was no visible difference between the glasses she had yet to take down and the one she had just put back. But her insights about cleanliness, including personal hygiene, went far beyond what the eye could see. She took the phone receiver in hand, pressed the on button, and in a muffled, raspy voice, because she hadn't yet spoken with anyone that day, said "Hello." Then the mayhem. When she was younger, she'd kept a level head in a crisis. Not one to panic, she'd quickly pull herself together, but as she aged, and what with the wringer we'd put her through, her equilibrium failed her. All sorts of things raced through her mind, had she misheard? A wrong number? Someone pranking her? With the receiver on her ear she staggered mindlessly around the apartment, repeating the same questions: "What happened? Lucija? Where is she now? How? Where do I need to be?" The person at the other end of the line was probably more than familiar with the panic aroused by the sentence: "Ma'am, your daughter has been in a car accident, she's in the hospital now, we can't say more over the phone, please get here as soon as you can." And then she'd repeat the same sentence calmly, distinctly, as many times as needed, and meanwhile, during the pauses, inspect her fingernails or doodle on the calendar at the front desk. The panic only swamped her after she'd hung up the phone; she wasn't sure she remembered which hospital she was supposed to go to. Then her old clarity in crisis kicked in, she flew to the bedroom and took a large bundle of money out of her nightstand drawer, not because she had any clear idea of what need there might be for money, but because the bundle was her black-day cache. For years she'd tell me while I sat across from her at the table, "There. In the drawer. For the God-help-us days. The black days." And here we were, the black days. There had been others, but this was clearly the worst, this was the time to open the drawer. Now she felt better, once the drawer had been opened, after all these years, in the most unexpected way.

In our family, black days were handed down the maternal line—always and without exception. Granny had received the black days from her mother; they'd been tucked under the bedbug-ridden mattress in a little one-room mudbrick house, knotted in a linen kerchief. I remember her, my great-grandmother, she lived till I was twelve. Several times a year we'd come to pay our respects at her bedside, a domain under siege, marked by the rank smell of urine, and there was the time when, already plagued by dementia, she delivered, with a hand resembling the pincers of a praying mantis, her little bundle, while everyone around gave sour little smiles. Her faded bills, the currency of a bygone era, had already been trampled underfoot by politics, but the fear of the black days was so relentless that it traversed time. I was nudged closer, hair neatly combed, a lace collar around my neck, to her domain where she half-sat, a braid hanging motionless down her back, so I could recite to her. After my every recited verse the old woman clapped dryly with the sides of her hands and opened her pale pink maw. Once she was gone, the black days were lodged in the bedroom of my mother's mother. More precisely, in the wardrobe among her funeral clothes, the nicest clothes she had. Granny called them her travel wardrobe. That's what she'd tell me while—as if lowering a newborn into a warm bath—she'd smooth out the black sleeves of the silk blouse, and under it, as if she were dressing for a dance, she'd arrange the pleated skirt, fifteen denier nylon stockings, and add: My toes won't poke holes in these. Under the clothes wrapped in thin white paper in the recesses of the wardrobe were her black days, stowed away in a little wooden box she'd purchased at a village fair. She skimped from the gray days for her black days, from Grandpa's drinking, from the scarves for his mistresses, from herself, and tucked them into the little box, as if at an altar. For us, the black days were what we lived for: life was the means to that end. Each year she lived less and less, staying with her daughter during her dotage. Prayers hummed from behind closed doors on her radio and she'd perch, trance-like, fingering the plastic beads of her rosary. There were times when she sat and stared. Straight ahead, at the wall. She'd prop herself up on pillows and stare for hours, with an inward-looking focus, into herself, her past life, or nothing at all. Hers was a blank stare, neither moist nor dry, almost reconciled with the moment like a tree in a forest. This was perhaps the most memorable and terrible thing that has stayed with me about her. Now it would seem that her condition was handed down to me, skipping a generation, when I reached the age of thirty. Once she'd gone, the dreaded black days found their new home in the drawer of the nightstand next to my mother's trimly tucked, well-aired bed. And then there she was, reaching for them. All in one painful, trembling gesture through which coursed, like a silver thread, a thin stream of pleasure: the black days were here at last. She had been poised, waiting for them for as long as she could remember; she was ready. There was no question whatsoever that she'd misremember the hospital where I'd been taken.

# 3.

I cannot see out the window. My eyeballs—which I'd never so much as noticed before aside from when a bug or a mote of dust landed on one of them and chafed—can move only vertically. Among all the dimensions of the world that have been shut out of my life, my left and right sides have vanished. Gone is the luxury of rolling my eyes, so mercilessly exploited in the past, gone is the spherical sense of being wrapped in images; the world has shrunk down to the ribbon of reality visible right there in front of me. Or above me, depending on how I've been positioned. I see the most when they put me in a special wheelchair and prop me up on all sides like a rag doll that stubbornly refuses to sit properly. They turn me to face the window: in its rectangle is the day. If they fix my head well so it doesn't tilt too much to the side, then the narrow ribbon along which my eyes stroll, scamper, or stumble becomes an endless path leading into the wild greenery of the park. I live in a castle, repurposed at the turn of the last century to become the Provincial Hospital for Ailing Children—as it was then named. You'll always be my little one, she tells me while she strokes my cropped, slicked-back hair. Today this baroque phantom building serves as a temporary or permanent home for people trapped within the vestibule of death, also known as the Special Hospital for Continuing Treatment and Palliative Care. Most of those here are elderly patients brought down by heart attacks and strokes. Convinced they're doing their patients a good turn when the weather's nice, the nurses sometimes wheel them twice up and down through the lush trees and bushes of the grounds, and then park them by the entrance to a building that has the words "In Knowledge Is Salvation" carved over the door. Most of the courtiers in the castle are short on both. This reminds me of those bizarre marathon runners who come together all over the world in springtime. I have never understood these earnest runners who dedicate their efforts to people in wheelchairs or patients in the clutches of disease. There is something deeply ironic in such actions. I don't find anything particularly merciful about taking the seriously ill elderly out into May's untamed nature. The chasm between the garish greenery around them and their clouded cataracts can only inflict even greater pain. I came late to a love of nature. For a long time, I found it tedious, and I preferred to go headlong into the fray and flee to the company of people. I loved being close to others, I longed for them to look my way with a friendly, if brief, glance, send me a nod. Once, when I was five, I danced before a gathering of family friends in our living room, wiggling my bottom. I wasn't aware of how suggestive my movements were, I was proud of the bugging eyes and fixed attention of the guests, until Mother, discomfited, hissed, "Enough now, out you go to play." Nature was indifferent to me, paid me no mind, in our youth we don't understand air or water or leaves, we just hurtle into relationships.

It was with you that nature touched me and right away we began escaping to it precisely for its indifference. That's when I realized that indifference is a good thing, indifference is not out to do us harm. The first time we went out we met at a park on the edge of town, again—early summer. The dark was coming on, its contours pearly and blue; we sat side by side on a bench and if this were one of those stories, I'd say we conversed in intimate, hushed tones, but since I cannot speak, I'm condemned to the truth. We did not converse. We didn't know how. The time passed between us painfully, haltingly. Still, we gazed into each other's eyes with hope, stubbornly seeking answers there, any sort of understanding. Conversation eluded us, we weren't using the same language, from different times and planets, we stammered, attempting to reach the meaning of the encounter, the futility was poignant. Meanwhile, something deeper than thought and more real than the words uttered nailed us to one another. I was captured by the space at the corner of your mouth and the flash of white tooth that broke through while you laughed, I don't know what about, I don't remember. Even before that bench, after we'd gone out together only a few times, I leaped into the dimple on your cheek and fantasized that I was running the pad of my thumb over your shiny, black eyebrows and that I was pressing the space between them with my lips and feeling the tiny, invisible hairs. I surprised myself, but I was still feeling playful, still steeped in simplicity, still more or less intact. As the pearly hue of twilight slowly quieted, we relaxed, our conversation faltered and we moved imperceptibly closer. The smells are what I'd like to retrieve but they simply won't come back. Everything else does. Your smells were not alien to me, they were tender, silken; it was almost as if they were mine and so there was no need to fear an unfamiliar abrasive tang. And besides they were tucked into your lotion for nourishing dry skin. The next day at the drugstore I tried all the lotions on the shelf, hoping to find yours. We leaned cheek to cheek without pressing too hard, I don't know where our arms or legs were, I can't remember, I know we spent a long time moving our faces, somehow honoring one another, we touched with the tips of our noses, lightly along the edges of skin and hair. We didn't kiss; that, we agreed, we'd leave for later, another day. Without a word, this was the degree of our understanding and why we stayed together. When we stood up from the bench the day was already dark, we ambled off slowly toward the center of town. We strolled along the main street and noticed something odd at almost the same time. People edged away, they circumvented us far more than necessary. Though we weren't even holding hands, I do think we were glowing. It's easy now for us to pretend we know what that was, but I'd say it was our story. Our shared future. We radiated potential that was thwarted from the get-go. Misfits. We betrayed decorum, and decorum is to most of our lives what water is to an organism. Our desires spilled over the limits of the permissible. Our bodies betrayed us and the leaking commenced in all directions. People edged away. We were unbearable. This is where nature came in. Parks, lone spots in the woods, a hill above the city where a tree grew out from the ruins of a church. This is where we liked to lie, right under that tree. By then we'd started talking. You noticed a special insect that was always flying in place, we adopted it straight away, ours. So much effort and struggle, the flapping of wings, sound, energy, all just to stay in place. We always looked for it when we stopped by there and we always found it or its offspring. This species, ours, expending all its energy to stay in place. I'd love to see it again, but that tree is far away, the bug is small, and my eyes are getting tired.

# 4.

Waking, it's as if waves are washing me ashore. I don't remember the shipwreck, but I was cast adrift on the painful, jagged crags of consciousness for weeks. A wave thrust me up against the rocks, I saw a brief flash of light, felt searing pain and my head spun, and then the undertow pulled me back down below. There I was suspended for the day, in the dark belly of the sea swell of the unconscious yet again. The image of her face often surfaced with my pain, probably because she was standing there by the bed. She'd greet me with a grimace of horror, leaning over, trying to retrieve me. She called to me, rightly sensing I could hear her. Or was this a memory from my past life? Lucija, why are you silent? Why won't you say anything? Speak to me, I'm your best friend, you'll never have a better one. Where are you, say something, why are you avoiding me? I started lying to her early on; she was unaware of this for years. But now, when I wanted to scream the truth, my voice box on the best days produced only a sigh a little like a choke. My silence had turned against me and chosen to exact its revenge for all the times I'd used it. I couldn't bear her look of disappointment. It was all because I did not like meat, so I'd chew it until it turned into a gray sponge and then spit it into my napkin—so delicious, Mama. It was all because she was sad all the time, so on my way to school I'd splash around in the puddles on purpose; I'd cook up lies to amuse her, a little dog peed on my foot, isn't that funny, look, Mama, how wet it is. It was all because I liked boys more than I liked her, so she'd slap me when she spotted a white stain on my pants in the dirty laundry—I'm not going out with anyone, Mama, you reek of sex, Lucija, you're letting them jack off on you. It was all because I'd outgrown her son and lied about it to boot, saying, he's just a little odd, Mama. I'd only just moved out, she hadn't spoken with me for weeks, though the little apartment I rented was only a ten minute walk from hers. She sobbed over the phone. I began stopping by evenings around six, after work. "Here, this is what I'm having for supper." She'd push over a bowl of porridge and in it a mashed banana. "I'm no fan of bananas, but when I mash it in, the oatmeal's easier to get down." This was not about the porridge, or the banana, or the supper, it was about her relishing in the ache of misery and something she was confusing with humility. It was about taking masochistic pleasure in making life a hell, even those rare moments when it wasn't. I imagined knocking the porcelain bowl out of her hand, the porridge dribbling down the walls. And then I'd simply grin and say: "Terrific, great for your health, Mama," Food dribbles straight into me now, I guess this is a case of what goes around comes around. A catheter was wormed in through my nose, it traveled down my throat and all the way to my stomach, and there it pours the food in so I don't die of hunger. A brownish liquid high in nutrients which, counter to every natural law, is keeping my body alive. I have never liked eating. Now they feed me constantly. Tubes connected to a pump issue a substrate into me at regular intervals all day long.

When I was small, eating felt like a tremendous waste of time, except when I was eating something sweet, the only kind of food I liked. Sweet things were enjoyable and safe, there was never something animal-based lurking in a sweet dish. I couldn't bear the thought that I was gnawing on somebody's ligament, that there might be someone's cartilage crunching under my teeth, that the feather follicles from somebody's former wings were poking into my palate. My stomach would instantly churn and up my gorge would rise. I left the room while Grandpa chomped on head cheese with his big stubbled jaw, while someone's hoofs and organs quivered inside the transparent cube of oily gelatinous aspic. During the autumn days when hogs are butchered, I went down to the end of the street wrapped in a thick shawl and kicked around in other people's yards so I wouldn't have to see the torrents of blood pooling in the plastic tub, gushing from the upside down hog. The stink of simmering hog brains overpowered all else with a supreme horror and emanated throughout the neighborhood. I was flabbergasted by how hunks of just one butchered hog could turn up again and again for a full year. The animal hadn't seemed big enough when it hung there in the yard, but the amount of meat swelled. It filled the freezers of relatives near and far, no matter how much bacon we ate, we could never eat it all, there was always yet another slab turning up, more cracklings to munch on at dinnertime. In this meat-eating family, I was the butt of sly mockery, I'd sit hunched over a bowl of soup for hours—duck's giblets swimming in it like little islands, my tears dripping down their gentle slopes. My family couldn't understand me and I was incapable of explaining myself to them, I ate as much as I could, and, when it wouldn't go down,

I'd sob. I don't remember anyone ever asking me: Would you prefer something else to eat? About the time I started school they took me to the doctor. My eating disorder was explained furtively, the way shameful, secret things are talked about in a family. The doctor was old, dry, he had bad breath when he leaned vulture-like over my tiny frame. Into my mouth he shoved a wooden stick, with the hard callouses of his thumbs he jerked down the skin under my eyes, pinched me on my lower arms, and all the while he wore a sneer on his purple lips. Mama stood in the corner of the doctor's shabby office and with every facial muscle she was abject in her apology. The long-anticipated diagnosis came out in two sentences: "She's small. And too lazy to chew." He tossed the stick into a metal cup, on it the word "used," and slapped me on the face once more. "So, what should we do?" asked my mother, almost coyly. "Nothing," answered the doctor, aloof, "she'll get used to it in time." And that's exactly how things went. This was one of the first times I was told to get used to something and it settled into the pit of my stomach like oil, creating room for all the others to follow.

Soon I started first grade, and this gave me more room to negotiate what I would allow into my mouth, and gave me more room for my lies. Nobody kept watch over me while I was at school. My school day alternated weekly: our class met in the morning one week, and in the afternoon the next. When we had afternoon school and my mother's and brother's shifts at work meant I was alone at home in the morning, I savored the warm buns and yogurt, and the possibility of picking the thick slices of stringy salami out from between the slices of bread with my fingers and delivering them to the waste basket.

It made me happy to see how they plopped in among the scraps of paper and the pencil shavings. But the next week, when my brother was at home to see me off to morning school, my stomach would start churning first thing. Seven years older than me, he prepared our breakfast. "Eat," he'd bark, coldly playing at authority. The hotdogs lay there steaming on the little plate and I'd start my whimpering. "Eat, stupidhead!" and then he'd be louder and louder, while I sniveled and phlegm dripped down all over my clothes as I sobbed and gasped. "You will not move until you eat this," he'd practice on me with a grim satisfaction as if he were a grown-up—like a greedy puppy licking shoes with an intoxicating feeling of power—while popping a third of the hotdog into his mouth at the same time. "Eat!" he'd yell and then he'd whack the plate in front of me so the hotdog bounced up and dropped, rubber-like, back onto the plate. I stared at the floor, drenching my neck, chest, clean, ironed shirt in tears.

"So, you won't, eh? Open up!" Once he tried to jam the pink meat through my clenched teeth. After pinioning my arms to my back with his big hand he sat on me. I held him off for a few seconds, but when I ran out of breath I reflexively opened my mouth and he jammed the fork partway down my throat. I started to choke and cough, his grip released, and having pulled free, I fled from the table. Then, after I'd coughed up what was in my mouth and rage replaced my fear, I uttered for the first time the only two words I could muster: "Cunt fag." I had no idea what they meant, my face beet red, my eyes puffy, I grabbed my school bag and raced out of the apartment. Tomislav stood there in the middle of the dining room, his empty fork pointed to the sky, and laughed. When I came home, nobody said a word. That evening I couldn't fall asleep for the longest time, I called to Mama while she was talking on the phone in the hall. Softly and persistently, pleading with her to come and sit by me till I dropped off to sleep. I dreamed of her face bending over mine and stroking me with her hand, I wished this would always be the first thing I'd see every morning when I woke.

# 5.

She's always scheduling you for appointments on Tuesday at 11:00 a.m. That's how I picture you today, my love, while my doctor makes her rounds, when she asks the two medical students she has in tow: "Is today Tuesday?" the girl says nothing; the boy answers, "Yes, it's only Tuesday." Only. I've already been processed. In the early morning, two pairs of strong hands shift me adeptly to a cot parked on the right side of the bed where I live, a strong man and an even stronger woman. They immobilize my head with a splint, I don't open my eyes, I pretend to doze, which is how I make their unnatural closeness easier to bear. The woman is at my head, I'm already familiar with the way the wrinkles on her neck merge as they plunge toward her large, wilted breasts, the gold chain necklace with a biggish Christ on the cross dangling toward my head, it swings over my shaggily cropped hair and never touches me. She shoves her meaty hands under my armpits, firmly clasps my torso, skillfully arranges the tubes of the respirator and catheters, says "Hey," with a glance at her colleague who is down by my feet. Her breath smells of tobacco and cheap Turkish coffee, I like inhaling it, I nourish myself with smells like these, the only tastes still available to me. My nightgown is hip length to make performing my body hygiene all the easier, they do not change my clothes here every day, even though the doctor did once give a little talk to a group of students about how devastating the depersonalization of patients such as myself can be, the vital importance of human dignity that must be preserved by dressing the patient every day in the clothing the patient likes best, attuned to their style and personality. I always liked short skirts, the casual kind, over Doc Marten high-tops; I loved pretty dresses, long and flowing, stovepipe jeans, comfy knitted sweaters, bare shoulders, a slender waist, lots of shoes, boots, sandals. Now I have this short nightie and faded purple slippers, crocs that someone brought me, they're only there next to the bed because someone else helped themselves to my floral slip-ons, ones Mama brought, that were more like orthopedic clogs. Not that I need them, I won't be running away any time soon, but they were holding the line of defense for me in my valiant battle against depersonalization. When I was rolled out into nature, they'd put on my slip-ons. "Hey," says the medical technician and they hoist me in no time over to the cot like a sack of wet cement. They roll me over onto my hip, and there is an arm—I don't know whose—stabilizing me gently, because, I assume, otherwise I'd roll off. For an instant my gaze is aimed at my bed and on it, before the nurse gathers up the first layer of dirty bedding from the plastic sheet, I see brown stains. They look as if they're regularly spaced a little like a snow angel, where the arms, the hips and the legs go. Maybe these are bed sores, or the stigmata, maybe he touched me after all. Today is not a day for bathing, today is only a rub-down with a washcloth, then ointments and lotions, a declarative swivel of a stiff, frayed toothbrush in the oral cavity and a hairbrush pulled through the slicked-down brown hair.

Then back onto the white snow to leave my tracks there again. Out of the whole morning procedure, I like it least when they talk to me, when they actually address me, so I've developed the defense of feigning sleep, though they probably guess I'm awake. But to deal with their "Now there we go!" "My, my, you'll be smelling fresh as a baby now," "Will you look at her, good as new!" means being planted royally on the throne of humiliation. When they shift me back onto the bed their work is done, and until the rounds and the physical therapist, nobody else comes by. Though I feign sleep, they crank the bed up into a different position, I cautiously open an eye, they're still pottering around the room. Once, while there was still a second bed in the other corner, two janitors appeared: "This is the room with the woman who can't move." After prepping the extra bed, they took it apart to move it. They didn't notice me watching, but I saw how they'd lined up their screw drivers, wrenches, a spray bottle on the sheet covering my legs. They picked up their tools and set them back down right on me. I breathed to myself.

Now, when the doctor makes her rounds, I can no longer keep my eyes shut, I stare ahead and every so often the medical students and their professor swim into view. They observe me intently, the boy with a shade more audacity and a tinge of fascination. The professor, who comes to the ward once a week, is leading a new tour, all she's missing is one of those red tour-guide umbrellas. The trio stops a few feet away, out of courtesy, as if I won't hear them or I haven't subscribed to the educational program. "This one is an unusual case, I mentioned her earlier, a person who has locked herself away, our term for it is 'locked-in syndrome,' also known as a 'pseudocoma.' It is recognized as a permanent vegetative state resulting from a traumatic brain injury. It usually comes about from a hemorrhage in the pons or an ischemic cerebral insult that disturbs and damages the areas of the brain mediating the horizontal gaze." Then she stops briefly, comes over and tugs the sheet up higher, toward my breasts. For a time she studies me, then steps away from the bed and continues in a conspiratorial tone:

"Such patients have intact cognitive function and they may be awake, they open their eyes, and their cycle of waking and sleeping is like ours. They cannot move the lower part of their face, chew, swallow, speak, breathe, or move their limbs. Vertical eye movements are possible; they can open and close their eyes and blink a certain number of times in answer to questions. The diagnosis is primarily clinical. An MRI of the brain helps us search for what caused the injury and will show any changes over time. The EEG findings are normal both in a waking state and in normal sleep phases." All three of them stare at me, I refuse—on purpose—to blink, I am using every ounce of my strength to keep myself from communicating with them. I am calm and glass-like, maybe I'm dead, maybe the two medical students will die, maybe the boy will be run over by a car. The professor opens the door, ushers them out in front of her, her clogs clatter on the linoleum and she chatters on freely, professionally, excited by the rare jewel she's leaving behind in the room until her next visit, and as she is on her way out she says: "The mortality rate is high, many who suffer from this die within a month. Recovery to independent function is rare, but possible within the first few months when the precipitating factors are partially reversible, such as with tetraplegia resulting from Guillain-Barré syndrome. Positive diagnostic indicators include early recovery of lateral eye movements and detection of responses evoked after magnetic stimulus of the motor cortex. Patients up to the age of eighteen have been known to survive locked-in syndrome. She has been here for about three months." They are all quite excited, the last such specimen was treated at Rebro Hospital in the mid-1990s, but he didn't live as long. Now the female medical student, quick and bold, asks: "Is she being treated for anything? What does her treatment entail?" Without emotional engagement, but still quite caring, the professor continues: "We treat to prevent systemic disorders such as pneumonia, urinary tract infections, we monitor the feeding tube, do what we can to minimize bed sores and pursue physical therapy to prevent contracture. Logopedists have been able to help establish a communication link using the blinking of the eyes. The cognitive function is unimpaired, so patients ought to be making their own decisions about medical treatment, as long as communication can be established. Our possibilities here, of course, are limited. Her mother visits and was put through the training, so at some point, if Lucija's condition remains stable, she can be moved to home treatment. But so far this has been a rough ride, the improvements have not been significant." Her voice faded into the distance, replaced by the ticking of the wall clock across from my bed, the time only ten, only Tuesday.

You must already be standing there at the train station, my love, though all you need is fifteen minutes to get to the hospital, you arrive a half hour before your 11:00 a.m. appointment, you're never one to be late. You board the commuter rail train, sit across from a woman, usually a woman, men still unnerve you. You study her face, clothing, the way she's holding her bag and you understand everything. How anxious she is about returning home, what her husband looks like, whether she has children. Is she sad, shallow, aloof? You've always known, you had to if you were to survive, you've been forced since your youngest years to scrutinize human nature. You have maneuvered your way through the labyrinth of other people's expectations, moods, and quirks to get by as unremarked on as possible, and when that wasn't possible, you'd adapt to the point of self-effacement, internal dying. Your painstakingly acquired skills delighted me, and sometimes we'd play diagnosis, especially while we were on public transportation. You told me stories about the people sitting around us. Once when we were on the train, though at the time I had the impression you weren't one hundred percent sure, you showed me a boy who was sitting across from us. Nodding in his direction you mouthed: "One of mine," with warmth, but also with a tinge of scorn in your voice, and sometimes I caught sight of something deeply hidden. The young man you were indicating was in his early twenties, and though a little smaller in stature, he looked like all the young men around here, ordinary and unassuming, a crew cut, wearing a loose short-sleeved shirt, jeans, and sneakers. "How do you know?" I asked, surprised. "By the way he moves his hands," you said. I still didn't get it, but then I saw how his fingers were pinching his T-shirt and holding it away from his stomach, as if he were too warm though he wasn't, and then the slight hunch to his back, he glanced around and with this specific gesture eliminated any suggestion of the space between his chest and the flat surface of his tee shirt. "There, that's what everyone does," you said.

You knew better than anyone what gestures tell us, what's

going on when someone eyes you, how the young men with shaved heads in the park walk when they come over to bum a cigarette, and how they walk when they come for you. That was long ago, and I knew little, hardly anything, about those days, days you talked about when you were taking the train, maybe like today, to the hospital. And though there's no longer any reason to, I know you still travel as if you're invisible, as if you're wrapped in a magic cloak, often behind dark glasses. Though your beautiful, narrow, almost noble face is hard to ignore—your large dark eyes, your striking curved eyebrows, your pale skin and the shining mid-brow furrows of pain that appear when you concentrate, furrows that switch to brightness and show a rascally spark when the corner of your lips twitches into a grin. In your thirties, slender and good-looking, with the old-fashioned poise of a fencer, you look a little younger, spry yet melancholy, blending extremes; things emerge from this blend of yours that people don't know how to describe so they call it beauty. That you are so beautiful, as I only later realized, was bound to make you a handy target for the rest of humankind. The aura of perplexity that shimmered around you until you emerged from yourself and surfaced in the last period of our life together—until you'd adapted your body to the boy who'd been crouching in the brightest darkness of your soul for twenty years—affected people in two different ways. The first group was drawn in by the resonance of the exotic. Unthreatening yet inflammatory, it was as if they were standing at the zoo in front of the cage of a magnificent Bengal tiger, resting easy in their knowledge that they could observe with impunity. From their superior position, they knew they could toy with this unknown, potentially dangerous thing, and, most importantly, they could step away whenever they cared to. It wasn't you who mattered. It wasn't the tiger that mattered. It wasn't the cage that mattered. A few, an offshoot of this larger number, wore their friendship with you on their lapels like a medal, to show off to their less open-minded friends and elevate their importance in society. By socializing with you they hoped to deck themselves out with the accolades afforded to an ally. They saw you as an endearing moron, forever in their debt. They, too, could step away whenever they cared to. Again, it wasn't you who mattered. The second group, the ones you saw as less dangerous but potentially more aggressive than the first, were outraged by your aura. A single glance at you that might show them some of the complexity of your being was enough to provoke them to revulsion and panic. The very fact of your existence gutted the image of their straitened world, in which nothing foreign could exist or survive. Indeed, the world for them existed only if it was exactly like them. They feared you with a divine fury, like a punishment arriving in the form of a disease, as if your very existence signaled their end, and they were prepared to do everything to destroy you. But this is now all in the past; the gazes these days are benevolent. As you step off the train platform, go down the steps into the underpass, and walk toward the Vrapče psychiatric hospital, you still carry your shield. You also carry scars on your soul. The arborway and benches lining the path are charming, there is something soothing about the path toward the always-open iron gate of the institution for treatment of a wide array of psychiatric disorders.

Still, the first time we went there together I cried the whole way. You held me by the hand and almost pulled me toward the building, my steps were leaden and with my whole heart I wished I could run away, but somehow I kept up with you. I was ashamed of my weakness, I was scared of everything, even the derelicts sitting on the benches, and all I could think of was Mama. What would she say if she saw me now, what would she say if she knew the secret I was hiding? You were quiet and pulled me along, I don't know how you managed it all, your persistence always won me over; once we'd made it to the door to the doctor's office, I was able to breathe more easily. Soon a petite woman with short blond hair and kind, bright eyes came out. She greeted us briefly, asking us to wait for a few minutes until she'd finished with her students. This sent me off on a crying jag again. I don't know why exactly, except maybe the thought that the students would be talking about us. We walked out, holding cigarettes that were wet and gluey with slobber and tears. And then, from behind our backs, a scrawny, translucent pajama-clad arm thrust out from between the bars and swayed there gently. "Gimme, gimme me one. Pretty puhleeeeease…" the older woman pleaded repeatedly in her scratchy voice. In soundless steps she moved all the way over to the window so her underarm was pressed against the iron cage. Her gray hairs floated off her head and her papery, lined face remained in the shadows. We looked at each other, startled, unable to decide what made more sense just then, in our world, in our life: choosing an act of mercy that sets us free from misery yet brings with it uncertainty, or sticking with the permanent certainty of prison. I don't know whether you are thinking back on this as you stand there today in the waiting room, I'm guessing that Irena opens the door for you right away, you've known each other for several years by now. You haven't seen each other for a while, maybe it's my locked-in condition that has sent you back to her. "How are you?" she asks. You say nothing. She fills the void. "Have you been to see her?" and gently, with no trace of pathos, she goes straight to the point. She's like that. You still aren't saying a word, but this time you shake your head, perpendicular to the direction my eyes can move. Left, right, and the bodily fluid for moistening the cornea streams down your face. But you're brave, you'll find the crack through which the words will seep, just as they did that morning when we finally stepped into the doctor's office. That's when I first heard you speak about *that*.

"I remember a scene I've never spoken of to a soul. I was quite small. Maybe five or six . . . I was home alone and came across a tennis ball. And I was really interested in seeing how my underpants would look so I slipped it right in there and felt how snugly it fit. I remember the feeling, I think I'll never forget how gorgeous that was. Suddenly strength hummed through me. As if I'd hooked into my main battery, if we think of ourselves as machines. Or, as if I'd never had a center of balance and then suddenly found it. The point is that this is something elemental. And after that comes the shame. Like after ninety percent of the things you do and want in life. Our body, our worst hell. Everything is fine while you're small, more or less. Nobody can tell, you're on the beach in the summertime, you're wearing a boy's swimming trunks and everything's great. But what matters is knowing that in the games you play with the other kids, in the scrambling around on the beach, in absolutely every appearance and action, you know you're lying. And then, again, the shame you feel because your buddies see through you. The worst part is when the other kids start pestering you with questions: 'So how come you tell us Ivan is your name?' And everything you've built, or rather haven't built but have come to by nature—by being naturally male—comes tumbling down. Gone in a flash, and then who are you? And absolutely nobody gets it, but instead, to make matters worse, they ply you with silly questions: 'Hey, Dora! Why so sad? Why have you been saying your name is Ivan? Hey, come on . . .' Then the rage starts mounting, the anger, the grief, a gaping hole that won't stop spreading. And spreads still today. And after all this Granddad shows up and is so utterly clueless, the insensitive type who prods you where it hurts the most. No mercy. We're sitting there, watching German RTL's top list of the ten weirdest people in the world. 'Granddad, what does the word hermaphrodite mean?' I ask and he peers down at me from above, and says: 'That's you.' Dad's not around. Never is. At work or who knows where. Mother is always on edge or maybe she's okay but with undertones of 'I'll be okay for your sake, because I'm your mother and you come first. I will subordinate everything to you.' And I'm sad. There's nothing to reproach her for because the situation clearly was bad. Whatever . . . only they know what they were feeling. That's all I can handle right now, I'm not doing very well."

I was dreaming. Noise from the corridor roused me. Mama's after the nurses again, accusing them of stealing my nightgowns, saying that I'm wearing one that's torn and washed out, that they took the new ones home for themselves. She's surly toward the staff whenever she comes, yet when she speaks to me, a spark of joy gleams in her eyes because of the care she'll show me, care I am unable to refuse. Back we've gone to the beginning. Because she thinks I can't fully feel her touch, she

35

touches me the way an infant is touched, the way the helpless are touched, who are being tended to with a profound lack of regard. Like when babies are held by their crossed ankles and hoisted into the air so their diaper can be changed, and their eyes bulge. This is the same cruelty as her arranging my pitiful nightgown. But before she can reach me and fix me, she must first break through the phalanx of her fury: at the hospital staff, at the situation that led to this, at this tragedy of hers. Her immobile adult daughter, one more pearl, the shiniest, on the string of the misfortunes she proudly wears with every outfit. This is why she almost always swims into view, howling with her sword drawn. The rising voices from the corridor creep into my nightmare and pull me up into reality, into the light of day. Ever since I've been in this condition, I dream the same thing, these are not dreams about walking or running. I never dream of myself in motion, I can't see myself and don't feel my arms moving, I am not making my way across a room, I am certainly not flying, and I'm not touching anything. I dream I am unable to speak. Someone addresses me, requires an answer, urges me along, starts yelling, I know the answer, and I know that I know it, but I cannot spit it out. I open my mouth, the sounds lodge in my throat or roll off like pebbles into a well of silence. I am horrified by my own helplessness, but at the edge of my horror I know this must be a dream because how could I be left with no voice? I give up fighting and wait for the moment when I'll wake, shout, whisper, retrieve myself, as if I'm nothing but silt pulling myself back to the dimension of noise from the noiseless sea. Only then do I wake. The double blow of the deception floods me to the point of choking.

I was often silent before. I could have spoken, preferred

not to, didn't feel like explaining myself, didn't care to waste words. I castigated myself with my silence. I bit my tongue, and with every swallowed word I stepped farther away from myself. My silence underwent big changes. The first stage was almost childish and lasted the longest, and it didn't include vast silences. When I spoke, I was nimble with words, I manipulated, blithely I'd twist the truth, and when I grew tired of it, I'd stop talking and walk away along with my voice. That is the ordinary brand of silence. Most of us have the option of turning ourselves on and off as the spirit moves us. That is why we chatter on, we adjust reality with our voices so it looks how we'd like it to look, we change and adapt the same story depending on whom we're telling it to. We absorb normality during our youngest years, we repeat phrases, we don't think, we just spew syllables, imbuing them with all sorts of meaning. "Don't ever hold yourself apart," Granny used to say while she pulled me along by the hand down the street on our way to my nursery school. My ponytail was done up with a red silk ribbon, my bobby socks with the ruffled edges around my slender ankles, I walked stiffly in white patent leather shoes, taking care to do nothing to spoil my outfit. The day was warm, autumnal, my heart was pounding in my chest, the neighbor's terrier was barking at us, its body pressed against the chain-link fence. "Scram!" snarls Granny at it as we pass by, and then in the same loud voice she says: "Got it?" I nod and the word "apart" rings in my nodding head. I still don't know, nor does my Granny, that "apart" is an adverb and means exclusion. She had only been through the fourth grade of primary school, at the age of ten she went into service as a maid, yet though neither of us understands the role of the adverb in the grammar of that sentence, we both know exactly what "not holding your-self apart" means. I am supposed to go where everyone else goes, do what I'm told to do without asking questions, look like other people, think and want the same things all children think and want. It isn't difficult for me to steer away from "holding myself apart," I'm a cute, well-mannered little girl, I like my porridge with cocoa, I'll even eat spinach, in this sense my life proceeds unhindered. At school I even edge away from Selma, the Muslim girl in our class, who sits out in the hallway on the stairs while the rest of us attend catechism, I won't hit her on the back with my slipper bag, and I'll even smile at her secretly sometimes, but I will not "hold myself apart." Don't be first or last, stick to the middle. The only thing I do is keep my brother at arm's length, he's always teasing me and upsetting my har-mony with the world whenever he's nearby, with that look like he wants to make me cry. Granny never warned him not to "hold himself apart" because standing apart is fine for boys, that's how they learn to fend for themselves. And even when he kicks Granny hard in the shins and she cries out in the yard so loud that the neighbor comes over to see what's wrong—she tells me, while pulling up the feather quilt when she tucks me in at night, "Don't breathe a word of this to anyone. Not even your mother. That's what boys do." There is plenty of being quiet in avoiding "holding myself apart," but nobody keeps track of that kind of silence, it is part of living in a place, it shapes us so that we fit in. And then there are cases when there is no choice, when your essential existence is already being "apart," when the struggle for you to fit in anywhere begins with the contours of your first reflection in the mirror.

You were expert at keeping mum about that. I coaxed you

into conversation, circled around, but nothing surfaced. As if there weren't words for it. When I came closer, you'd shut the door and turn the key. I was jealous of your Tuesdays and Irena.

"You'll get back every last one of the nightgowns, don't you worry now. Today you're looking well." She says this while she bends over me, and I am silent, not because I can't speak, I'd be lying if I implied that. I'm silent because I don't know what there is to say. I think of the ice cream dripping from your six-year-old fingers, my love, while you sit at a plastic table and stare at the soggy cone while the children from the beach stare over at you, united in their surprise, crowding around you in censure and mockery—the strongest glue in all human communities. This is where your silence begins. You are afraid to look around, shame is rooted in your soul, and even though you know nothing because you're only six, you've nevertheless figured it all out. Unlike you, I am only now seeing people, their putrid souls, now when I can't feel anything and when I can no longer speak, I see how she strokes my unmoving arm while she takes out a packet of moistened wipes and wiggles them in my field of vision. Today I seem better, much better than last week, immeasurably better than last month. She is employing a strategy of concern that is spilling all over the bed, she's almost humming as she arranges the boxes, face creams, new pillowcases. And she keeps touching me, my body that is finally obeying her and not me, my body, my worst hell.

# 6.

It's a true miracle that she survived. She could have died. The worst is over. She was so lucky. She's through the worst of it now. Like an echo, in any number of versions, the outrageousness of this miracle of mine rebounds and ricochets against the cells of my inner being, like the battered plastic balls bouncing against the worn rims of an old, abandoned pinball machine that will never again light up, left behind at a club with broken windows on a concrete slab beach nobody goes to anymore. Not for the sun, nor music, nor fun. Nothing inside the machine will ever again make that pinging sound, nobody will jostle it anymore, grab it, ram it fervidly with their hips. People pass by unliving things in silence. Unliving things are not spoken to, they are here to complete the world, people use their concern for the unliving to launder their conscience the best way they know how; the unliving don't talk back. During the first month nearly all of them, over seventy percent, die. I dangled for several weeks on the slenderest thread, sepsis was taking my body to pieces, it spread through my veins, released its poisons, my organism rotted from within, but powerful doses of antibiotics coupled with a pugnacious streak in my spirit—something in me that refused to be yet another statistic—brought me back to Middle Earth. What extraordinary luck she had. They had no idea at first just how immense that luck actually was. Lucky thing that I couldn't respond to them though I heard them and understood what they were saying as soon as the condition of my immobilized body stabilized.

The first days after my miracle I often sank away into darkness, but equally often I surfaced to make some sense of the constants in this world that was becoming my only environment. Aside from Mama's soft and unremitting sobs that reached me from up close, he, too, was here. Then there was a high, thin voice that came into my room each day belonging to the doctor who did not smell bad. The voice was accompanied by the jangle of her bracelets, the click of her ballpoint pen, her throaty laugh into her cell phone. "I'll be able to get away for two days, no more, look I mean it. Because of the kids I can't, no more talk about this. If you want us to see each other, this is the only way." When she came to my room to talk on the phone in the early evening, knowing no one could hear her or look for her, the clothesline along which the doctor's voice was hung out to dry stretched between the flirtatious little girl, through the restrained, yet deeply moved lover, to the mortified penitent who could not believe what she was doing yet nevertheless was planning a two-day getaway to Lake Bled. Almost as if she were on stage, she paced back and forth across the room in front of me, stopping now and then before the chipped hospital room mirror to check on the perfect arc of eyeliner above her lid. I've never gotten the hang of that, women who can draw such a perfect line are uncommon; their lives have always looked a little different to me. After the conversation she dropped the cell phone into the pocket of her lab coat and stood, lost in thought, for a moment, then she sighed deeply and glanced over at the bed. But she wasn't seeing me, she was seeing herself, so she didn't notice my eyelids. She had no strength just then to break through to me. Her condition was every bit as serious as mine. I was buried alive inside myself, but my realization that she was probably worse off rose like the tide each time she left the room. With every day, she heaped upon herself shovel after shovel of pulverized limestone, burying herself amid the people she lived with, whom she loved and looked after, until one day there'd be nothing left of her, no trace. "What I told him is that I am attending a symposium with you and we'll be leaving from your place, yes, if he asks. Yikes, I don't know, please don't, that's more than I can manage. No. I don't know. Things are as they are now. Hey, don't ask me. What couple is still sleeping together after ten years? Look, I can't imagine breaking this to the kids, I can't imagine walking out on them and on my father-in-law, who has supported me every step of the way, I see him at the hospital every day, I can't leave the apartment, I can't go back to renting, not on only one salary. Can't you see? I can't even think about this yet. But I know I've never felt this way. Alive. It's not just the sex, my friend, it's everything. All of it, being with him, the sex, the breakfasts, the showers, and sitting together at the conference, reading the fucking newspaper, every bit of it. Can you understand? Yes . . . Who saw us? What did she want to know? Come on, there are always stupid stories making the rounds, but fine, I'll be careful. Ah . . . I am looking at this woman lying here in front of me, and I know, it's awful, but sometimes I think, one day all this will pass, all of it will be behind me, nothing will matter anymore, strange to think that way, but a relief in a way. Yes. Okay, hon, I'll call, don't you worry about a thing." She bends over me once more, looks straight through me, leaves a cloud of Dior above my motion-less head, and leaves. She walks over to her office, sends off a few messages to her lover, the weekend is coming, he writes to her exactly what she needs to liven her up by the time she gets to the car, something theirs alone and unique. The minivan with the nice new car smell slides through the cold, rainy evening, she puts Diana Krall's "The Look of Love" on repeat, this gives her strength, the brief moment in the day when she is by herself, her own person, then up the stairs to their apartment. Nobody says hello, her boys are on their PlayStations, is Dad home, nope, a rush of relief. She'll get into bed soon, within a few hours her husband—whom she loved for two years, like loving the silhouette of an idea without much emotion—will drop into bed beside her, with no foreplay or intimacy he'll try rubbing up against her for a while, and she'll just lie there motionless, like me. Then he'll give up, get up and go into the bathroom, after a while she'll hear the water flush. When he plunks back into bed he'll clear his throat, and she will be even more brittle, more buried, under today's new layer. She will be me, but I can no longer be her. That's how it will be tomorrow, the day after, and after Bled, and for years to come, until her boys move out, until her father-in-law, the head of neurology, dies, until her husband finds a younger lover. But by then no time will be left, just mounds of pulverized limestone on all sides. No one will be able to hear her, all she has clung to for so long will turn out not to have mattered. But if she could know this and feel it now, her true desires would be stripped of their importance. I see this so clearly now, and sometimes, in these early evenings of ours when I watch how chronic locked-in syndrome begins, I utterly forget myself. I listen and wait patiently for her to find a crumb of space for me, she could do that, she'd know I'm here, if only she eased up ever so slightly, if only she opened herself up just a little.

On Monday morning, after the weekend, while she talks with a colleague about how a gastrostomy would possibly be preferable to the nasogastric tube that has damaged the tissue of my pharynx and which, she thinks, might push me to contract pneumonia again if only one single tiny, microscopic bit of food goes down the wrong way, she looks deep into my eyes. I push every ounce of life force in me toward the paper-thin skin of my eyelids, I squeeze, I go wild and howl at my eyelashes, I force an ocean into my eyes in hopes that it will gush over all the dams. As if I'd been left unattended for a moment by my kidnappers in a dark cellar, when I happened on a crack leading to the outside world. All the noise I make evaporates into silence, but still she leans over and suddenly speaks to me directly. To me. After two months of non-living, someone speaks to me with four words. Four ordinary words, short, so often uttered. They assume the shape of a bright red life preserver above my head: "Can you hear me?" I jump up, prance around the room, lunge animal-like to grab the life preserver, squint as if the whole sun has come down into my face, my pulse throbs, she becomes more and more convinced, looks at the screen, and says: "Slow now, slow now, if you hear me, blink. Oh. My. God . . ." Now she has turned to fully face me, she opens space inside herself and sees me. Excited, she says: "I am going to ask you a few questions. If your answer is yes, blink once, if your answer is no, blink twice." And suddenly, through the crack in my eyelids shines a slender ray of light.

# 7.

I cannot choose. It is not mine to decide whom I'll see. People pop into the room whenever they feel like it, assuming I'll be so happy and grateful for their visits. I have no way of sending anyone away, I can't turn the key in the lock, or wedge a chair under the door handle. Entering a room housing people who are immobile is like violent penetration. They lift my nightgown, push my legs apart, open the door, raise the bed, peer into my face, cry, whisper, grimace in sincere or faked pity. I cannot even turn my head away when I know they're faking it, instead I have to suffer the self-congratulatory expressions on other peoples' faces because they have made time for me. Ever since the doctor discovered me, there has been turmoil in the ward. I went through several exciting weeks. One after another I was put through MRIs, they rolled me around the floors and wards, I jounced around on the elevator in anticipation of any number of tests, teams of doctors arrived, I was touched by women, men, they spoke to me in various ways, they talked about me as if I were a she-ape in a cage, they were thrilled by signs of intelligent life in one of the many useless bodies expending the resources of health insurance. The excitement ebbed, I reckon, after a month, after they'd all taken turns with me and extracted the material they needed for their scientific articles. The diagnosis was unchanged, immobile, so to speak, the consciousness of the patient was preserved, present were signs of depression, her reluctance to cooperate with healthcare staff had been observed, the possibility of regaining independent function—negligible. Her caregiver mother insists that the patient should be allowed to go to a spa to convalesce, but the medical opinion is that this is not currently feasible with her diagnosis. In other words, she'd be taking the place of someone who actually has a chance at recovery. The recommendation is that she remain at the hospital for extended treatment and palliative care for the next three months. Once the caregiver is properly trained and medical staff has been assigned, it may be possible to arrange for home care in the foreseeable future. So back we went to old times. Between her sighs and fidgets around the nightstand with the fragrant candles she quickly replaces, she shows me a catalogue with hospital beds. If I'm lucky, we'll choose one. Her voice takes on the texture of butter while she laments in my ear about an intelligent relationship among price, quality and additional features. She coos over the pressure-relief mattress to combat bedsores, available for a mere 554 kunas. Aside from her, others kept coming after the first exciting month, drop by drop. In order of appearance: the psychiatrist once a week; the speech therapist, three times a week; the physiotherapist every day; two friends, each of them for one visit; your shadow, my love, every day.

"Please, have a seat, sorry to keep you waiting." I sat for a long time in the ward of the Rebro Hospital psychiatric hospital and listened to music, waiting for the psychiatrist to see me after I'd come to her through the recommendation of an acquaintance, without having to seek a referral from my doctor. Valentina, a former colleague from the university, loud and intuitive, who had been a student of psychology, was the psychiatrist's cousin. At the time, in those first months when you and I were together, I'd distanced myself from everyone. Mama had taken to lurking, evenings, by my front door, and when I refused to open up for her she'd threaten to kill herself. Tomislav's reaction to me: Fuck her life choices, she's dead to me. Then I ran into Valentina. "You don't look so great, honey, your complexion is positively gray," that's what she said. "What's up?" "It's a long and tragic tale," I was trying to be witty without offering anything of substance, and a few minutes after we'd each gone our separate ways, the screen on my cell phone lit up with Dr. Marić's phone number and the message: "All of us need a tune-up now and then, I know this best of all. Give her a call, after two conversations you'll feel better, guaranteed." So that is how I ended up in the psych ward. I pretended to be engrossed in what I was reading, while out of the corner of my eye I was checking out the people around me. They all looked pretty normal, and I did my best to give the impression I was a nonchalant medical resident, waiting with a question for Dr. Marić. The room was well-lit, and the doctor had on a rust-colored woolen sweater with a bow on the back, like one I'd seen at Zara. She was short, dark-complexioned, pointy ears, a long nose, and seemed disinterested. I didn't know where to begin. "I don't know where to begin," I smiled awkwardly. "From the beginning," she said in a serious tone and knit her fingers together. "Why did you feel you needed to come see me?" "Well, I ran into Valentina," I had this habit of tossing off witty remarks when I was feeling troubled, to spare others the discomfort, to come across as appealing, to be left alone. "Okay, now, be serious." The doctor didn't want me doing that. "Well, I have these problems with my mother and brother . . . I feel as if I don't belong in my family, as if they don't understand me, maybe this will sound too serious, but it's as if they despise me for being different from them. And I know I'm not the first or the last, all I need is some advice about how to deal with it," I blurted out in a single breath. "What about your father?" "He died," I said as if anchoring for the TV news. "Their scornful attitude has to do with my choice of partner." "Back to your father," insisted the doctor, "When did he die and what did he die of?" "That's not what matters right now," I wasn't keen to waste time, "he was sick, ten years ago, but there's something else I'd like to say . . ." She interrupted me, almost shaming me: "It's not advisable for us to skip over such a major life event as the death of your father." An awkward pause followed, it is not advisable for us to skip over your dead father, I nearly laughed aloud at the weird sentence structure, at myself for sounding so foolish, and then the doctor decided, after all, to urge me to go ahead and say what it was I'd intended to say. "No please, speak freely, what is the problem here?" A storm raged through my whole body before I spoke, distrust crushed me, I strode along a straight, uninterrupted path against my better judgment, deciding to ignore intuition and be rational. So I told her about you.

Suddenly the rust-colored wool came alive, and the bow shimmied on her back. She began digging for details, licking her lips like a mangy, half-starved fox. "Do you feel womanly with this person? Have you always been with such people? What is your relationship like? Like two women or different?"

To each of her questions I responded sincerely, sinking deeper and deeper, I didn't know how to hold my own against her, I hadn't yet found my footing. "And what was your father like? How did he treat you? Think, might it be that your mother and brother are merely concerned about your wellbeing?" With her predatory claw she passed me a tissue across the desk, by the end of the session I was covered in stains, my clothes lay ripped in shreds all over the floor, and raising the torn scraps into the air, the doctor circled around me. She peered into my holes, took my measurements, and listened with her stethoscope to my femininity. She thrust herself into my face, peeked into my panties and mused on where the heart of our perverted relationship lay. She charged in with brazen questions, and my answers satisfied her very little. She could not fathom how it was possible for the two of us to feel fulfilled by holding hands or when you lie face down on the couch and I make you into a deck chair. I lean my bottom on the back of your shins, arrange pillows on your back, and rest my knees on your heels. Or when you make me into a puddle—a small puddle or a big puddle—when I'm a little sad and when I want to kill myself because of this world we are living in. When I am a small puddle, I sit in your lap, on your crossed legs and you rock me like a little girl. The big puddle is when I lie on top of you and you make a circle around me, I cry, and you croon to me softly. Or sometimes, when there is no way forward, and you say: protect me. Then I feel womanly. Now I feel raped. I leave the office, the hospital, the entrance ramp. You're sitting in the car and waiting for me the whole time with excitement because I'll feel better, because I'll find a way to agonize less over everything, because

I won't leave you, because loving each other will be easier. Full of happy anxiety you ask me, how was it, my love? Okay, I say, I swallow, okay, beloved. I'd like to go home now.

# 8.

I imagine myself turning to the wall. She is talking to me and I just roll over onto my side and stare at the oily green wall paint. And then I pull the sheet over my head. This would be most glorious act of defiance in the world. A meter and a half up from the floor, the wall is painted in a shiny green, while above, toward the ceiling, it is whitewashed. Maybe this is so the walls are easier to scrub and wash because of the scuff marks left by the patients. I don't know the real reason, but I can't turn over anyway, I'm not up to such a feat. On the other hand, I also can't keep my eyes shut all morning long, this is why I crumble quickly and easily, I join her stream of consciousness and try to switch off my own. "I was over at Manda's for dinner on Sunday, I didn't want to go, you know me, I don't like going over to other peoples' places. But what can you do, she was so insistent and tiresome, called me every day, and called Anja too, because of everything that has happened I shouldn't be so alone. She made some soup or other, then Zagreb cutlets, but using turkey, with breaded cauliflower, you know how we used to fix it with eggs and breadcrumbs, from the oven, and stuffed tomatoes, God help us, I mean she really cooked up a storm. And again, that cooking of hers, not to complain, but what she prepares doesn't taste right to me. You know that smell from the frying, so wrong. And her soup. My soup speaks ten languages. It's like she tossed in a bone, then took it out, and, why not, stirred in a pinch of Vegeta to liven up the flavor. That is not the way it's supposed to be. When you put it on the stove at eight in the morning to cook with a nice cut of veal, but not at a rolling boil so you'll be done sooner, the cooking needs to be slow, three hours at least, and you stand there right by the stove, scooping off the foam that forms on the top with a strainer to keep the broth from getting murky, or all muddy. You know how you were always asking me, how come when you make it, the broth isn't clear? Well, it takes time. But fine, anyway, they sent their regards, asked after you, how and what, maybe they might stop by one day, and I told them, later, not now, God willing you'll be home soon and you can see them then. I think they're decent folk, they're good neighbors. Though, again, what has happened is something they cannot understand. Manda has no children, what does she know? Anja's kids have been living in America for years, so she's used to them being away. How could they know . . . When the little one you bathed, kissed, carried while she was no more than a moppet ends up like this. I tell them: how many nights I spent in vigil by her side, on foot to the doctor's in the dark, then watching over her homework, then her studies, keeping an eye out, steering, you have to be her teacher, her nurse, her psychologist. You hope she'll become something one day. You praise her to the stars, and then look what happens . . . " At this point she starts to sob and turns away, we've practiced this several times already, ever since she found out I can hear her. She dabs her face with a tissue, spins back around, pats me on the head as if I'm a dog and says, "Well as long as you're with us, even if you're like this." She is heating up with the excitement, I can see her brow beading, and she moves to pull back my covers, because if she's feeling hot, I must be hot. This is parenting. I am burning only with the desire to no longer be alive, but this is not yet an option. Mama pulls the sheet back from my breasts and rolls it down, then she shrieks so vehemently that I am nearly catapulted from the bed. She covers her gaping maw with her hand and, grimacing, screams for the nurse. Like a panicked hamster she scampers back and forth between the bed and the door, waiting for help. Soon the rhythmic thump of clogs can be heard. The older nurse comes in with big, firm strides, asking everyone and no one: "What's going on here?" "Where did all this blood come from?" wails Mama, gesturing to the red stain with its intense smell, her discovery under the sheet. A luxurious, garish flower is pooling there, below my pelvis, I feel a mild gust of air on the wet, exposed skin between my thighs, my nostrils are filled with the smell of metal. The nurse catches on right away, she is still a little miffed by the panic my mother is forever raising, but she speaks with a professional demeanor. "Ma'am, this is just her menstruation, someone didn't put the diaper on properly." Mother stops, this was the last thing she'd hoped for from me, her re-born baby. Bleeding from my reproductive organs was beyond all her expectations, a betrayal by an organism, which, maimed in every possible way, was still geared for reproduction. The miracle of science cares not a whit for what is up with the rest of the body—the head, the heart—it does all it's supposed to do each month, like a self-sustaining factory, producing ova that wait patiently to be pierced by the corresponding bearers of chromosomes. They crouch there in the dark of my apparently dead and useless pelvis, carrying in themselves all the potential for a living and ambulatory future human being. They treat me like a warehouse from which they'll wriggle free as soon as possible, after taking all the food and shelter they can muster. Cells care nothing for my desires, nothing for your desires.

There was one time when we were lying there on the couch, at the very beginning while we were still in hiding. We'd stolen a few hours from a day and our hands were everywhere. At one moment, you were stretched out in front of me and I burrowed into your back, into the smell of your skin that radiated through the warm cotton of your tee-shirt. Your bottom was in my lap and we tried to find a position where there wouldn't be even a centimeter's gap between us. I nuzzled up against you, hugging you from behind, and my hand slipped into your pants. I wanted to crawl in there, into your warmth, soft and close, but you firmly took me by the hand. For a while I smiled to myself, trying to work my way in, but the grasp on my wrist was not playful. Then I heard only a dark, "Don't." I drew back and asked you gently, "What is it, love?" Shame sifted through the strainer in crumbs, choking you. "You're smart, figure it out," was all your bent back said. I don't know whether you'll ever be able to understand this, but it hadn't crossed my mind that your body had betrayed you that way. Not once did I think it would be capable of such a thing, to betray you so totally. We made it through that moment. At least wordlessly. By the end of the day you'd pulled yourself together. A whole man. As for myself, I grieved for your pain, full of admiration for the courage you manage despite a life spent in your prison. Only later did you tell me, explaining this dimension of a world I hadn't known—all about disbelief and humiliation—

with moments like the time when you were in fifth grade and as you were squeezing through between the window and the shelf where all the art materials were stored you happened to knock the window frame with your chest and you realized that something was hurting differently. Grief for childhood, such as it was, and the beginning of losing the body that had protected you at least partially until then. Pleading with the few girlfriends you had for them to wait in line at the cash register in the drug store and buy your sanitary napkins for you. Bloodied again each month. Your embarrassment and attempts at getting closer, those strings of misunderstandings, were taut at first, but relaxed in time and produced much more agreeable sounds. We became so much closer that we entered one another, easily, more easily than ever, and at times we turned our insides out to that pain, and then found it weightless, even amusing. The "trouble" caught me off guard once—that's what we called it, we had our own words for almost everything— when I was in town and started bleeding at that old movie theater we most loved going to, on a Sunday afternoon, angry and in pain, and not a drug store or kiosk in sight. You took me by the hand and gave me your backpack. "Go to the restroom, you'll find everything you need in the inside pocket. Where else could you find such a boyfriend?" And then you even shot me a wink. My heart spilled over because of the wall you'd jumped over, because I felt on the surface of my skin how we were changing and becoming normal, how we loved each other with trust. Nowhere, my love, nowhere.

Only then does she start sobbing bitterly, realizing what else she'd lost "what with all that happened." Grandchildren were spilling in crimson over the sheets, into the diapers for incontinence, heading irretrievably for the hospital garbage dump where they'd join the amputated limbs, surgically excised growths, and all the rest of the detritus of human bodies. The nurse wheels the cart in with clean linens, steering Mama toward the door and from there I can still hear her sobs.

People who have children seem the loneliest to me. Maybe theirs is an entirely different kind of loneliness, which people without kids cannot know. In the period of life when you have your baby, you probably think you are finally done with loneliness, you think you've brought something into being, you've given yourself and the world a justification for your life. This is a time when you are able to look beyond yourself, to the needs of the most selfish creature you'll ever be bound to. For the next few years you live under the romantic-religious illusion that all the sacrifice you're making will be compensated, that the people who are made of your very own flesh and blood will truly care for you. It is in their nature, however, as it is in yours, to survive, to take all they can get to secure for themselves better living conditions. And this is as it should be. But the fact that this is as it should be is the greatest disappointment faced by people with children, and that they must nevertheless accept their children as their own. Most parents make it halfway down this path and stay permanently disappointed by their offspring. A very small number faces this head on and lets their children go far away, as far away as possible. People without children mainly entertain a kinder view of parenting—fancied and embroidered with the most charming fantasies—than do those who have real, deficient children. We dwelt between these two worlds.

I don't remember how exactly the thing with Lupko got started. The way I remember it, we were lying on the mattress in my apartment, watching a show on our laptop. A rabbit-shaped stuffed animal with one buck tooth peeking out from its snout, an attractive grayish color, a little worse for wear, a relic of my childhood, had been dumped in a corner of my room. You stretched to reach for another pillow to make us more comfortable, and along the way you grabbed him, Lupko, so we could push him under our heads. As we nudged and nestled, he ended up between us and suddenly, in the glow of the computer screen, we were a rabbit family. Daddy, Mommy, and Baby Bunny. The same thought coursed through our bodies, I saw it flash by as it was born, Lupko wiggled its paw, and we looked at each other with a crazy spark in our eyes. Thumbelina, Pinocchio, Lupko, beloved children all over the world are born from the same sources: a flower, a tree, polyester. They do not come about in the usual way, their parents are already elderly, they're alone or, like us, they are fairy-tale monsters. Though I was quite sure of what had just happened to us—we'd had a child—I took Lupko by the paw, looking deep into your eyes the whole time, and lowered our little one into your lap. You whispered softly, "Is he ours?" I answered, pressed up close against you, "Our very own." "He has your cheeks," you said, stroking the synthetic fur, and I saw in this our unique alliance. "And your big feet," I added, teasing you and pinching Lupko's pudgy paws. "Well, he had to take after me somehow," you agreed, feigning disappointment.

The days that followed were the most wonderful of our parenting, we often had to spend time apart then, go off for weekends to satisfy the needs of the families our government acknowledges, travel for work, and one of us took Lupko along each time. He had our smell, we couldn't get enough of it, in the fur below his chubby neck. Whichever one of us was more alone or on a longer trip could hold him at night. We took him with us everywhere in a backpack, when we were traveling by train we'd unzip the pack just enough for him to enjoy the view; we could see him, convince ourselves he was real. We noticed how he was growing, on the good days when we spent a lot of time together, and when we were alone, Lupko would be bigger in the morning than he'd been the day before, we teased him about getting fat. On those other days he'd pull away from us into himself and start looking like a twenty-year-old stuffed animal. So it goes with children; when there is a lot of love around them, children flourish, their mark on the world deepens, they become unique human beings, and when there is none, they seek a crowd, meld facelessly into the masses, fearful to march to a different drum. Their averageness shields them from their lack of courage. Once when you had him in your backpack and didn't have time to go home, you took him to work and I teased you about what might happen if he fell out in front of your colleagues. You said, "So what, I'd put him back in, I wouldn't be ashamed." That was you being you. Sometimes I wrote him a poem, a children's poem, but when my friends came over, Lupko waited in the closet. That was me being me. Maybe Mama would have been glad to know about him, to know we had a child, that we weren't the most lonely people in the world. Maybe she'd be willing, if she could understand, to bring him here, to the hospital, he wouldn't mind. Maybe she wouldn't moan and groan so much about her lost grandchildren and be horrified by my wayward body which, immobile and vulgar, discards my ova. Maybe if she put him next my head I could still get a whiff of my motherhood and our evenings on the couch. Maybe you could take him, if only I could reach you, take him from the closet and keep him in your backpack.

While I am imagining the quantity of dust that has by now probably eaten away at him, I have been changed and cleaned, as if nothing happened at all. "Whoopsy daisy!" says the nurse while she flips me over on my back, and my gaze slides to her floral clogs which have finally learned to walk after their short spin on my dead feet.

# 9.

The ceiling at all times of day, the light, depth and meaning in an array of shades, seasons. The wooden window frame painted with the brand of white paint used for finish carpentry, peeling in spots, the curved iron window handle held in place by a solitary nail, a hole yawning where the other nail used to be—all this when the right-handed head nurse, Ružica, and Buddy change my clothes, and when he and Silvija flip me over—the nightstand with the scented candle, an open St. Anthony two-page booklet that fits in your billfold, and between the pages a colorful plastic sheet depicting the saint holding a bald infant who looks both like a baby and an old man. To its right, on a crocheted doily, stands a little radio that never plays, a plush reindeer with a red-green scarf, and Zagreb salve in a stick. As for clothing, I have two pairs of Benetton sweatpants, I know this because Mama made a point of telling me when she'd bought them, dark blue plush and gray cotton, she held them up for me to see and rubbed them with her thumb and forefinger; only then did she bite through the plastic tie attached to the label. "I'll bring them back once I've washed them in our machine at home." They put them on me so seldom, really only when they wheel me out into the yard, and this is only when we hit a day when the nurses are in a good mood so they're willing to take the trouble to push my long stiff legs through the limp pant legs. Two bathrobes that I'm guessing are knee-length; living people have height, while the dead have length. One of them is snow-white with embossed designs, and the other a gray-pink plaid in flannel. A coarse terry-cloth glove by my head on the pillow—used by whoever comes by to wipe away the saliva that starts dripping from the corner of my mouth if my head is slightly tipped—it is yellow with pink edging. Several baby doll nighties of indefinite shape, gray on gray. One hairbrush and a matching mirror the size of a tablet, framed in white plastic, stowed in the drawer of the nightstand. My worldly possessions. All the material items I own. All that sets me apart, the patient in room No. 17 on the second floor, from the other voiceless creatures in human form living in this shared home of ours. My possessions used to include the floral clogs, but now their soles are being worn thin up and down the corridors. Ružica with the meaty hands is in charge at the hospital of people and property as she finds them. So be it. Of my already sparse belongings, few were in any way remarkable, and, of these, fewer were the ones I'd chosen myself. The ceiling, the window frame on which I know every wormhole, the salve, the terry cloth glove, for instance, could hardly be counted among them, almost all of us had those. Most of the patients, in their conscious or unconscious gaze, retain an image of their ceiling, their window frame or the edge of their nightstand. In all the wards, the hands of those near us slather, with merciful strokes, layers and layers of Zagreb salves onto dry, impersonal lips which damp tongues can no longer moisten, but the reindeer, the plush toy Mama brought, now that is something that used to stand on the shelf in only one childhood bedroom. He is unique in the entire hospital and whenever I spot him, as they turn me toward him while rubbing my bottom with gauze, I know I am still me. I see my reflection in his brown plastic eyes and remember how I loved to lick him, how we threw him at each other on my birthday and he fell into the mayonnaise, and how I lathered him up in secret in the bathroom sink and dried him with the hairdryer. How I shoved him into my panties and danced to "Whole Lotta Love" by Led Zeppelin while my girlfriends from school clapped, how I wedged him between my desk and the wall so the desk wouldn't wobble and scrape the wall paint. How I abandoned him to spiderwebs, grew up, changed, buried Daddy, stop speaking with my brother, moved out, told everyone to fuck off, sat in a car, and, what do you know, here we are again, he and I. The St. Anthony booklet belonged to Granny. When I went to pass my driver's test she tucked it into my hand and, while standing with me at the door, said: "Cross yourself each time you get into a car, the instant you turn the key in the ignition you're one foot in the grave." He came with me that night when they brought me here all smashed up from the car wreck, he was in the billfold my mother dug through and she placed him near my head. There isn't much that sets us apart here, in this way of life, personality is fragile, in much greater jeopardy than life itself, exposed to all the sepses, embolisms, blood clots that crawl like vulturous worms toward the lungs. There is no longer any material evidence here of our lived lives, the things that make us special find no reflection in anything but the horror in the eyes of others, those who do not visit us every day yet go on living through all sorts of belongings and clearly defined roles.

Martina heard. She heard that I'm conscious, and then everyone else heard, too. They all heard. She ran into Mama, they stood, holding each other by the sleeves of their coats for a few minutes, patting each other tenderly but not too intimately, while they shook their heads, have you heard, I've been meaning to let you know, it would be good, said the doctors, good if you came for a visit, if you can. Martina was not my best friend—she was a friend. We met when we were students, she had all the print-outs, the reading lists, markers in all the colors, she wrote group emails, saved me a seat at the seminar while I cruised through on my way elsewhere, slightly above ground, happier to hang out with Lada who, out in front of Café Limbo during the lecture, recited Bukowski and told me how she'd had an abortion during her senior year of high school because of her philosophy teacher. Between two sips of Badel brandy, she told me how her dad threw her out of their apartment and she spent the first night in a park, how he kicked her in the back. We laughed like crazy women, while the early dark of winter was falling and life hadn't yet begun to happen, we left them all behind. Lada disappeared at some point in our second or third year, sooner or later all the Ladas disappear; the Martinas stick around. They organize birthday parties, email groups, dream up an exchange of holiday lingerie as gifts among girlfriends, spend Friday nights attending pub quizzes, concerts of poorly known indie singers, in their spare time they read Lacan, the books on their shelves are organized by genre and alphabet, once a year they see their gynecologist, one dentist visit, they discreetly blur their profile on social media, they click and share Pride, they straighten their hair with a light balayage, and whenever you're really a wreck, wearing an especially worried smile under which seethes a geyser of happiness, they ask, "So, how are you doing?"

I hadn't thought of her even once until I heard from the corridor, at the threshold to the other world, a greeting sung out as only Martina could. "Hey there!" The "heeeey" stretches out, and then shifts to a higher register, lighter, more melodic, and so synthetic that there's nothing left in it of a greeting meant especially for me. She comes cautiously over to the bed, horror gleams at the highest level, but she channels it so smoothly and colors it over with her markers, her face is perfectly calm as if we'd only parted ways a month ago after she'd told me all about taking part in a knitting workshop. "How aaaaare you?" She knows I can't speak, and she doesn't expect me to. Like a hipster-version of Mother Teresa, she pats me on the head, pretending this is how we've spent our lives, she in her designer leather jacket and her made-to-order handbag, which because of its chain strap keeps slipping off her shoulder and slapping against me when she leans over, and me there like a mummy. She keeps jerking the strap back with a nervous twitch, she's afraid that if she sets the handbag down somewhere in the room she'll be leaving a piece of herself, but the chain has a mind of its own, it keeps slipping and rubs against my gray nightgown with the Varaždin General Hospital seal. How cool is this, to have friends like me in this discrimination-free world. I clearly see in her eyes how devastated she is by my condition and appearance, I only saw myself once, a month or two ago, and I no longer care to, it took me days to forget the mush where my face used to be and the several clumps of bristles on the back of my head. I think she's pulling back from the smell, too. Despite this she pretends that absolutely nothing has happened, her reaction is the result of her decision to behave precisely this way while she was chatting with Sandra over coffee about how she was coming to see me, they broached the topic only minutes before they were about to part. Then they came up with a few of the remaining knee-jerk clichés: "I tell myself, I'm going to see her once a month." Then she took out her almond oil hand cream, squeezed a pea-sized droplet on her upper arm and massaged it carefully in. Now here she was. After she patted me, at a distance, on the shoulder, she stepped back and found some space where she could reclaim her fragile sense of self at a safe distance. As she'd predicted, we couldn't pass the time with conversation like we used to, and she also predicted her own discomfort, so she'd come up with something truly exceptional to brighten the encounter for both of us. She looked around for a chair, in three steps she reached the corner of the room and drew it up from there to the bed. She sat down and began rummaging through her handbag, took something out, and then then with a bright chirp held two books up in my range of vision. I was supposed to choose. "Blink which one you'd like me to read to you." She waited, confused, for something to happen while in front of my eyes loomed the books of poetry. Danijel Dragojević and Sylvia Plath. Blinking doesn't afford the option of selection, clearly this was something she hadn't thought of, though if I'd been able to, I would have been happier choosing a dagger to my heart than to have her read me verses in an exalted tone that had nothing to do with me and even less to do with her, except as hollow bricks for erecting her self-image. I closed my eyes. She probably thought I was tired, she certainly hadn't expected such pitiful, essentially non-existent communication. In movies about the paralyzed this isn't how it looks. They blink and blink and everybody understands. I tried to defend myself with my eyelids as best as I could, but my ears I couldn't close, no, they let in the fractured verses that split me in half. No horror could have hurt me more, I barely exist as it is, my body has been ground up, my soul displaced, and at a certain level I have become used to having other people dress me, wipe up my shit, handle me roughly. However the beauty of the poetry, the words linked with such extremely polished insight, wounded me deeply. I didn't look at her anymore. While she was reading about apples in a foreign city, about August, about a moment of round and shining freedom, I was erasing all my memories of her, all I remembered, preserving only one, the time I told her about you, that memory should stay. She was the first person I confided in, this was poor judgment on my part, I'd been drawn in by her inauthentic breadth of spirit—an artificially created illusion that she was capable of understanding complexity and life's depth—that brought me that sunny afternoon to her apartment. She listened to me open-mouthed, very pleased, she said this had never happened to her before, but she understood how everything is possible, what mattered most was that I am happy and who cares what other people think. Then, in the end, after we'd finished off the last drops of the pelinkovac, after I'd left my armor at the door, after so longing for a friend I'd finally felt something breaking free inside me, she asked, giggling, "But hey, aren't you going to miss cock?"

Maybe I really did drop off to sleep, I don't know how much time passed, but when I opened my eyes, she was gone, the books were gone, the dark had begun creeping into the room and the ceiling was in its twilit variation. My worldly possession.

# 10.

You, too, ended up with no worldly possessions. I became
aware of this on the morning when I helped you pack up after
they released you from the hospital. You got up slowly, you
were feeble, only a few days had passed since the operation and
only a few hours since they'd removed the drains from your
armpit. Open holes remained, direct passageways into you.
You moved like an old man, your hands moved, robot-like,
slowly and away from your body, you struggled to pull on your
sweater, but under the tense grimaces on your face, under that
first sheath of physical pain, a light was breaking through, a
new smile. With slow steps you went over to the nurse's station for them to write your discharge letter, and I swept into
a plastic bag the crumbs of cookies, the blackened banana, the
moist wipes from the nightstand. Your mother brought you all
that. She showed up and talked for a long time about problems
at work, you asked her to help you, rub you down a little with
the moist wipes because you weren't supposed to bathe yet. This
was strange for both you and her. She hesitated to touch your
bare skin, and you said with a hollowness in your voice: "I can't
recall her touch, I can't recall it from before." She rubbed your
back while staring at the metal legs of the bed. After she pulled
your tee shirt down over the bandage, she remained another

68

minute, two, and then left. I retrieved your slippers from under the bed, I opened the cupboard you used, I took out the shirt you were wearing that morning when you came alone to the room. I was ill, running a fever and full of anxiety, maybe I was also feeling a little uncomfortable, loving you had pulled to the surface all that was pathetic and cowardly in my nature, I left you by the entrance to the hospital. From the shirt wrapped up in a ball on the floor fell a bra. It wasn't a proper one, it was a sports top, two sizes too small, the armor you lived in from your earliest youth, we called your bras "black devils," there were also gray and white ones you wore under lighter-colored T-shirts and white undershirts.

Once you called to me from behind the shower curtain: "Could you please pass it to me!" "What?" I didn't catch what you'd said right away. "The black devil!" you shot off in the direction of the top that was lying there, black, on the washing machine. So we wouldn't have to use the word, we had the devils. So it was that you found yourself losing many of your belongings, and even though you hated them, when you lost them you lost your past and never again would you have the right to claim it. No matter how awful it might have been, your past was you and you were it. Your childhood days were etched into your being. They were days filled with anguish but also with growth, with the carefree spirit particular to children whom life has exposed to unfathomable pain, but also they were days of little victories, with strides that finally brought you to where you are today. In one small part, this past of yours was built on the us we found right at the very moment when you were ripping yourself up inside, getting ready to emerge through your skin, mucus, blood, and stitches. Everything leading up to the moment of transformation was supposed to be soaked in gasoline and set on fire so that for once, the grass would grow up green, and later, entranced by the most beautiful living green, nobody would ask what lay beneath. But I didn't have the heart to jettison our past into the depths. So I preserved the images that made us what we were from our first days. When we sunned on secluded beaches in summer, when I rubbed your back with sunscreen, when I tucked my fingers between the edges of the straps on the black devils and your skin, when I kissed you along the transitions in the shading of your suntan. When I held a towel around you so you could change, but we were wobbly and a little groggy from the sun so both of us almost tipped over, you were tangled up, trying to strip off the black devil, and I choked with laughter, trying to hold back a spurt of pee so I crouched and in the end heaved the towel at your head. We looked like two maniacs in front of the families with children, in front of the chiseled bodies, in front of the need to be a perfect man, a perfect woman, perfectly superficial. When I watched you from the rocks on the shore as you stood knee-deep in the sea, two months before the operation, that last summer of your larval stage, with a plastic frisbee in your hand and a grin that summoned me. From afar I could see how the drops of water gleamed on your skin, how your wet and lustrous black slicked hair glistened, how alone you were in front of the boundless seascape, how you stood there like a marine demigod, radiating beauty, fear, and awe. And then I thought, I'll never be able to describe you as I truly see you, and I'll always feel sad about that. Maybe you were the most beautiful to me then, maybe that's when we loved each other the most.

For almost a year you didn't let me lie across your chest and caress you. If I started to move in that direction you'd take my hand and lower it to your belly. Only sometimes, late at night, when we'd come closer than close, when the whole world went still and nobody alive could hear us, you'd nod when I said in my softest voice: "But I love it all so much, all that's you." And then you'd add from the dark, "You are a very strange girl," which always angered me, maybe because that very feeling of wholeness we had was what felt the most normal to me. Today, when other people are getting to know you as a young, attractive, talented man, a photographer, when they ask about your remarkable work, about the rays of light you capture in your lens as if instead of an eye you have a magic globe, when they ask you something about yourself, you're a person without a past. Full of generalized stories about growing up in a small town, the younger brother you roughed up, leaving home early, your grandfather's Leica camera that gave you a window onto the world, a world hidden beneath the world and which, with your dislocated point of view, you drew into the right angles of photography. This is more or less all you have to say about yourself. A greedy cast-iron stove reduced to ash all those years filled with  wrong ways of responding to your surface, your stabs at retraining yourself to fit into the gears of  other peoples' expectations, all the black devils you strapped yourself in with until you were out of breath, vanishing into the chasm of the non-existent, along with your childhood fantasies at your grandmother's house when you dreamed you'd wake up one day in your right body, and how at the age of twenty-five you'd be sitting under a tree with your girlfriend, with a moustache, sipping Coca-Cola.

Smoke devoured all of it. You are without a past, I, without a future. You are standing now in another sea, less vast, less terrifying, no black devil, with slender lines of scars across your heart, which, and only now I can see this, you can sport as a badge of courage from the goriest battle. If I could, I'd tell you, don't hide. But now I'm afloat in the dark of the hospital night. I am letting the scenes that live inside me flood the verges of my consciousness like pleasant waves without end, without wanting, I have separated me from myself and am allowing my life to live. I think I'll die tonight, I feel I'm forgiving them all, but isn't exasperation what keeps us alive?

# 11.

"Good morning, sunshine!" she says in a joyful voice and leans over me though I haven't yet even opened my eyes. Sunshine, that's what I was years ago, in lower school, when I brought home a certificate for good comportment, with the comment, "never any problems with her." If I'm being addressed like this, something remarkable must have happened, apparently I haven't died, maybe my condition is so stable that my next bed will be in Mama's living room, the room with the chandelier and its four downward-facing cup-shaped shades, my castle with its elevating backrest, with the mattress encased in crinkly plastic sheeting, with apparatuses of gleaming metal that will always hold me in life, even after everyone I know has died off. My tower high above the ground from which I'll never again descend, and every two months she'll trim the hairs that keep stubbornly growing from my resting head. Her breath smells of coffee and cigarettes, a smell I recall from childhood, which I used to love so much that it would transport me to a state of elation. Now I hold my breath and refuse to crack open my eyes. The defiance of my eyelids has remained the sole remnant of my identity that can be manifested outside of the shell in which I live. When it dwelt in an ambulatory package, my selfhood interested her hardly at all and now, chances are, it interests her even less. The ways I have found to rebel against her have invariably been smothered through a combination of her bitterness toward me, the sorrow I provoke in her by being who I am, and the guilt this brings for me, which has always ended up spitting on my ridiculous attempts at emancipation. The precepts that guided her became the measure of my horizon. In formal and legal terms, once I came of age I was no longer owned by her, but I walked the world bounded by the sentences she had been pounding in with her velvet hammer, one by one, along the perimeters of my being from the age of baby talk. Ever since her lucky break, since I've been lying here, it says on paper that she is in charge of me, but I can protect myself with my eyelids and I see, especially when they're lowered, into the very core of her being, woven of a fear that has the density and flammability of petroleum, a shame that guides every step she takes even before her foot hits the ground, an envy that devours her flesh from within. Envy of all those who are built differently, who are not shaped by fear and shame. "He's coming this week for a visit!" Gleeful though still holding back, she declares this near my ear. First I think she's referring to you, but it hits me that this tone of voice cannot belong to anything that has to do with you. The indeterminate someone she is speaking of so solemnly, half in trepidation and half in saint-like adoration and rapture, can only be Tomislav, son and brother. Once a slimy little lump emerges from its mother's womb and between its legs it has that nubbin of dangling flesh, the aura hovering over the brand new baby boy is similarly rapturous. For instance, when I was born, as Mama told it, there was nothing dangling between my legs, but instead I had a bump on my forehead, a largish one, resulting from difficulties during the birth. My father's mother—a dry, unfeeling, and vulgar old woman whom I recall scrubbing me so hard with a snotty handkerchief that the skin around my mouth chafed red—was already sorely aggrieved that her daughter-in-law had given birth to a girl. Since there was no way to hide the bump, and its shrinking couldn't be hastened, with her belly still warm and her perineum freshly stitched, my young mother pleaded with the on-duty doctor to explain to the malicious old woman that the bump was not a malformation or a sign of mental retardation. If the baby had been my brother instead of me, a fuss would have been made over how best to help him, feeling a little sorry for him along the way. The night before I came into the world, my grandmother announced: "In this house there is room for only two women, one to do what she is told, and the other to command and take charge when there are no men around." Even before I came, these positions were occupied. To her great disappointment, a bumpy female head arrived and with disdain she scrutinized first the head and then Mama, and once more she drove home my mother's failure and her own superiority: "If I were to give birth a hundred times over, I'd give birth to a son every single time." We ran behind all those sons, brothers, and grandsons, their shadows. Our childhoods were formed and invaded by their imaginations. Racing for their approval, we competed furiously in following the path they left us, no matter how pathetic it might have been. What we did as children, we went on doing as adults.

Like the mark my brother made and then boasted of before a holiday dinner back when the two of us were still communicating, arguing mostly but, nevertheless, talking. He and his new wife, while on vacation in Prague at one of the hotels, sneered at the Czech hicks, will you look at their haircuts, their language sounds so ridiculous, how gullible they are, even though they're more affluent than we are, they're more pitiful, dense, inferior. So, every morning, my brother, to make his mark, would take a shit in the toilet in their room before he left for the day, and he wouldn't flush. Then he and his new wife would sit in one of the Prague cafés and howl like hyenas with laughter, picturing the maid who'd find the massive feces waiting there for no one else but her to clean. He didn't plant his shit next to the toilet bowl, not that, he couldn't have people thinking he was a psychopath or report him, no, he did so decently, but leaving an unambiguous message. He was a superior being and the woman who cleaned would have to be aware of the difference between them.

At the dinner table his new wife simpers as if this story makes her uncomfortable, but I know it doesn't, I see by the expression on her face that she's proud of her husband and I see her eyes shine at his violence and stupidity. The rest of the time she smokes, stares blankly, and does what she's told. Mama can't make up her mind, she shakes her head, she finds this a little distasteful but, like in a fairy tale I once read about a serpent bride, Mama has no choice but to accept her daughter-in-law such as she is, she can do nothing but join in, opt for her own distaste instead of a life without her son. I get up from the table and go to the bathroom. I flush the toilet, I sit on the edge of the tub and feel my gorge rise. I choke down the bile, go out into the hallway and pretend to be talking with someone on my cell phone, I signal with a wave that something urgent has come up and I leave. I work to cleanse myself of the blot of his feces; I think about the woman coming every morning to work a job that barely allows her survival—after she has seen her children off to school, after she has pulled together dinner for today from what was left over yesterday, after she is criticized every day for all that can be ascribed to female failings—and then she finds the feces left by my brother, a young man who takes a crap on others for fun. I imagine how her life sickens her and I'm conscious of every nuance of pointless pain and anguish in this world, which he has made only worse. I am also aware of why my father is not here. Ever since I'd known him, he had been enveloped, more than anyone, though he was taciturn and withdrawn, in a thick web of nerve endings protruding through his skin. There are times when I think he knew everything, that this was clear to him from the start, that precisely for this reason things couldn't have ended differently than they did, but perhaps I am projecting my own traits onto him, perhaps I only want to belong to someone, to know how I came to be who I am. The features of his face are blurred by now, but a picture keeps coming back to me, they only showed us once, he is kneeling on a deserted basketball court under the hoop, on a taut rope. He could have stood up.

By chance I open my eyes, I've been awake for a while now, they inadvertently pop open and I see Mama and her face—radiant, dreaming of bringing her family together around her again. Sure, for only half an hour, sure, in a hospital room, and with a daughter who is closer to mummy than woman, but the precious idyll of the family portrait, the gathering, no matter how we treat one another, ranks high on the scale of values. Even Tomislav will make the effort, now that he has found God, as sometimes happens to people at the extremes, people lacking the courage to be comfortable in themselves and the uncertainty of life, and so it seems that after his outrageous behavior he has met the Almighty God—an ornery one, with a penchant for bizarre rules. I believe he has acknowledged me again as his sister in His name; I believe he's doing all he can do to face my immobile, ugly body; I believe He has given my brother the strength for this, because Tomislav would never have been able to manage it on his own. Just as God gave him the strength to stand, with flushed face, last spring, by a booth in the center of town, plucking people by the sleeve, urging them to sign a petition that would legally define you, my love, as sick, brand you as a degenerate, lower status, dehumanized in every possible way. He sought to brand you as someone thanks to whom people can feel superior, people cannot face themselves without the help of God. Glory to him. Family Day has been declared, for the first time in a while I see she cannot elude true joy, so vast and sincere that she cannot hide it. Somewhere deep inside she is profoundly aware that my immobility has brought her back to life.

This knot that holds us together is the dark heart of the family, which I have spent the better part of my life trying to escape. And the harder we tug the ends of our ropes as we flee, the smaller, tauter, tighter the knotted heart becomes. The ropes slash painfully across our palms, if we tug hard enough, they may snap and we'll finally be free, but left with no heart. This is why you and I kept feeling our way back along the ropes and worked at untangling the snarls. When you talked about your family, I'd hear mostly things having to do with Irena; you'd talk about your brother too, but differently. "My constant was my brother. Whom I systematically tormented. Probably because I envied him. I know I loved him a lot and always stood up for him, I

78

often beat up other kids when they teased him, but I beat him up, too. There was a lot of violence in the family. They hit us a lot. Nothing or scarcely anything was resolved with words, more often with a wooden spoon, a belt, hands, and endless yelling. Worst of all are all, those ugly words that were always used. My mother to my father, he to her, she to us, we among ourselves . . . always. Now I see that along with this I acquired no insights from them. Our mother was always obsessed with appearances. In my head I was forever hearing: 'What do you look like?' The first thing that occurs to me when I think back to growing up is: 'You aren't good enough and you're always pretending.' So you have to prove yourself. First that you, too, can do everything they do, as boys. You see that you and they are the same, but it's like you belong elsewhere. The girls, with whom you clearly have nothing in common. You do not share a single interest, they don't like anything you like, so it's tricky to communicate. They absolutely trample you. So you are afraid of them and stay away. With the boys it's super because they play soccer, play war, a thousand things, but you don't belong there either. Because even though you love all that, it's not who you are. And they're constantly reminding you. The boys think you're great up till the moment when they decide they have something to settle among themselves that isn't for girls. And then abruptly, you're out. The point is that somebody else always controls the story, your place, your freedom. Each thought or action you have must pass through an approval apparatus. You always aspire to be good enough for someone but you are absolutely, constantly under threat. Of course, along with this comes sensitivity. So someone's bad day is seen as your failure or as if you did something wrong and hurt that person.

"I remember my attempts at re-educating myself. When I think about this, I feel it was all for my mother. We were in Čakovec visiting our grandparents, and before the visit my mother and I were in Helin, this shit store for clothes. I really liked loose cuts in kids' clothing when I was little, skater style, that's what was cool for me. And then there, at that lunch, something playful inside me said: 'Why not try that green jacket with the fur trim? Maybe I should start dressing like a girl. Why is that so bad? Wow, why maybe I could be as pretty as a girl . . .' And here we come up against a problem. Whenever I thought about my beauty as a 'girl' it didn't ring true. I couldn't see it. The expected beauty never passed muster. Not in pictures of me or what was inside me. If you don't have beauty, there is no social life, especially in primary school. You have to be cool there, we all know that. Of course, they always teased me: 'So are you a boy or a girl?' That really hurt. I don't know why. I don't know which side of me was hurting. And so goes the story of the total gray zone of belonging. You're good to the girls up to a point because you're a little odd and you're a lot like a boy, yet as far as category goes, you belong to them, so they, again, are the ones who decide. But they speak a strange language you can't figure out and mostly it hurts you. They were quite nasty in the way they went about things. The boys started coming on to you more and more because they were discovering their own bodies and you don't belong there anymore, as a part of that whole thing. You start liking girls. Innocently. Like, she's so pretty. But you know that's impossible. There was no talk about homosexuality back then, but if someone told a person you're a fag or a lesbo, that was the worst disease, one you definitely didn't want to have."

# 12.

When they knocked out my two front teeth during those first days—I was suffering from trismus, a spasmodic clenching of the jaw—to introduce a plastic catheter tip into my mouth that helped me breathe at first, I saw him standing right there next to the bed. It was rough going, I had healthy front teeth with long, sturdy roots. The doctor's face flushed and swelled, someone grunted and swore, men's hairy hands flashed by my gaping mouth, and then a sound broke through like when a half-sawed tree comes crashing down in the forest. A sound that lets everyone know something that was healthy and strong is snapping, something that ought to be standing upright, alive. I think I fainted from the sound and the pain. When I opened my eyes again he was lying right there on the bed next to me. He was naked to the waist, young, my age, with a hole in his belly the size of a newborn baby. He laughed softly, looking at me, and asked whether I'd seen the little chicks coming out of the hole, he thinks they skittered off under the bed. I tried to get up and look around for the yellow fluff balls. By some miracle I managed to clamber out of bed. I crouched on the floor and began peering into all the corners of the room. I wanted to find at least one little chick to make him happy, so I could ask him why he hadn't told me anything, why he hadn't straightened his legs and stood up. Night was falling and his face grew darker, it became sadder and sadder as I rolled around on the dirty linoleum, but I couldn't see much anymore. They must have caught them all, he said absently, I tried to persuade him that maybe the chicks had run out onto the corridor. We could ask the nurse to search for them. I felt we had to find them, otherwise all would be ruined. I was scared that because of the lost chicks he might do again what he did before and leave me with no answers. "I saw how they were carrying boxes full of chicks and they chirped so loudly, then they cast them into this huge funnel where they ground them up and then their juice poured out into vertical pipes," he said. "Don't go," I managed to say. He didn't answer; in his eyes I saw I was losing him.

At first, I hallucinated frequently, the images were so alive that for months afterward I couldn't tell what had been real. I saw Daddy more often than anyone. And he was always lying next to me, in my room. This was a familiar image. It came from a time at the beginning of the war when Tomislav and I spent four months each year with him at the Krapina spa, a hot spring. He managed to recover somewhat while we were together. Before all that, there was the morning when the on-duty student came to fetch me from class and take me to see the school counselor. All heads turned to watch as the teacher escorted me out. I was excited and a little happy to be getting out of class. I didn't realize this had to do with him. He had been off at the front for two weeks already, but he called us pretty regularly. When they took me to the counselor's office, Mama was standing there, awash in tears, and my ashen brother, on whose face I noticed right then, maybe because he was so pale, maybe because I was con- centrating on not looking at her, the tentative, black whiskers he had started to grow. Mama hugged me and said we had to go see Daddy, that he'd been wounded and they didn't know if they'd be able to make him better. Out in front of the school there was an olive-drab car waiting for us that drove us to the hospital. He was lying there, all bandaged up, around him spread the smell of iron and urine, I didn't want to come closer, but then again, I wanted to hug him. His only reaction to us being there was raspier breathing. In the days that followed we learned that he'd been "shot through with shrapnel like Swiss cheese," as the doctor said. In the months that followed we learned he'd come down with hepatitis C along with the entire volunteer corps, which was among the first to engage in defensive action. Of the thirty of them who'd stumbled into the ambush, only ten made it out alive. The wounded received blood transfusions tainted with hepatitis because there hadn't been time to test the blood supply, so on top of their becoming invalids they were plagued with this permanent affliction. Of the ten, today scarcely three are still alive. Of the seven who died, four of them, including Daddy, chose their own death. My stays among the maimed, wounded men, among the smashed glasses and the bar where the janitors with purple noses cleaned up every morning, among the children whose limbs had been blown up by shells and who were my only friends there, these stays were where I spent most of my school vacations. Lying on the black, inflated tires the children floated on the pool, and I pushed them and turned them around. I quickly got used to the rounded, red stumps of their limbs, there was no difference between us until we saw the pitying gazes of other people. "That's enough, Lucija, let them be, you can see they can't do everything you can do," the nurse would say, without realizing they could do what I could do if only they'd wanted to. Then their eyes would go dull, and I'd leave and kick around the compound's abandoned playgrounds on my own. Maybe this was a mysterious forecast of my own finale, here in the hospital bed for long-term treatment and palliative care, but at the time, with great interest and a feeling of intimacy, I lay on the edge of Daddy's bed and watched the world around me. The patches of flesh of different colors, the stitches, the deformed bodies, they are all around us, we just like to pretend they aren't, as if their differentness is a punishment, sin, or misfortune they deserve and we, too, could catch it.

You stand on the cold tiles in the bathroom, for the first time you are going to have to change the dressing by yourself. I am standing outside the door in the hallway, I want to help, I knocked twice already, but all I can hear is the buzz of the fan. Until now you've only let me see the bandages, you're afraid of how I'll react, most of all you're worried about whether you'll be repulsive, weird, unattractive. "Fine, come on in," you say with a somber ring. I open the door slowly, I notice you've turned out the light above the mirror and you're looking at your feet. You're standing in profile, short sharp sutures protrude through your skin, you've been stitched horizontally across the middle of your chest, with a short break between the incisions, but the real wound yawns open across your whole body. I come up behind you carefully, run my hand slowly over your shoulder blades, move on to the shoulders, all the way to your collar bone, I turn you toward me. For the first time I see you naked, though you're dressed from the waist down, everything is for the first time, though you still can't feel touch on much of your chest. But because of this first time, everything from before is gone, erased. Your attempts at finding intimacy as others have pressured you to, all the rough treatment you've suffered with as a person who is different and so deserves such treatment, the bruises on your back left from when you tried to be "normal" so you let a kid from juvenile hall press you up against a wall at the back of the little park. The only boy who ever wanted to be with you, when I asked what he was like, you said: "He killed his younger brother with a shotgun, by mistake." I erase all of that with the tips of my fingers. "This doesn't disgust you?" you ask, I don't want to speak, I smile. I lift your T-shirt, with one hand I unclasp the bra on your back, the tightness releases, I lean tenderly against your skin. We look at each other for a while.

Those first days, I don't know whether I was hallucinating or not, I saw you next to the bed. You were somehow unreal, your eyes were red, and there were purple flowers growing out of them that probably weren't real. I remembered them from a poem. But the touch I felt on my face, careful and always imbued with a certain fear that you'd squeeze me too hard, I'd swear even now, that touch was real. Were you here, did you know I could tell? Do you know I tried to tell you?

# 13.

"Whoa, are you squeezing your pussy so tight 'cuz you think we're out to snatch it?" guffaws Ružica and tries to spread my stiff legs as if I'm squeezing them on purpose. Buddy laughs and with his fat fingers he unrolls the clean diaper while his belly bounces around near my head. Suddenly from behind his back appears the doctor who entered the room unnoticed a moment before. A pulse oximeter is attached to my finger, the apparatus starts to go wild, and, noticing the frequency, she snaps: "Get out, both of you out! Right now!" Ružica and Buddy get serious, they flip me professionally and quickly start putting on the diaper, but the doctor won't allow even that and yells so loud that her voice cracks: "I said, now!" They leave, crestfallen, without finishing their job. The doctor sighs deeply. I am half naked, concerned about my condition as much as I can be, the moment lasts a long time, then she pulls up a chair from the corner of the room and sits down nearby. Her eyes are sad and moist. We look inside each other, I see that deep in my pupils she is seeking a well of reason, and I do everything I can to sustain that thought, even if I can use no words. I feel the cold air moving over my lower abdomen and, as if she reads my thoughts, she stands up and bends over me. I am confused by the sincere tenderness I feel on my skin, she slips her soft hands under my bottom, arranges the diaper neatly, and firmly but comfortably, fastens it with the adhesive strips. Then she pulls down my nightie and smoothes its edges and covers me lightly with the sheet. I gaze into her pupils to see what happened. She raises the level of the top half of the bed and asks me, "Is it good like this?" I blink once. Whatever you do is good. "A little higher?" "Yes," I blink once more. Today she doesn't have eyeliner on, just a little black mascara and pink blush on the tops of her cheekbones. Her lips are chewed and pale, her big blue eyes wander around my body, I cringe at the thought of how she sees me. Although she's looking me over closely, it's as if she's not engaged with my exterior, but is continuing our conversation. "You understand everything that's happening?" "Yes, I understand," I answer. Again she sighs and in a fraction of a second I can see there's something pulling her two ways, I see her making a decision, a decision that has not been well thought out or considered for a long time, but is deeply rooted in her intuition. "I'd like to help you, I think you could be doing better." I don't know if this is a question, but my vocal cords respond for the first time in months with a startling sound that comes from my dry, raspy throat. I gurgle as if I'll choke, and then with all the force of my body I articulate something that sounds as if it is coming from the dawn of the cognitive revolution, from the birth of the most important desire in the universe. The desire to communicate. The doctor is surprised, she smiles and gives a slight nod. "I know a young speech therapist, we could bring her in for a time, maybe a few months, to help you a little, so you can find a way to communicate. Would you like that?" I blink, I raise the blinds. "And we can crank up the physical therapy, too. But first I want to know what you want and with whom." This last sentence of hers doesn't make sense to me, how can I tell her that I don't get it, I don't get it, ma'am, what I can want and with whom, I don't. She stops the flow of my thoughts and goes on: "Your mother is very concerned about you and she is making a huge effort to learn everything she can about your condition, to overcome the bureaucratic and technical obstacles, to have you moved to home treatment. But I am not so sure, having watched this, that her efforts with you are producing results." She halts and is tentative, chooses her words, come on, Doctor, you get it, my mother doesn't care much about my wishes, she's happiest with her big newborn baby who, of course, requires a great deal of care, a lot of time and attention, but what a baby offers in return is invaluable. Needs to attend to all day long in an otherwise empty life. A medal of good motherhood that shines to the skies, that is why, Doctor, you're right. She found life with me before much harder than it is with me like this. And that I can't speak has turned out far better than she dared hope, this has turned out to be just a regrettable turn of events, not yet another disgrace for her to bear. I transmit to the doctor my flood of thoughts, and there is a decent chance that she understands them, but even if she does, what other options do I have? What. Other. Options?

The answer to each of these questions is like the story about the wrinkle in the bedding under my back when they are sloppy in getting me ready for bed in the evening and when I have to put up with the pain all night long. People have no idea, ordinary people who shift their position forty times on average during a night of sleep, what it's like spending an entire night lying motionless, your thinned skin pocked with bedsores, on a folded lump. It's as if you're lying atop a mountain chain. So until morning you moan inside and wait for Buddy and Ružica, and when they open the door it's as if you've caught sight of God and you're so happy that you'd even like to laugh at their jokes about your squeezed pussy, because then, in another minute or two, they'll smoothe the Alps under your back, and after so many hours of torment they'll change the position of your body and everything will be dandy. These are my options.

She seems to see my mood darken, my gaze wander and she decides to explain and be concrete. "Okay, in the beginning, when they first brought you in for intensive care, a young man, Dorian, came to visit you two or three times." The traitorous monitors go wild and she realizes she is on the right track, that in addition to losing the possibilities of movement, speech and control over all other bodily functions, I have been denied an important part of my world. "Fine, fine, steady now," she says in a soothing voice. She continues, "I was wondering about this, I'll tell you what I know, then we'll see how to proceed. At first you didn't react, we couldn't establish what the extent was of the damage to your brain, until that day we assumed you were comatose. Afterward they moved you in here, during one of his visits I saw your mother and him arguing in the corridor, in fact I interrupted them, and then he left, and when I asked her what that was about, she said he is a problematic man with whom you used to be in a relationship, an odd one, he was sometimes aggressive and she didn't want him near you. He calls sometimes and asks about you but because of what your mother told us, we don't give him much information." Now she is no longer looking into my eyes, I know she can't bear to, I push her with my gaze fixed on her shoulder, I plead with her to find me, I want her to grasp how huge this is. "Would you like to see him?" I blink. Immediately. Clearly. Then I start to cry, I blink twice, I don't want him to see me like this. Then once, because he has already seen me. She lays her hand on my arm, fine, slow down, we'll work this out. We are silent, at the bottom of a pool of powerlessness. Then she gets up and opens a little cupboard door and from there she takes out a small clean towel. She runs water over it and soaks it for a long time. She waits for the warm water to come so that when she presses it on my face it won't be cold and unpleasant. She gently rubs my forehead, eyes, rests it against my cheeks, lips, squeezes a drop of water into my mouth. I'm grateful to her, there are two groups of people in the world, two groups that are more inclusive than all the rest, whether ethnic, religious, or gendered: those who assume that people who are paralyzed don't care whether you use the same towel to wipe their face and their ass, and those who get it that in that little piece of cloth lies the essence of human dignity. She opens the other drawers, finds the hairbrush, brings it to my head and I can see that she's dismayed, but nevertheless she brushes me. She notices that I've noticed this so she says out loud what she is thinking: "I'll bring a hairdresser by one day to clean you up, your hair is really thick." It's as if I can feel it on my shoulders, its weight, how fragrant it is after being shampooed twice, you can barely push through it, there, by the neck, your whole face is buried in the long, wiry, buoyant tresses, you push your face in, here, you say, this is where I'd like to live.

# 14.

And then there were times when I was a royal pain. The circle of people we hung out with, especially at first, was small. There were two, three who knew we were together and accepted us without reservation. Two of them were Olja and Dijana. You met them as part of the "Remembering the Victims of War" project when you spent several months photographing elderly women and men in half-ruined homes on the margins of our country. Both women worked at a center for trauma treatment, Dijana as an attorney and Olja as projects coordinator, on the frontlines of the battle against forgetting. They signed you on right away, as soon as you sent them your work. In the photographs you submitted they saw that you could see and that was enough for them. They were a few years older than us, they lived with Olja's mother and two dogs, and walked around town arm in arm. No, it hadn't been easy for them to reach that point, we got to know them when they had already torn down all the obstacles. At first, they hid like everyone else. Friends. In their strolls through town, on summer vacations, at the movies, at twilight on their walk home, only when nobody was looking, love, in a dark entranceway, fingers entwined, a quick kiss on the neck. On Monday everyone at the office talks about where they were with their partner or family over the weekend, where they went out, why they had a spat, how they made up, but you say nothing. You have no one, though you live in the same world, sometimes marvelous, sometimes ugly, every bit as human, and you'd be glad to share it with them, but you have no right to the little things that make a life. Taken from you are your family, the Sunday dinners, the quarrels about the dust, the sag in the sofa you created together that doesn't exist in the real world. You're the one talked about in hushed tones. Then one day Dijana said she'd had enough, she didn't want to spend her life like this, then Olja's mother threatened to kill herself. There was a lot of drama, she didn't kill herself, but she did get cancer. Watch out what you wish for. She had only Olja, whom she'd slapped multiple times before Olja's twentieth birthday over girlfriends, I know what you are up to with them, called her a freak several times before she turned thirty-five, but when the cancer came for her, the freak-show changed. Dijana had a good job and a few other gigs on the side, she was a respected attorney, smart, emotionally and socially savvy, dedicated, and not the slightest bit devious. If you have a little luck, sometimes that is enough for you to make your way. She showed up in front of Olja's mother's apartment, Olja chewed her lips until they bled, wringing from herself the guilt that she carried about her mother's cancer, something she had never admitted to anyone. Dijana marched straight into the living room, stopping in front of the sofa on which the gaunt, wiry woman was lying under a blanket, while in her lungs abnormal growths were multiplying. Dijana sat down next to her, Olja stood in the corner of the room, her eyes red, like the twelve-year-old girl who had spent the whole summer in Tučepi chasing two-years-older Natasha, fatally in love with Natasha's bangs that came right down to her eyelashes and her suntan lotion. Olja already knew for herself that she wasn't normal, that she was sick and that one day her mother would get sick because of her. Dijana asked her: "How are you doing?" and Olja's mother glanced, confused, over at her daughter in the corner of the room. Dijana took out a little bottle of hemp oil she had brought from Slovenia and a file with papers setting out a treatment plan from the best clinic for lung cancer in Sremska Kamenica. A specialist had examined her case closely, much more serious cases had recovered, all she had to do was pack up her things by the day after tomorrow, the two of them would take her and they'd get a hotel room for the next two weeks, as long as the cycle of therapy took. Mama's face began to crumble, the nearness of what inevitably lay ahead came back to her like the slap, she couldn't lift her head, her gaze moved across her arms, legs, feet, and wherever she looked she felt she was seeing something freakish. She only nodded and said, softly: "All right." Dijana stood, went over to Olja, still there in the corner, hugged her, though not as a friend, and announced to them both: "Now Olja and I will have coffee and you'll have a green tea." The cancer retreated, the transformation was correct and complete, Mama went back to her violin, and Dijana and Olja to their shared jobs and plans, and there was no longer anyone who could hold back their hands when they walked through town.

I often waited for you out in front of their office, then, once, Dijana invited me in. I still felt guilty, it's difficult to explain why or maybe it's too easy. Truthfully, I would have liked it to be more complicated than it actually was, that way I'd be less petty than I am. I was ashamed of myself, even in front of them, who had been bearing this stigma their whole lives. "Come on in,

Lucija, no need to freeze out there. Dorian will be done in five minutes, it's just something we need to go over for the show," Dijana said in a lighthearted voice, drawing me in by the hand. Tall, dark short hair, and an openhearted brow, she radiated the kind of appeal possessed by people who are upfront with themselves and those around them, no matter what price they paid for it. Olja was her opposite—blonde and shy, quiet and steadfast; her unobtrusiveness transformed everything she set her heart on. While Olja was full of bleak forebodings, dread and darkness, these bloomed in Dijana's eyes like sparklers, their only residue being memory and laughter. Dijana carried Olja's jacket, kept track of her cell phone, organized whatever was needed, while from one year to the next Olja saved dozens of people whom the entire country was bent on forgetting. You still had half of your wait to go, with several months left before the operation, you were eager to change your documents and were given your first dose of hormones at around that time. We were often in tears, every day someone hurt you, every day you asked someone not to speak to you in the wrong way, frustrated by the feeling that your happiness and integrity depended on the good will and judgment of others. When you spoke to a woman behind the counter at a bakery, a teller at a bank window, your voice dropped and you'd assume a pose that turned you into a heavy stone block and, yet, there was no question of your gender though sometimes they spoke to you as someone younger and unimportant. Your friends had the knack of forgetting, or they'd rely on habit, punching you in the gut just when you managed to stand up straight. Some were confused, I'd close my eyes and hold my breath each time you told me how you'd told so-and-so not to address you the wrong way. I'd steal a glance at your face and couldn't discern what other people saw. Again and always, for me, you are just incredibly good-looking.

When I first saw you, I recognized the pain you held. Diagonally, across a whole room, you were sitting at a table, quiet yet alive, more alive than anyone else around you. As if the world were in black-and-white and you were the only person in color. Our gazes met and lingered a second longer than expected, a spark touched my mind, I wanted to get closer to you. It was a Saturday night, that early, chilly summer, three weeks before the park bench, before nature came. We were at a jazz concert in the cellar of a club, gazes flashed over the heads, through the cracks between the bodies, your company was boisterous and large, while I was bored by the women I knew from university. When we connected, the thread went taut and pulled us out in front of the club, onto the road. At two in the morning, we went out for a smoke, I bummed a cigarette off of you, you said, how many do you need, we laughed, giddy, you began to sing "My Funny Valentine," you climbed onto a hollow brick on the street, I stood below you, the cheering audience, your trench coat cast a shadow on all that had already happened and what was to come, I thought, good God, where did you come from, what's this crack that your embers are glowing through, then this boy came out, said, "Doks, girl, what the fuck, where the fuck did you go with those cigarettes," and it was like your gaze nose-dived into the abyss, a boundless sorrow took ahold of me, *here I am, fuck it, here I am*, shrieked a red darkness from inside you, the moment passed, passed forever, you thought, you stepped down off your stage where you'd blazed so splendidly for that one second, you were a little drunk, a little dead, *I am still here*, I took you by the arm, you didn't resist too much, just a little, I wanted to hold you more firmly, hey, watch out you don't fall, our faces were close, I breathed your air, then we looked long into each others' eyes, there in the middle of the street, your drunken crowd pouring out of the club, they tugged you by the coat, one winked and shouted, "Hey little girl, you'll fall," you looked at me, sorry, all of you were rolling off through the gloom, your slender, restless figure turned, the film rewound, you stuffed a slip of paper into my hand, "My cell phone has died and I'll be joining it soon, get in touch." "Of course, I will, I want to hear the rest of the concert," I wasn't wrong, this was you, I knew it, still diagonally then, for no reason at all, I recognized the pain, "Helloooo, come ooooon, damn it," they called from way down the street, but time had somehow ground to a halt, it stopped for only a few seconds on that corner, in that square meter, just long enough for us to find, in the illusion of continuity, a hole, deep, dark, with the shine of an invincible mind and in it we embraced. And that embrace in the middle of the street was the collateral for our next two years. Steady and all-powerful enough to cover everything, especially the times when I was obnoxious.

The book with your photographs came out, we went to the launch together, Martina came along with us and spent the whole evening eyeing you as if you were a butterfly stuck on a pin. The exhibit was a real occasion for people who suffered from the illusion that they were a cut above our violent and conservative society. Poseurs fighting for human rights, artists with a Facebook following, actors from the front pages of the tabloids who recorded video statements for the Center for Facing Trauma, but not without a make-up artist and a manager's blessing. Their opinion mattered more to me, it turned out that evening, than anything. I ran into old friends, kiss kiss, I lowered my purse onto the chair that stood between you and me, and you moved away. They looked you up and down with a surprised glance and then back at me, inquiring; my nonchalance arose from the most selfish pit of my personality, where I rot in fear, worried only about the lie their lips will spread further, "Oh yes, let me introduce you to my girlfriend, Dora," I laughed hard while waving around the broken rose you'd given me that evening to mark our three months. After that my friends concluded that you didn't mean much, at least to me, and they looked around for something more interesting than my girlfriend Dora who looked a little like a guy. Out of the corner of my eye I saw how you shrank during the evening, your eyes went dark and you glanced over at me less and less wonderstruck, until all that was left of you on the third chair was your oversized suit jacket with the rose I'd thoughtlessly left behind, sticking out of its sleeve. A man across the room was jabbering on loudly, talking in my direction, engaging me, trying to make me laugh and amuse me, I accepted the ambiguous signals, this is nothing serious, we'll forget each other by tomorrow, even though your photographs were featured, nobody spoke to you, so I, too, stopped. At one moment a man sat next to you and spent the rest of the evening talking to you about the price of real estate in the western part of town, and I thought, well good, at least you're finally talking with someone, now was that so hard, totally and lucidly aware that you had no interest at all in the man or in real estate. I had a little to drink and I was tipsy from the attention I was getting, a fiction I interpreted as meaning I was worth something. We got up to go to another bar, you got up when I did, you tried to help me on with my coat, I looked at you, no, don't do that, you walked a few steps behind me and carried the fucking rose. Jasna, someone I knew from the theater, inserted herself, half-drunk, between us, we'd relaxed by now so this was the moment for a heart-to-heart. You know how it is when people get drunk. So, hey, Dora, Lucija, either of you getting any action in the romance department? "Nothing here!" I declared, at the ready. I had heard a lesbo was spreading rumors about how I'd come out of the closet, and it hurt me badly, frightened me badly, what would Mama and my brother say, nothing ever again. We drank the rakija, we stood in a crowd at the bar, and you were still there, flower in hand, I had the urge to kiss you, to devour you, I had the urge to shove you out the door and never see you again. I couldn't stomach this impotence of yours, I couldn't stomach my own cowardice, I didn't want to be in or out of the closet. I had the urge to drink myself silly and then push us under a car. The manifestations of our life are entirely different from the manifestations of our internal world. This moment in which I now lie, after lightning blasted my fuse box, as urine dribbles from me without my control, as feces and blood issue from me, while I'm a mere statistic in the vestibule of death, all that I was gains color, taste, and meaning for the first time. The truth takes shape, not subjective nor objective but relational, the truth in relation to this distorted image of myself, of the relationship: this is me, I love you. One cannot penetrate the intimacy of consciousness, on the outside nothing has anything to do with anything. Thinking that is born, thinking about myself, about us, remembering us as we were, has nothing at all to do with how information is stored. I cannot reach that depth. That is why I was angry at you. I am not authentic enough. Shaped by someone else's image of my pitiful existence, I rebuffed you each time you looked over in my direction.

We were driving to your apartment, everyone had dispersed, their importance dispersed, a chasm was opening in the middle of my heart, I leaned forward and with blind eyes I studied my misshapen, disgusting face. Please, I have one request, don't ever call me your girlfriend again, you said, without looking at me.

# 15.

Someone was taken ill last night. If that is even possible to say because we are all sick all the time here. Taking ill, the continuous form of the verb. This meant commotion in the ward, the on-duty doctor was summoned, the nurses huddled in one of the rooms across the hall. They prepped me for the night in a rush and didn't remember to fully draw the dark-green curtain of mites and dust. So now, ever since daybreak there has been a golden rectangle punching me in the head. The distant star is casting its blazing light on my face and I cannot evade it. So I wait to see what will happen. Either someone will move the shade or the sun will explode—an event forecast for roughly ten billion years from now; we'll see which happens first. "Oh, damn it, the sun woke you up," says Ružica in her raspy voice. Today she is being noticeably reticent with me after the doctor chased her out of the room. She fiddles listlessly with the diapers, rubs me roughly, with brusque movements she cleans and arranges the tubes. As if I were the one who hurt her feelings, she snorts and doesn't offer her usual comments, she vents her frustration on me because of her difficult and pointless existence. Where else can she vent? She finishes up quickly and leaves the room without a word, thank you, goodbye. Soon I hear the tramp of steps in the corridor, steps from several different feet, shoes that are heavy, medium, and light with a heel are approaching my room. I hear muffled laughter. First enters Mama, acting like a child who is sneaking into a hiding place she's built by herself on an untended field behind their apartment building by piling up boards, branches, nylon bags, and assorted trash, a place where she tends to a mangy little kitten. Half proud, half anxious. The other children file in after her. The boy who thinks he's God's gift conquers the space with his pompous self, he assumes everything belongs to him and he has the right to it all. Behind them comes an airheaded little girl who builds her sense of importance at the side of a boy like him. She is convinced she is not someone who can have finer qualities and has no need for them, except lipstick on her lips and a sly toady up to those who are stronger and more aggressive. A couple from paradise, a couple from hell, Adam and Eve, stupidity and the rib, the prototype of man and woman as envisioned by one of the near-sighted authors of the most influential book on this awful place called Earth. Still, the pompous boy freezes in horror, fear, and disgust when faced with the sight of his mangy car-wreck of a kid sister. The core of this Holy Trinity is society's acquired and violent reaction to nonnormative bodies. Bodies that determine destiny. The skull of an albino child—smashed to guarantee a good harvest, skin color as the alibi for iron shackles, hips too narrow to give birth banished to the outskirts of town, paralysis of the limbs as a ticket to the sanatorium, compulsory medical intervention on babies whose future life hasn't yet begun to take shape. The scalpel for normalcy. The noose for those who don't opt for the normal. Long is the history of attempts at correcting those who don't fit in. A history built on the wooden beams of the gallows, on torture devices, in concentration camps, gas chambers, ouster to the very edge of society. Rich and varied, yet the same everywhere on Earth. My brother was swept up by it at just the right moment, there he stood on a street corner, lost, already halfway through his life's journey, without firm footing within himself, desolate and, to be fair, endlessly sad, as empty as a black hole in the universe. This time, history comes in the shape of a mob that fears you. A mob that over the years emerged from the wartime traumas of a small tribe at the edge of a jungle, a tribe that after a brief period of progress reverted quickly to instinct, to the dark age of myths awash in the fragrance of incense. My brother was given the opportunity to stand at a booth in the center of town and volunteer as a member of a movement of people who had declared themselves the guardians of moral order in society. He had the honor of gathering the signatures of citizens so he could push for a law that would abolish the rights of a minority. Lacking their own center, obsessed with the lives of other people, they launched an attack on the intimacy of others. Marriage belongs to us. They are free to register. Dijana and Olja are the target, their bond reduced by the law to a dry linguistic phrase used for regulating the ownership of a new vehicle. My brother distributed leaflets saying that we face extinction because of them, if we allow them to use our words for their relationships. My brother plucked at the sleeves of passersby and asked them to sign the petition he was holding, because if they signed it they'd be protecting their families. My brother laughed with his healthy, white teeth, he waved to people, gave balloons to children in strollers, my brother felt important and good, he was on the front line of the defense of our families and our values, he was upright and righteous, for fourteen days he battled his opponent—who was a hundredfold more threatened than he was—he fought with all he could muster, if need be he'd repeat lies thousand times. Around his neck he wore a crucifix, the rear-view mirrors of his car flaunted the checker-board insignia of the Croatian state, my brother was obsessed with the idea that if Olja's and Dijana's love were treated equally with other loves this would mean stripping our country of God and Homeland. It seemed as if the Almighty and the Homeland were so fragile that a tender caress between two women could reduce them to dust. He was fighting so that if a person as righteous as himself were to throw a rock and hit them in the back while they were walking arm in arm, the attacker would be applauded instead of being charged with a crime. "Last spring," he said, "when we showed those fags their place . . ." paved the way for years of violence. The new struggle, even greater and more vocal, this time oriented toward your minority, my love, within the minority, began at the same time as that unstoppable warmth was blossoming between us. A closeness that created rifts around us on all sides, with dense and uncalculating warmth that melted our skin and made us liquid and vulnerable, a warmth that gave rise to life itself.

"Son," Mama pats him on the cheek, consoles him while he stares at me, trying to soften his bad feelings at having to see me. "Would you like to sit for a minute," she asks him gently. He stands there as if turning to stone, Mama scrapes a chair over the floor, I can't see him clearly, but I feel his stifled energy, I feel how he can't take even one step toward the bed; broken and immobile women are the most terrifying monsters for courageous fighters like himself. He brushes her hand away roughly and goes on staring at me. His wife stands behind him, she takes a few steps in my direction, leans over the bed as if leaning over a coffin, and presses a paper tissue to her mouth. She finds me appealing, I feel it, I appeal to her the same way people rubberneck traffic accidents, horrified, yet at the same time almost erotically caught up in the wrongness of the scene. This sort of lurid fascination springs from the disjointed fantasies of people who have never outgrown early adolescence. I see straight through her, through the perfectly coiffed hair, through her little leopard-skin patterned coat and the fashion-brand handbag she is clutching with her long fingers and gel nails. I see the little girl who got stuck, who never fully grew to what she could have been, who walks through the world like an empty mirror of social reality. Ironed, superficial, malicious because of the feeling that she is missing out on something, but too lazy to make her own way. She counts on my brother, acts as if she might faint, tries to draw his attention, but he doesn't actually care about her. This is all just a game. Then it's as if she pulls herself together, opens her handbag and takes out her rosary. She drapes it over the drawer handle, without asking anyone whether that's okay, she just slips it through the handle and tugs it tight. "She's actually not in such bad shape," says Mama, uncertain, I realize her enthusiasm has faded a little because she has suddenly seen me through their eyes, on her own until now she was used to seeing me and forgot what I look like when someone is seeing me for the first time. Her comment receives no response. Tomislav sighs loudly, and all he says, through clenched teeth, is: "Fuck life," forgetting, or maybe not forgetting, that I can hear, "She should be released from this torment." Mama starts to cry, "Don't say that, Son, she is my child, too . . ." she sighs and sobs, and his wife merely stands there and stares blankly, her mind has already wandered off. The family moment isn't quite as idyllic as imagined, Mama sobs louder, and he starts snarling at her, unable to bear the picture in which he finds himself. "Come on, Mother, she's no longer alive like this." I feel for him. I am always wondering, ever since I found myself in this condition, what kind of an impact it has on people—being faced by someone's boundless isolation. To bear something like this you need to be strong as an ox. It's easier for me, the isolation is mine, in some ways now it is getting easier and easier. Mama sobs, the air becomes loud and thick, I hear light footsteps from the corridor that somehow reach my hearing. In comes my doctor. "What's going on here?" she asks gently but firmly, clearly taking my side. Mama goes on wailing, my brother turns to her and, with his usual pompous tone, asks: "What are her chances, how long can she go on like this?" I see that only now my doctor fully understands, she needs a few seconds to pull herself together, swallow her fury and disgust, and then she says to him, equally brusquely: "Sir, I must ask you to leave, your sister needs peace and quiet, she'll be fine." She stands by the door, the moment is frozen, I have the impression she is raising her arm like a switchman at a railway junction, shunting them to a side they weren't expecting: "Come on, now, all of you, out you go, please, leave. Visiting hours are over, she needs rest," she says loudly and implacably. "But we only just got here . . ." protests Mama, "and you said we can visit her whenever we like!" Her tone rises and she prepares for a fight. "From now on, that will not be possible. Please." Him first, he can hardly wait, and after him, his wife, he'll probably give them a piece of his mind, he knows what needs to be done. He should be asked.

# 16.

Your eyelids were often bloody, my love, when you woke up. A thin line of crusty blood would etch itself on you during the night like a young black moon arching over your eyes. I was startled by them when, not fully awake, I saw you in the semi-dark. The dry air and an atopic dermatitis made your skin crack along folds. Like a negative of the night sky studded with stars, the white sheets would be speckled in the morning with brown droplets. A skin disease that had an internal logic of its own. In the places where your skin needed to stretch, the blood would flow, where your skin was thin and poorly pro-tected, on your neck, in the folds of your elbow, on the silken spots above the knees, there were patches itchy to the point of madness. One morning you sat at the table with the neck of your T-shirt pulled up over your face. That was how we drank our coffee. You brought the cup to your lips from underneath, you wouldn't let me see you, but it wasn't the red skin, it was your inner struggle surfacing. "Imagine," you sometimes said, "all these people, they don't even get it that they have skin." At times you'd show up and be so decisive about never scratching yourself again that I'd believe you that instant, as if the itchi-ness weren't real, as if it was all in your mind and you could control it. All that mattered was that you must not scratch.

All that mattered was that you must not irritate. Your skin and people. This would last for two or three days, you'd remark that you were feeling so much better, like you used to, and then you'd wake up again with the bloody lines arching over your eyes. You pulled your sleeves over your wrists, so whenever we held hands there was a piece of cloth between us. You freed them only when you picked up your camera and assumed your stance behind the lens. Then you'd forget yourself; your eyes were busy seeing. I urged you to go to a dermatologist. At first, I didn't get why you were so dead set against this, there would be therapy, a salve, you'd feel better. "I will not go to a doctor," you repeated as adamantly as a sleepwalker. I thought about how stubborn you are and how you were suffering for no reason, always panicked about whether you had remembered to bring you skin cream in your backpack, because if you'd forgotten it, you'd crack clear open and bleed to death somewhere along the way. We almost fought over this, and then you said: "What if I have to take my clothes off? What then? I'm not stripping for anyone!" How immersed are we in our own reality that despite this interwoven, shared life we are incapable of seeing things through the eyes and spirit of even those we're closest to. What for me is merely a boring sit in a waiting room among people with problems who are passing time there, what for most of us is a routine gesture of pulling up our undershirt so the doctor can listen to our lungs, nothing more than proudly pointing to the place on our body that hurts and needs treatment, this, for you, is yet another betrayal of your entire being. Yet another potential humiliation mischievous nature has in store for you. Its record of your body is mixed: slender wrists, the dark little hairs above your navel, chivalric eyebrows and a powerful jaw, plump breasts and a broad back. But a clear sense of yourself. You cannot simply pull up your shirt and drop your pants; as soon as you expose yourself, they enter you, they inquire about your divided inner self, they are impolitely surprised, knead your insides, do with you whatever they like, completely forgetting the complaint that brought you there. What for most people is an unconscious gesture for you is moving mountains. "Fine," I say, "okay, my love, you don't need to go, we'll figure something out." I hug you, sheepish, aware that the cure lies elsewhere entirely, not among the skin creams on the shelf of a pharmacy. My brown specks are now much larger and more serious, bedsores are tricky to treat, especially for someone in my condition. They progress through constant pressure. Pressure that becomes so strong and intense, so smothering that the circulation of blood and oxygen is interrupted, so the skin there becomes first stiff and red, and then soft and purple. I, for instance, was red for a long time, but when I lacked air, I became purple. Those who are not capable of preventing the pressure of a hard undersurface on their flesh are constantly at increased risk of bedsores. This was a risk I already felt as a child, I was not resilient. Our tissues are able to sustain a great deal of pressure for a brief time, but if they are exposed to it for longer, lacerations begin. My bedsores had been developing for years. They weren't from this bed but had their origin a great distance away. Television and the internet, from the fliers my brother handed out. I got them from random passersby and neighbors, from former friends whose looks stopped my circulation. They arched back all the way to the worst pressures from family. Little by little, the space around me narrowed, the mattress of well-intentioned concern pressed down upon me from above and up from below, and that's how I came to be here. Treating bedsores, as is the case with treating atopic dermatitis, is expensive and time-consuming. But before this terminal phase, it wasn't always so extreme. There were brief stretches when I believed we'd make it through, when we learned to be both happy and unhappy, to be ourselves. You would come to me, abruptly roll up your sleeves and extend your arms: "Look, my love, it's gone!" Then I'd run my hand over the soft new skin and together we'd admire it. In the places where you'd had lacerations, summer would leave you with tiny spots of pigmentation, and on your shoulder you had a golden stain the size of the palm of your hand that looked like a meadow in impressionistic sketches. I'll spread out a blanket there and we'll have breakfast. Your vulnerable skin brought us many things. For instance, the ritual of applying lotion after a shower, we sit on the bed, talk and rub in the lotion, the door is double-locked, we are clean and naked, you're all better, we travel back to us as six-year-olds at the beach, we've excluded everything but our own reality.

Our time is distinct from the ordinary flow of time. In our parallel world we control every moment, we know the causes and effects, we move with confidence and freedom. We understand so much. For instance, that we have more than other people have. So many more ways we can make love, I recognize the moment and then I try to explain it to you as much as I'm able. Although you're doubtful, you seem able to hear it then, you understand, my love, with you I have only more. Compared to you, everyone else is boring, unidimensional, predictable, and they touch, unseeing, they think they know what and how. Then, excited, I begin quoting the ancient peoples of

India, hey, look how smart they were, relying on spirituality with a speck of pure reason. They believed that someone like you had been granted profound insight into all of humanity. And you sit, curled up in a ball on my bed, you grew up never knowing which side of you hurt more, you hide yourself from yourself and insist on giving me what I don't need. Hey, don't go all dark on me, this reality is simply a wrong dimension we happened to fall into, next time we'll do better. I run my hand down between your shoulder blades, under our skin we have the same skeleton, it's just flesh between the bones and the surface is so taut that I don't know how you feel at all. You're here, yet you aren't. Maybe with laughter. "How do you even live, young man?" I ask you this while I swing my hair low over your back, I enjoy biting you from time to time. "Well, I don't know," you say, "At five percent capacity, the remaining ninety-five percent is caught up in handling my complicated personality, babe." "Well, you're doing fine with your five percent, give me another five, love, make it ten, then the next five you've never given anyone, laughter does it, laughter is love, and laughter is freedom." The flesh under your skin relaxes and you let me in slowly, I raise my flags, let loose my hair, close my eyes, calm my breathing, stand before a tall gate, in front of thick walls and endless hedges, and I wait for you to beckon me in. The blackest dark is inside, nobody has ever been here before, I advance, wary and quiet, I can't judge whether it's that you desire me so you're giving me yourself, or you love me so you're letting me in. I know you love me, but you are some-where in there deep down, deeper than the depths I've known, and I realize that for my happiness you are walking along the very edge with nothing on. I need to find you quickly, because if I'm late, as I often am, you slip away and drop a few levels farther. Then I start making too much noise, I start shouting after you, running and breaking all the fragile parts of you on the inside. I no longer know what I'm doing, in my desire to merge with you I become nervous, say stupid things, pressure you, why are you resisting so, darling? I cannot do this anymore. We breathe in the dark, you've pulled the covers up over your head, the duvet trembles in an irregular rhythm. Will you ever stop hiding? We fall asleep. Night sinks even deeper into time. We float between sleeping and waking, slumbering deeply enough that our fear sleeps, awake enough that we're aware of one another. I feel you come over to me, we don't open our eyes, we leave awake only the good in us, what can be given and believed, all without words, without a single thought that will divert the concentration from us, from our beings who love each other. Hidden from ourselves, we find ourselves before the break of dawn. I wake up slowly and see your profile as you bend over me, groping around the nightstand in the half-light, I hear the lotion squeezing into your hand, your dry skin drinking under your fingertips, you search for your slippers on the floor, I hear the water from the faucet, the flint striking and the gas hissing, the rattling of cups and saucers, I've already opened my eyes, good morning, you're bringing me coffee in bed, a smile so radiant that I choke with pain. On we go, ever onward.

## 17.

Once a week I'm given a bath. A real bath, they strip me naked. That's when the acrid stench of my immobility hits me. Then they lay me in the bathtub and sponge me down. The water laps over my shoulders, and my arms, legs, and breasts move under the surface. I feel alive. When they lay me in the special tub, if they think there isn't enough water, they turn the faucet on right by my head. They don't know how the hot droplets pelt my face, get into my eyes, pierce holes in my skin—my skin oozing with memories.

I walk in through the fogged-up glass door, the air inside is hot and heavy, you can only gulp it, not breathe it. It smells of green tea, stupefying and dense, the light allows only contours. When my eyes grow accustomed to the gloom I take a seat across from a stone trough in the middle of the room that holds aromatized salt—this is why the room smells as it does. Before I take my seat, I scoop up a handful, as if this is something I do all the time, and rub onto the skin of my shins and thighs coarse crystals to exfoliate my dead skin. I haven't had a look around. I pay no attention to you. Nothing is ever enough for you. You are petty, hard, and you shut out everything around you. Something always threatens. A woman and man are sitting across from me; she, like I, is wrapped in a thin cream-colored towel, tucked in under her armpits, reaching halfway down her thighs. She is sitting with her legs crossed, massaging her neck. Although she has done her hair up in a ponytail and wiped off her makeup, I recognize her from the hotel restaurant. By now I can see better. He has thrown a towel over his lap, sits down next to her, raises one of his legs—bent at the knee—to the bench and leans on his arms behind his back. He is big and strapping, she—all soft and small.

So go ahead, lie down all alone in our room and savor your limitations. I was all wrong. I'd thought that out of all this time that had broken us we'd grow a protective shield, but here you go, reverting to the old ways. Back to the room, to loneliness, to the box. Will it ever be possible to leave this behind? Will you and I, the two of us, be the two of them across the way who are simply sitting there in a sauna, without obsessing over every nuance of their shadow, without longing for approval in the eyes of random passersby? Can we feel the warmth of the air on our skin and let our pores breathe? Can we lead normal lives? This is what I was thinking then, while you were waiting for me up in the room, while I was thinking that a total immersion in loyalty could heal everything from before. I also assumed that other people were normal. I resented your reflex, I worked to understand it, nourished it, held it close, pushed it away and then resented it again. Blaming you that my loyalty in joining you inside the stifling box you have chosen for yourself hadn't done you much good. For me, immersed as I was in our anxious pseudocoma, everyone else looked as if they were lounging on a rolling meadow with their arms raised high and legs spread wide. But when I took a closer look, I saw his hand traveling between her legs. I saw how he rudely pushed her towel aside, pulled out her breast, and kneaded it. I saw how both of them were looking at me. He, with brazen arrogance, she, embarrassed, but with a flicker of hope. At first I was confused. I didn't want to look away, I felt awkward about feeling awkward. I felt awkward at her awkwardness and I was furious at his brashness, at the easygoing way he tugged the towel off her breasts, so confident that everyone else was prepared to bow down before his erect prick. I felt ashamed about you, though you were lying in bed several floors above. In the end I stood up, confused, a demonstrative attempt, through the dark, moist air they couldn't see how abrupt my movements were, and the glass door with its pneumatic closer couldn't be slammed shut. What was I after here? Even if this offered a certain flavor of freedom, on the edge of murky swimming pools, through the nakedness, everything became clear and transparent. The women who, frowning with worry, pinch their belly skin while sucking it all the way back to their spines. The men who pat their flabby paunches with tenderness and pride. The world is mainly divided into these two and a few others in between, while you were waiting for me there in the bottom of our room, beneath all the gut-wrenching divisions.

# 18.

"Forgive me, forgive me, please. I was off for a few days . . ." She waltzes in and launches into a cascade of words from the threshold in place of her official greeting, instead of her usual glance at my medical chart with my basal temperature, and, spinning on her heel, she addresses me as if I've been waiting for her for an hour in the center of town by the clock on the main square in a snowstorm, as if we're aware, both she and I, that I'm hurrying and haven't much time. She experiences me as if so much depends on my forgiveness. Could I ever not forgive her? It's as if I'm not lying here like a bump on a log, used to being forgotten by everyone. "Forgive me" no longer has such a familiar ring. It's as if we're friends, when I still had friends, as if she needs me at least as much as I need her. This is how she talks to me. And then: she comes straight over and instead of stopping at least three feet away like all the normal visitors do, she rests her hand on my forehead. I blink once, yes, then I look at her, I'd blink more but then that would be a no, and I don't want no, it's just that I want to express something to her. To give her my blink, my utmost. I don't know how she sees me, when I've found it difficult to see myself recently, but whatever it is that she sees, she addresses me as if I'm responding to her with exactly what she needs. "Forgive me, I was moving out of the house, something unplanned came up so I took part of the week off to sort things out." Then she stops and I blink again. I know, I knew that everything was headed in that direction before you did, and it's good, it will turn out fine, nothing terrible will happen, believe me, if anything, use what you have: get up, turn and go, that's rejoicing. They will all be fine, they're equipped for it, and your sons who walk through life permanently shielded inside the aura of your concern, nobody can touch them, and he will find his feet without a hitch because this world is tailored to his measure, that is why the only thing that matters is that you're good. Good to yourself. Nobody else will be. I tell her all this with my vertical gaze, and suddenly she shudders, she has remembered our beginnings. My room—her refuge, my consciousness, and her secrets. Then she momentarily slips into confusion, I blink again. "They all hate me," she says softly. I know, I answer, but it's not that they hate you, it's childish frustration because of they can't reckon with the idea that you're slipping away, this will be an unforeseen obstacle they will overcome, a lesson that will help them understand something about taking people for granted, a growth opportunity for them. How many insights I have. How far I've had to come to find them. How late I've come to know my own strength. How I no longer feel afraid. How I'd love it if I'd . . . But along with all this, I can clearly see how the impossibility of emancipation was written into my genetic code, as it probably was in hers.

My DNA is knitted into the little mudbrick house where my great grandmother lived, a twenty-two-year-old widow with four children who earned her living by serving as a maid in other peoples' homes. The children went around bare-bottomed, just a smock in winter, and sent to school in wooden clogs that Great Grandmother stuffed with paper. That is how the older daughter lost her leg to amputation, rotten from frostbite, and Granny made it through four grades of primary school just so she wouldn't end up the same. Who would want a girl like that? And then Granny also went into service, as a ten-year-old she looked after children in the finer houses, she'd fix them breakfast every morning: tomato sauce, cream of wheat, and fresh bread. And when something burnt to the bottom of the pan, she'd be rapped on the knuckles with a poker. The war went on and on, they survived on eggs and hootch, forever delousing, waiting to see which army would pillage what was left of the village this time. Then Granddad appeared, he showed up on horseback, he had curly hair, and that was why Granny didn't ask any questions, she climbed up on the old nag, she didn't know where it was going, anything was better than the musty cellar, the tiny children and the mattress covered in coarse cloth and stuffed with putrid straw. At the age of nineteen she buried her first son. As the women in the village said, he didn't quite take hold the right way. Yes, she gave birth to him, but soon after he was lost. Nobody mourned him, she was still young, maybe a little unruly, Granddad watched her out of the corner of his eye, should he have swung her sister up on the mare instead? Well, he didn't break her after all, my mama came along, she wasn't particularly happy, but at least she was healthy, at least she wasn't tainted goods, God willing there'd be a son by the next year. God willing. Husband willing. She just received and accepted what they willed for her or denied her. Mama had grown up in the kitchen among the women, aunts, old women, she was bored and ever since her childhood she had been given menial tasks, sometimes she'd run off when her father came back from work drunk so she wouldn't have to cover her ears with her hands. The noise level kept rising, Mama was left an only child. They moved to the city, she ventured out on her own to find a school to enroll in, no you don't, what good will all the book-learning do, hitch yourself up to someone, get yourself in the family way, don't you go out wiggling your bum around town, but she wasn't one to give up easily, she loved reading, she liked to sew herself a skirt, she liked going to dances, far away, as far from the crocks of sauerkraut as she could get, from the greasy towel on Granddad's pillow that Granny changed every two days because his head was so oily, from his stern look that made her wet her pants when she was little. Once he thrashed her so hard she didn't go to school for a week, she'd been hopping around the yard while bringing a bottle of rakija up from the cellar and it dropped from her hands and smashed. She barely managed to get away. My father was not, perhaps, the best choice, but he was the first to offer her a way out without cursing or swinging a cane. The only thing was how quiet he was a lot of the time and that he didn't ask for much. So she, hemmed in as she had always been by abuse, didn't know what to do with him except to belittle him. But he didn't give her enough reasons for that. How could she deal with good after a whole life of bad, except to turn him into what she knew best. Luckily, Granddad's ornery character lived on in my mother's mind so in my brother she created a little tyrant who'd give substance to her suffering. All the cringes that had stayed with her from Granddad's creaking incursions into the house came back to her through her son. All the cringes from the little mudbrick house, the constant fear and shame also fashioned the links of my chain. How to shrug them off? How to be free of myself? And how to bear all this when, having come to know you, I was able to see it all? Your kiss was a little like breaking a spell, but it also had the opposite effect. First it freed me, then it trapped me by showing me the unimaginable dimensions of a world I had never known, which hardly anybody knows. A kiss so enchanting that with it came both exhilaration and a curse. We just wanted to be free. I dragged you down, I know. I was scared my mother or brother would see me on television as I marched by your side in the Pride parade. You talked for days beforehand about what an exhilarating feeling it was to march in the parade, my love, it let you forget those who wanted to pelt you with stones from the sidelines, this is the day when you walk with head raised and are borne along by a marvelous river of people, one day each year when you feel normal, love is love, people are people, and you are thrilled at how everybody looks at you so nicely, the way we all need to be seen, it's colorful and alive, you can hold hands with anyone you like, it's liberating, just imagine. I moped all morning, I was as gloomy as a January afternoon though it was June outside, smelling sweetly. A thousand times, what's wrong, love, a thousand times, nothing. We got into the car, we listened to the radio announcing the lead-up to the parade and the route it would take through the city. This year there would be more police than in past years, this year my brother would be standing behind the police cordon brandishing his rosary. Maybe he'd be shouting. We drove in silence, my strength was draining away, and then suddenly I realized we were on the entrance ramp to the highway. I looked over at you, puzzled, you said nothing but gripped the steering wheel, we drove right out of town, I didn't dare ask where we were going, but I saw that we were on our way to the Mrežnica River, to our refuge, nature, cascades, and the wild river. All in silence. There was hardly a soul there, this early in the summer. The rivers are still icy cold. You took a blanket out of the trunk, there was no anger in your eyes, I walked behind you. We came into a place that was like paradise, sprouting river reeds bent over the path we took, the reflection of the sun on the river painted the air with shine, water murmured in the background like life's soundtrack. You found a spot on the shore, soft with ferns and hidden by bushes at the water's very edge. We sat down, I looked over at you, I was ashamed, leave me, go back to town, to the other river you'd hoped to join, leave me. You hugged me, too bad we don't have a frisbee, you said.

"Is this too cold?" I blink twice while she wipes me down with a cold towel. I enjoy feeling something, I enjoy the coldness on my forehead, though the day is not hot, but I don't know why she is doing this, I don't which part hurts me more. The part of me that wants to hope there is something more, or the part of me, starting the car three months ago, that decided I'd had it with pain. And she still surprises me, this doctor, this source of impartial goodness I never entirely believe. What will I do with this now, she keeps drawing me out from my thoughts. "Hey, I have an inkling of a plan in the works, would you like me to lay it out for you?" She asks warmly, with enthusiasm. I blink, yes, let's have a look. Boy, do I miss sarcasm, I'd give my right leg for a single eye roll or to cock a brow at just the right moment, the look that hits the spot, but still clearly includes a ray of belief and benevolence. Fine, I don't need my right leg or my left, give me the plan. "So, we can run this as an experimental treatment protocol because of your age and the rare diagnosis. Otherwise, we'd never get approval for the spa in your condition, but since I will take responsibility for keeping track and putting together a study, in quotes, I'll get the green light, I've checked. And some funding to boot, and a few more doctors and experts who'll join us in making progress. So I can get you out of here for a spell. I'll explain everything later, if you agree. You'd stay here a little longer, enter into a much more intense phase of therapy, and if there are at least a few results, minimal improvements in communication, muscle tone and your general condition we can take it further. You'll go to the spa for a stay, that could really begin to help you, but till then there's a lot to do. And of course, I'll take care to respect your wishes. Tomorrow the speech therapist will come, and after that she'll be here every day. Come on, now, blink for me just once." She laughs, she's onto me. I wait, I wait for the tension to rise, I'm teasing her a little, and then I blink, nice and big, like I've never done before.

# 19.

They never actually caught on. My mother and brother, I mean. But I couldn't bear it any more. During your transition, as you were coming into your authentic self, you looked a little younger than me. This was enough to be threatening. Every digression from the cruel ideal, God the Father and the meek wife, gently weak-minded at the level of a child, caused, if not scandal, at least scorn. One morning Mama saw us leaving my building. Sometimes she'd pass this way and stare at my windows so she could glean something about me. "Why did you move out, Lucija, so you can drag snot-nosed kids to your apartment and fuck them? Hats off to you." My attempts at defending our relationship, at describing you as my equal, as someone with whom I'd found myself, ended with me leaving her apartment and sobbing in the elevator. Every Sunday after dinner we usually wound up spending two agonizing hours around the table in the dining room where she'd crush me little by little—nobody loves you like I do, why are you always so secretive, who are these weirdos you're hanging out with, did you have to leave me, was the roof leaking? You had cooked food and laundered clothing. If only you'd lifted a finger to be just a little normal, nobody loves you like I do, I never know what to tell Tomislav when he asks about you, you have school, you have a job, you need children, Lucija, and what would your father say if he saw what you're doing, what you're doing to us? Mainly I kept my mouth shut, there was no way to respond to any of it, a ton pressed down on my chest, my lie was too huge and too terrifying, it had a double bottom and through it I'd fall several times a day. Once she even locked me in when I decided to leave because I no longer cared to listen to the insults. I can still feel how I plunged my nails into her hand to get her to release the key so I could get out of there. It's strange when you're thirty and you can see, from above, two women, one young but already grown, the other on the verge of old age, wrestling over a key in the hall. Who will lock up whom? When I felt my nails sink into her flesh, into the tissue that I myself, had sprung from, I stopped, this was a border I could not cross. I released her hands and started saying over and over: "I'll call the police, let me go, you can't lock me up, you don't have the right." But then it dawned on me to retreat, I'd leave her the keys.

We took our seats for the last time at Irena's office, the worst behind you, my love, the worst ahead of me. My brother, even without knowing it, had leveled his battle axe at you. Such were the times, the society in which we lived. He had it in for people who had been molded differently by nature in its compelling diversity, who had been suffering terribly since their earliest childhood, unable to be who they were, and when they had the courage to step forward they most often lost what little false security they'd had. The family, job, often the apartment too, friends and every shred of dignity. People who, in the general population, have the largest percentage of suicide attempts. People who make up about one percent of the population and have no social, political or financial clout, people who, through life, in the best of cases, try to stay under the radar. And when they try to live in keeping with how they feel, this doesn't come close to bringing an end to their suffering. Because the point is not in this discovery, someone will figure out what you are, the question is about the agony that doesn't end, the quaking anticipation, the control others have over you your whole life. They decide. You exist in the light of their judgment. It is up to them to discern whether you are sick or well. They decide your fate. Having grown with you through our years together, I felt the same pressure on myself. Instead of it getting easier over time, this became increasingly hard. Posters went up all over the city showing people like you as if you were monsters, raping people in public toilets and brainwashing little children, like the plague of the modern age that will bring about the end of the world, like those who deserve to be exterminated. That Tomislav was posing to have his picture taken in front of these posters, that he was handing out revolting leaflets which subtly called for violence, this I somehow suppressed, we were no longer speaking to each other. But the day when you and I were walking around town holding hands and I realized he was there in the distance, walking toward us, that's what brought me here. My legs buckled, though he was still far off, he stared at us, I opened my mouth automatically to say hi and then realized I was holding your hand. A surge of panic swamped me, I almost began to run, you couldn't make sense of what was happening, softly I said his name, Tomislav, you froze dead in your tracks. "Quit it!" you said. "Hey, stop, we can't be doing this, come on, stop, cool it." I stopped only because I was no longer in command of my own body, I wanted to sink into the ground, disappear, take this burden with me to a place where there was nobody. Then he walked right by us while we stood there like that, me with my head bowed at your shoulder, you standing upright, looking straight at him. Nothing happened. Once he'd passed, I realized it wasn't Tomislav at all, just someone who looked a little like him. Irena said: "Dysfunction in a family rolls down from generation to generation like a forest fire, devouring everything in its path, until one person in the series musters the courage to turn and face fire with fire. That is the one who will bring peace to their ancestors and prevent the suffering of the children to come." This all made sense, but I didn't have the strength to be that person, I felt more comfortable choosing the path of my predecessors. More comfortable following my father, and, like him, I left no letter behind.

I came home, everything seemed unreal, I was unreal. The only real thing was my fear and my longing to be free. Evening was coming on. As if I were sleeping, I picked up the car keys, reached to take my jacket off the hook and then my hand stayed suspended mid-air. I sat in the car and drove for a while, I liked that dark stretch of the road before the tracks on the way to your place. I stopped by the lowered gate, the lights of the train approached, both fast and slow, and then I drove around the gate. I heard the blare of the siren, I thought of all the people who would be getting home late tonight, who'd fume and rage in their train compartments, I thought, they'll send out buses to pick them up, I thought of you, I'm sorry, this will be harder for you, it will be easier for you, beyond that I don't remember. I thought, free, finally free.

# Part Two

# 20.

There were certain rules I had to make in life: no more hard liquor. I wake up, it is day outside, I go to work, day outside, I go out for a drink, day outside, I come back to the apartment, day outside, and then that moment when, beneath the light, I could see the exact color of your eyes which I'd never been able to pinpoint. A blue circle around the pupil, melting into green, a green that was pierced with golden dots and violet fissures, gold that thinned toward the rim of the iris and transitioned to tree bark, all of it outlined with a metal circle. Why haven't you called? All you had to say was, love, you are so stupid. There are times when that's how I feel. A leftover. I can hear you saying I am nothing. You think I want everything to be about me. I know. I'm stupid. I get it. But sometimes I can't help myself, you have this long, see-through dress on, because of it your step is even lighter as you walk. Did you know I showed Filip a photograph I took of you at the beginning that caught you while you were walking? Of course he immediately saw what it was about. I said, see, that's her stride, it tells you all you need to know, look at her stride, between the bench and the wall, look how I caught the air between those long legs, her neck and the locks of her hair and the solemnity behind her smile, and all that in her stride.

And then we're strolling through town, he's strumming a guitar on the sidewalk, he plays well, not badly at all, "Unchained Melody." You told me once that you had a crush on Patrick Swayze in primary school, I am thinking of those big hands of his, I would definitely come back to you as a ghost, lift you up onto me and protect you, then you stop for a minute and listen to him play. You smile at him, your smile is a gift I would like too, you're holding my hand but that's not enough, I want every single crumb of you for myself so I start in on you. You know how I can be. Stupid, first of all, then sullen. I know you're simply enjoying the moment and the music, and there should be nothing nicer for me than to watch you while you're enjoying something. I have to admit that I'm less and less often like this but sure, sometimes I'm stupid. You take this way too seriously when it happens, we argue about it, "Look, there's no point in blowing up over everything," I say, "I just do it sometimes." "But what is the point if I don't take you seriously?" you say, "Come on, love, come on, we had such a brilliant time together, I only have eyes for you and I can't believe, you know, I can't, it insults me." You protest with such sadness. I make you so sad. Goddamn it to hell, I didn't want that, forgive me, all I wanted was the gift of your attention. Look, you have everything, why can't you see that, if you see everything else. We can't hear the music any more, now we're walking along to an empty rhythm, we're still holding hands, but not being ourselves, until at one point you stop and start peering around like an animal, like you're about to turn and backtrack. You pull me in some direction, I don't catch on right away. "Sweetheart, what's wrong?" I ask. You just whisper, "Tomislav." Then I get it that you're thinking of your brother.

When you showed me his picture I couldn't believe that you are even related. The big belly swathed in red-and-white check-erboard like the Croatian flag, the screaming of fans you can hear right through the pixels, a flawless specimen of manhood living in such a cramped cage that he can't even see it. I don't like it when you talk about him. Not just because he is, to my mind, an ordinary sadist who is only strong with his words, and mean to his sister and mother; I don't like him because you are so afraid of him. I know he's older, but the power he has over you is too much. I keep trying, we sit on the couch, I massage your feet, what small, sweet feet you have, and you're always walking around practically barefoot, even mid-winter, you wear no socks from April to October, so I reach for them whenever I can and plunk them in my lap. "Come on, tell me now, try to imagine this," I tenderly press the balls of your feet under your toes, "What's the worst thing that could happen?" "What do you mean?" you ask. "Well just that, simply put, what's the worst thing that could happen between you and Tomislav?" You puzzle over this for a time, you are wearing the same expression as in a picture you showed me from first grade: the other children are giggling and making faces, while you gaze off into the distance. A conscientious little girl, you don't want to disappoint, especially not the teacher. I can just picture you, so small, and I feel sure I'd know how to be with you, my little solemn one. You are still silent. "Come on, tell me, what's the worst? So maybe he stops speaking to you? How long has it been since he called? Not even once since I've known you." "True," you mutter. "Then what? Are you afraid he'll do some-thing to you? I'm here, you're not alone. And he wouldn't. Men like him are cowards, I know them." "He wouldn't," you agree, "but I'm scared of what he'll say to her, I'm scared he'll let her have it, she always allows him to rail at her, like, poor boy, he's been through so much." "Love," I try to keep it simple, "if that is her relationship with him, it has nothing to do with you." "Why are you being so mean?" again you're on the verge of tears, this is why I don't like talking about him, because I end up sounding mean, because you can't see, despite your visionary gaze, despite being my smartest girl, you're crying and telling me I'm mean, there, I can't do it. I relent. "Why don't we watch another episode. We can fit in two if you don't fall asleep." The stories of other people soothe us, detached heads float around the screen, a flight into fiction. I prever to evade your tempest, I want to calm you, to pop popcorn for you, to brush the popcorn bits off your shirt, the last time I made it I ruined the pot. You don't say a word, except: "I guess so, will you download the subtitles for us, too?" I will, I'll download whatever you like, but I can't avoid the fear. Again I'd halfway quelched the fire, it didn't singe us, but we'll go to bed with the smoke in our lungs. Every conversation about him ends that way, muffled, choked, smoldering. And now you're trembling in the middle of the street and burying your head in my shoulder: "Hey, quit it, we can't be doing this, come on, stop, cool it." I turn your stiff chin toward my face and hug you with my other arm. A man walks by us, he's not Tomislav, and only then do you burst into tears. "I want to go home," you sob, you're six years old and you're going to crawl under the bed. "Fine," I sigh, "let's go." "No, I want to go alone, I've had it with everything!" you shout in the middle of the street. "Sorry, I'm sorry for that thing, I'm stupid, I won't do it ever again." It's as if you can't hear me, as if it's not getting through, you push me off and leave. You don't turn to look back, you walk with such deep strides that you sink knee-deep into the ground, move at a clip, you're running away from me. You switch yourself off. Disappear. Hours pass, hours. Your cell phone is off. Try a little later. Hours. Your door is locked. All day. Two. Three. This is why I had to make the rules, no more hard liquor. It's forever daytime, I don't know which part, I pile into it all that fits, all the alcohol, no drugs, drugs no. Someone licks the screen of the television set in an unknown apartment, a man hugs me, another is bare to the waist, he kneels and whimpers, where am I, where are you, call me, please, I've lost my way.

# 21.

I don't go back to my apartment. I could take pictures of fractals in the lettuce leaves that glued themselves that day to the inside of the salad bowl, soaked with oil and vinegar, I could lie down on the bed without taking off my clothes, I could push my head into the toilet bowl. That is why I don't go back, I'm just stretching the day. My equipment is at the office at Olja and Dijana's, I'll crawl into my room there, work, curl up on the sofa, be awake and wait. You'll call me, first you'll send a message to ask if it's okay for you to call, always courteous while the world is crumbling around us, and then I'll call you. I'll go wherever you need to me to be. Like I always have till now. This persistence of yours is unbearable, the forebearance you are so proud of when we fight. You always win. You can stand hungry and in the rain for days, and the more difficult it gets, the stronger you become, you're nourished by your own hunger. And then you use all that powerful strength to run me over when we clash. You and I are both privy to the secret that you are capable of dying for trifles, you don't care how many victims there will be, but meanwhile decisions about the really important things you leave to fate. This is what I decided I'd tell you, once we talk.

"I can't live like this!" since morning you've been marching around the apartment, kicking my things which are, I admit, strewn all over the place. "This mess is killing me, how could it not bother you to be living in this dump? And get off that laptop of yours for once. We cannot go on living like this, you're behaving like a kid. We have no plans at all for today or for the rest of our lives!" Sheepishly I collect the socks around the sofa and close my laptop, I move into a corner, along with all my things that I am not leaving at your place. I feel like laughing out loud while I look at you warring with yourself like a fury. When the doorbell rings, I bound panther-like in three strides into the bedroom and hide behind the mattress because this might be your mother. That's the way we're living, darling. This is the real mess. Or when the phone rings, and you glance over at me like a lost soul, just one micro-glance in my direction before you start chattering, please, look, there's no one here, I'm alone, I'm reading, I'll be right over, five minutes. The implication is that I'll understand.

We have no plans, my love. We'd just started going into town. We were going to the movies, but your mother had a stomach ache. At the bus stop you turned the car around, drove right over the solid line on the road. Back we went. You spoke tenderly to me but not as tenderly as before. We made it to a later showing because you told her you'd be home, she asked if you were going out again this evening. Another car almost collided with us on the road, you raced off to the pharmacy, in record time you picked up Reglan, I waited for you in the parking lot in front of the building for almost an hour. I didn't dare get out of the car. Neighbors. I was as furious as a fire-breathing dragon. It happens in a second, it climbs up into my throat and I can clearly visualize myself punching someone until they bleed. My fists sink into their flesh, I howl and soften them up with blows, with my feet I smash bones, I could, no problem.

Then your face appeared at the car window, your eyes were swollen, under them you feigned a smile. I wipe the blood off my fists, quickly let you in, what happened, darling? I was so worried. First you were silent, then it came tumbling out while you fidgeted there by the window: "She keeps saying she knows something isn't right with you." "Why do you let her say that to you? Fine, you bring her the meds she needs, but when she starts going on like that, get up and leave, you don't have to put up with her." I spoke cautiously and no matter how I tried to be soft, you fled, retreated, isolated yourself and fell into your black hole. I couldn't reach you any more. I traversed ten kilometers of detours, I took you by the hand, no point in struggling. "We don't have to go to the movies tonight, we can go back, we'll find a series to watch, we can make crêpes. That's a good plan, too," I told you tenderly. You nodded, you hid behind your hair, we went back yet again. We have no plan, this is the mess in which we live, my love, we are behaving like children, all this went through my head, but what good was it? But what good was it? It was no good at all, or I should say it was only good when we stayed put in our little paradise of thirty square meters of mess.

A buzz, in my head or for real? I can't tell. Over the last few days I've been hallucinating the sound. This time for real. "So's it the same plan for tonight ☺?" The same. I respond. A few days ago I picked up Lana and Helena, I know them from before, they work with Filip. We roll through grungy bars as soon as the work day is done, Lana is never tired, she laughs aloud and talks fast, pushes things toward the edge, the glass is always right on the edge of the table. While I roll a cigarette, I see how she picks up the lighter and holds it without looking at me. She picks up my cell phone and takes a selfie, she hides nothing, snaps a close-up of her face, her neck under her hair to her chin, the palm of her hand, her knee, and her eye. She is creating an album called AhLana, she gets up, tosses my cell phone onto the table, and leaves, she's easy. Helena only laughs a guttural laugh while the smoke billows from her throat, from her eyes, from everywhere. They wait for me not far from the office where they left me this morning, her face doesn't look tired and as soon as she sees me, over she comes, thrusts her arm through mine. Her touch burns me, I don't want her there. Nobody but you has been there, what if you were to show up now out of the blue, I'd die. We don't go far, to the first station of the cross, as soon as we enter the bar I move away from them, greet others, faces I know from somewhere, puffy faces, faces that don't care, amicable faces, faces of smoke and numbness. We move on. It takes a while, but then everything sorts itself out, becomes bearable, even amusing. This man puts Helena's foot in his mouth and sucks her toes, there is always glass smashing, the noise is good because I can't hear myself, then Lana, the whirlwind, comes over and pushes me out. Out there. She looks at me close up with a broad, crazy grin. I've seen this before. A toxic particle of fascination. "Okay, so why do I always have to be the last to find out?" She holds me by the arm and calls me out, winking conspiratorially. I look up and sigh. Do I have to explain myself? I do, to everyone but you. Instead I smile. "So what was it you were supposed to find out?" I say lightly, just as she is light. "Well, you know, I find it so fascinating, the thing, you are an absolutely incredible guy!" People think they're paying me a compliment by saying this, but it's when everything is lost irretrievably, blundered, the moment they think I'm fascinating. She measures me up with a seductive glance, I always find myself out on thin ice, I give, and then everything is taken from me, my head separates from my body. Down below I hear only her laughter as if coins are dropping from her pockets, weaker and weaker, and then she leans even more into my face. "So how do you pee, anyway?" then she giggles like a little girl. "Cut it out, Lana, don't fuck with me," I say as kindly as I can muster, I pull out of her superficial gaze and step deeper into the chaos. In it I can be with you better. Never a single wrong question, never the slightest rough intrusion, not a single mistaken fascination, only ones that came from within. Fascinations with our inner worlds, our stories. With stories that gave us no pleasure; instead they gave us an eternal prison we will never be able to leave. Talk to me, my love.

## 22.

When I first caught sight of you, what I saw was your light. You were wearing a white shirt with long sleeves draped over your slender wrists, you shone there among a bored crowd, but it was clear to me straight away that your brightness came from absorption of black. That's how light works. Under a bright surface there is a sarcophagus of darkness, while a thin black surface glaze most often shields a flawless inner light. This attracted me. And then your gaze. No bottom to it, in place of the pupils only a narrow well of unease and a very familiar restlessness. Everyone else stood back a little from you, while Filip sat to my right, always to my right. We grew up together, he never pulled back, not when they watched me, and not when they chose not to watch me. When a pack of unruly kids appeared in the yard demanding an explanation for why I'd said I preferred to be called Ivan, he stepped in front of me and let them know he knew who from our street had put ground glass in the dogfood dishes so they spun on their heels and left. When I told him, "I have something to tell you," he only squinted into the smoke of the cigarette he'd pressed between his lips while sketching on a piece of paper. "Well thank goodness you finally said so out loud," was all he said, and we never spoke of it again. At the time when I was taking in your brightness, only he knew what I was preparing to do, only he addressed me properly, while with others I was always looking for a way to advocate for more fitting pronouns. Something closer to me. My name was in perfect discord with myself, so most people who knew me at the time called me by my nickname, Doks, at least that way they could somehow bridge the gulf that yawned open when we adhered too rigidly to form. I saw that you could see me. Why such sad eyes? I'd like to cheer you up. I'd like to drive you mad so the glittery gravel down beneath the murky water swirls up to the surface, so you throw out the shells, grass, silvery fish and crabs, so the surface roils and you pour yourself out. To spill onto me, flood me. You do not pull back from me. This is thrilling. As if I drink you in with each sip of wine I pour into myself. I go out, I'll wait for you. After two minutes you come out looking for me, though your eyes are elsewhere. Here I am. "Have a cigarette?" you ask. "So where have you been all this time?" I ask in answer. The sediment is starting to swirl ever so slightly. "Well I'm here now, couldn't get here sooner," you answer matter-of-factly, and a laugh bubbles up under your tone. We exchange looks, time passes and slows to a standstill, moves backward, there is no time. Time is merely a dimension that serves as a backdrop for us recognizing each other. This helps us connect the us from the past to the us now, and opens a way for the future us to move in all sorts of directions. I suddenly sing, you made me do it, from out of me comes music, I climb onto a podium, erect the stage set for our encounter and everything that will follow, I move close to your unhappiness, my unhappiness sniffs your fur, the words find their way, as if someone wrote them for us, we wrote them once long ago, "My Funny Valentine," you stand alone amid the crowd that has passed through life and you look at me, *your looks are laughable*, I look at you, *unphotographable, yet you're my favorite work of art.* "Doks, where the fuck did you go with that cigarette?!"

You're not going to call. I know you won't. I am way too much. But in the time we had I felt like we accomplished everything. The day after that first night I sat for a long time outdoors on the terrace, serene because I'd seen you, I didn't get up though my cell phone had been buzzing inside in the room for the last hour. Maybe it's jobs, maybe it's people whose picture should be taken so they can last forever; they don't know what forever is. Lazily I climbed down from my floating raft. An unknown number, the message: "Greetings, I don't know if I have the right number, but I'm looking for the Singer in the Night, I would like to find him, if you know how to reach him, I'd be grateful. L." I stood over these words, you wrote to me an hour ago while I was aloft in my serenity, in our serenity. Ah ha, so that's why. I answered you: "Dear L., you have the right number, the Singer in the Night is free every evening from now on." And then I wanted to add, he sings pop songs, plays serious music, Romany music, fusion and dirty jazz, and anything you desire. Then I erased the dirty, and then the rest. You'd figured all that out anyway. I have always been short on words, but in my thoughts—insatiable. Now I am sorry I didn't tell you more, that I didn't write, yell, sing, so much more, but I didn't dare knock down your walls. I have never been happier and never sadder.

You arranged it so Martina would walk between us, maybe so your friend and I would get to know each other, maybe so she'd see how nice and interesting I am, mostly—admittedly a little odd—entirely normal, and that she'd come to accept me.

And maybe so we wouldn't arrive at the exhibit as an obvious couple, so your friends wouldn't ask questions about me right away, to obscure the relationship between the two of us a little. Wanting to fit into the thing about arriving at an event, while you go around greeting and hugging people you know from somewhere, and I stand not far from you, wait my turn, and eye the purse you set down on the chair between my chair and yours. You are being deliberate, let everything be free of obligation, we're hanging out, we're open, different, but actually the only thing of value is the picture of us that all your friends will be talking about tomorrow. The better half of our crowd. Actors, intellectuals, writers, fighters for human rights who will be wondering the whole time where the photographer's prick is while nodding benevolently with eyes wide shut. Fuck me, sometimes things go easier with the worse half. Filip's grandmother, for example, who has known me since the dim days of childhood. When he told her, without looking up from the mlinci pasta she was cooking Grandma asked, "Is he a good man?" "Yes, he is, Grandma." "Has he deceived anyone, has he ever stolen?" "Come on, Grandma, you know him!" "Well then, what! Who cares about that if he's a decent man!" And that year like every other year she sent to Zagreb a jar of apricot jam and a bottle of plum brandy, each, for me and for Filip. But then the journalist who had been treading water for years in Women's Studies, an afficionado of an assortment of minorities, worms his way to peek at what we're drinking, peer into our pants, under our dresses, see what is going on there. He could smell something was up, he still didn't know me so he kept his distance, but you interested him, nothing similar had been associated with you yet, and when someone who is perfect like you is tarred with the brush of the bizarre, with a whiff of secrecy and tragedy, this becomes a cause for celebration in your whole community. I know how much this hurts you, it isn't easy to be in that place. Probably because you were bestowing all your attention on the knucklehead across from you who looked like Hugh Grant and played at being an artist—as if he understood things. And you nodded, approving, because you, too, understood things. The two of you were united in agreement and your understanding of nothing, sure and protected by your own appealing exteriors, with only a little more luck than those on the edge of town who were shaking their heads at the same time while above them hung the symbols of the state, religion, soccer club, political party. All of you understood things, except what it means to not belong. Radically. To anyone. Not to this crowd, or a different crowd, or any crowd for that matter. So that is why I felt bad for you. While we were driving home, when you started crying in the car yelling, "Sorry, sorry, but you just don't understand!" I understood that this hurts you, it hurts us, each glance, each time we go out, each venture. And then you and I were again alone and I knew you loved only me, me alone, and nothing could convince me otherwise, even your denial. This is why I was never happier and never sadder. The only thing I wanted was to free you, more than anything, that and only that.

## 23.

I dream that a building is collapsing on top of me. A horrible clatter, there's no way out, only chunks of concrete falling nearer and nearer, my legs shake, my body is too heavy, I'm out of my mind. I get up from bed drenched in sweat and look out the window, they're paving the road by the building, hence the noise, iron that grinds and smoothes; a young man pushes the machine. A mowing machine for a road. I lower the blinds halfway and go back to bed. I look at my phone, nothing. Everything is in a fog, the only thing crystal clear is that this is now the fourth day. My lungs are stinging. I can't get back to sleep. I lower the blinds to the sill. In the half-dark of the room the blue light of my monitor flickers. I have to get through this, you'll call. I know you will, you always do. I'll wait. Because I cannot accept this. I sit down by the computer, puff a lump of ash off the desk, get ready and off I go into the province of Skyrim. A hero born with the soul of a dragon who happens to find himself in the wrong place at the wrong time and is condemned to death. A true hero in the wrong body in the struggle against evil and multiple enemies. And a kingdom always on the brink of civil war. But there are enemies you cannot defeat until you resolve the quests they are linked to. It always comes down to that, observing and adapting. Combining magic and weapons. Should I call your mother? I'm worried. The quests related to her were always too complicated, not weapons or magic, though I did try my best. When you talked about her at first, you'd raise a wall straight away, not a chance, you said. So, absolutely no chance that she accepts this. But, love, when she gets to know me, I always charm mothers, no need to be so worried, then you punched me in the arm, what other mothers, you dimwit!

It was New Year's Eve, winter like in the countryside, every detail of the landscape visible. The whiteness was so rich that it transported us to a state of exaltation. Because actually, our eyes don't perceive all the colors that go into the color white. It is only when they are refracted, like in a rainbow in the sky, when raindrops are falling from dark clouds and the sunlight illuminates them laterally, that we can see the seven pure colors, which show us the true nature of light and the secret that white light is actually a mixture of colors. This is what I have been wanting to explain to you the whole time. People think they see white or black, they think they have a grasp on clarity, they think their faulty eyes have the monopoly on reality, but actually they can perceive only one dimension of the world. I knew at once that you knew this, though you may never have analyzed light, though you weren't interested in the way white looks white in photography only because the surface is reflecting light, and buildings in deep shadow look black because they are absorbing light. Which actually means, just like when I first saw you, my love, that black objects are full of light. Do you get that? And the white ones are full of dark because they repel light. You accepted this without surprise, the invisible rainbow, as if it were everywhere, as well as the fact that things are often the opposite of what they seem on the surface. We started drinking before noon, just you and I, in a little café in the center of town, we had no plan for how we'd usher in the new year, or rather the plan was just for us to be together. This was always our only plan. After a few glasses of wine we went over to Olja's and Dijana's for lunch, we watched them bustling around the stove and bumping hips, how Olja called her mother to come and eat with us, how Olja's mother didn't feel like getting up because she was watching Doctor Zhivago on the television set in her room, so Dijana and Olja rolled their eyes, teased her, laughing, and took a tray with lunch to her mother's room; we were seeing a family. We heard the cough from that same room and noticed the look the two exchanged over their plates of steaming stew. We were seeing concern and love, drank a little more and decided we would do the same. We went back to your place, slowly. I was driving. You know how I love to drive. And I love driving your little blue car, I always love driving you everywhere. Then you lay your hand on my neck. After a time you took it off and I said, more. We put on some music at the apartment, then we made an apple cake, I am a little clumsy at that sort of thing, but I do a good job of chopping, peeling, arranging, you just have to tell me how much and when, I'll do the rest. Then we got dressed up. I put on a suit and I think I looked dashing, I even wore a tie. You were marvelous. In a slim black dress with your hair up, then nice make-up, we stood in front of the mirror and we couldn't see anything wrong, nothing that we were could be held against us. Then you picked up the phone. I heard the little girl. "Hey, what's up? Are you okay? I see. Nothing special, some friends over," at first I was plural, "we want to stop by to bring you a little cake, if you'd like. Of course I know we don't need to, but still, I made it from scratch . . . Fine, okay, good, see you." The afternoon and day were still propelling you along, though you'd shrunk a little in the dress, but I kept lifting our spirits all the way to the elevator, and then I plummeted one hundred floors down. What if she says something to you, I think, I don't want that, I don't want to expose you, I always come with problems and I want you to be happy, not all miserable and green. You go up to the apartment, I stay outside. Then you come back to the stairwell and say, come in, come in. I step into the hallway where the light is dimmed. The whole apartment is dim, I see your mother at the back of the room, standing with dust cloth in hand by the bar. I walk in boldly, energetic, I put on my finest smile, I proffer my hand without a thought, there, chop it off if you like, I don't need it, I have another. She approaches, slow and cautious. She doesn't say a word. She stops an arm's length from me. This is a good distance for a camera lens. She looks me up and down with a vague expression, her gaze slides over me. Over my face, frozen in a smile, drops to my neck, hairless, stops on the scars under the shirt and eyes the shoes I'd wiped clean on the snow. My hand is left midair and instead of a clasp I'm given a question. "How old are you?" "Twenty-seven," I answer clearly, adding six months to make up for what my thin, pale skin takes away. "You're on the small side," she says huskily. "Come on, Mama, please . . ." you plead like a little girl who is feeling awkward, miserable, the way one pleads with authority, and at the same time I assume my oh so familiar mask of the joker and say something like: "I'll just have to grow some more!" all with a grin. You trade cake platters, discomfort rips the clothing off us with its teeth, we stumble and run out the door, Happy New Year, Happy New Year! We're silent in the elevator, we stare at the chewing gum stuck to the floor, and then somewhere around the second floor our eyes lock. We start talking at the same time, that wasn't so bad, well okay, we made it through, yes, now she'll start to see that there is no reason for her to be that way, well I think, but she saw you, you're charming, debonair, she still doesn't know you're also smart, you're teasing me, well you're no monster, after all your folks aren't Serbs, there's nothing wrong with us, look at us. We love each other so, but that is how we chip away at ourselves, I know all about it. We turn every lie into our truth, and this costs, you need strength for it. We didn't know then what all awaited us, what was ahead, exactly how much strength we had. Should I call her? Maybe she'll be glad to hear from me if she hears you haven't called. Every misfortune has at least two sides, every picture has its negative. Defeat.

I switch off the battlefield and switch on the news. Before my eyes across the top of the screen scroll news of corruption, the purchase of military aircraft, a priestly pedophile from Bibinje, the identity of a man who was nabbed with an incredible 16.5 tons of cocaine, in Split they tried to load an excavator, the cable snapped, they weren't able to load it, the woman who was hit by a train at a railway crossing is still in critical condition. There is a circle on the photograph around a smashed blue Renault Twingo. Shivers run up my spine, the last letters on the license plate are the same as yours. Last week I paid for parking with my cell phone. That car is exactly like yours. I don't know what I'd do if something happened to you. I scroll down and my gaze drops from the photograph to the brief text. Most people are horrified only by the visual, something primeval, they want speech, they want text, they want something unambiguous, they want an explanation. Not me, but this time I can't resist. "The police are reporting that a train smashed into a vehicle, a Renault Twingo, where a local road crosses the tracks. The crossing has a gate to stop traffic, and there are sound and light warning signals. At the scene of the collision the siren of the locomotive was heard blaring before the crash. The freight train only could come to a stop a hundred meters later at a difficult-to-access location, dragging the car along ahead of it. A young woman was in the car. Thanks to the timely intervention of the police and the emergency services she was rushed to the hospital. Her condition has remained unchanged for four days; she is in critical condition. Doctors are fighting for her life."

# 24.

The driver is a pinpoint that hasn't budged on the screen for five minutes. Then he turns into a wrong street. He can't find my address. I pace up and down in front of the building, I'd run, but I don't know where to go first. After another five minutes the app shows him arriving. A Mazda pulls up. The window lowers, he eyes me and asks, tentatively, "Dorian?" I get in and answer, "Yes." It's stuffy inside, he's bald, his arms are covered in tattoos, our sacred homeland. "What's up? Going to the doctor are we?" he asks without looking back at me. "I'm going to the hospital, yes." "So, you're sick?" he is personal and intrusive. A river of others like him is coursing through the city. They pick people up in front of their apartments and in the fifteen minutes you're in their car they want to know all about you. "I'm going to visit someone," I hear myself say. I am not. I do not want to find you. What can I be thinking? That I'll find you in the first hospital I thought of? The one I know inside out? The largest one, the one we went to together? The one where hunks of my flesh are rotting in their dumping grounds? Better I call her mother. "So who've you got at the hospital?" He is not giving up. "A friend," I answer. It's not you. You're at home, sore at me. You're binge-watching TV, reading, writing texts for theater catalogues, irritated by shoddy performances, leaving me to wait, to wise up. "So what's wrong with the friend?" he asks and asks. I'm feeling sick to my stomach and answer the first thing that comes to mind, so as not to bring on a curse. "Broke his leg." He works a cigarette out of the pack, looks straight at me and asks, "You don't plan to report it?" I shake my head. "How?" "Pardon?" I've briefly lost track. "How did he break it?" "Fell off his motorbike," I say. "Like, he got wasted? What does he drive?" You got wasted. I wasted you. I didn't find the key. I know exactly when I wasted you. The day when we came back from the Mrežnica, I knew you were scared, I knew exactly what you were scared of, but I couldn't help myself. I was angry at you because we'd missed the parade, I was bitter because we weren't your first concern, your fear took first place. While we sat there by the river you stared fixedly into the green water, I just wanted us to talk, but suddenly you weren't looking at me. If we'd at least had a frisbee or badminton rackets we'd have run around a little, our bodies would have come closer through doing something different, that's what Irena said: "When you find you can't communicate about a problem, when each of you is in a bad place, maybe it's wiser not to insist on conversation just then, wiser to do something together, play a game, take a walk, distract yourselves, and when you start feeling better, then you can talk. I didn't insist, I didn't, I just went cold. And my cold is immeasurable. It is so freezing cold that everything around me shrivels. And when I touch you with it, you're gone. When I brought you to the building and you were still silent, that is how we stepped over into the wasteland, you and I, your silence and my chill. Then we lost our way in the wasteland. "I'm not sure I need this," I said. The first and last time. I didn't mean it. You looked at me with such horror and surrender that for a fraction of a second I felt pleased. I enjoyed it that you love me that much. This is what wasted you, I didn't know better. I wanted everyone to see your love, our room wasn't enough for me. I wanted to show it to everyone. That's when the germ was born in you, the idea about being wasted, I added weight to the scales you drag around with you, weight that pulled you under.

"What's this, man, a fricking Latin mass? Yoohoo, we're here!" Baldie realized he was dealing with a madman, waved his fingers in front of my eyes, and when he withdrew his hand from my face I saw we were there. The white lab coats smoking at the entrance to the green building, diagnoses hobbling through the double doors, people entering, healthy for the last time. The whole building is full of half-goners, ragged and singed flesh, tumors, wrong growths, vertigo, stitches joining torn skin, rotten lungs, all in one place, each one of them having started with the germ of something that, when denied, began growing deep inside them and then mushroomed into a disease. My germ, on the other hand, grew up with me. With my first awareness of myself came the awareness of wrong growth, denial took the shape of my shadow. This is why it was harder for you, you were pure. Your purity is what touched me. At the reception desk sat a sculpture. A female sculpture in her late fifties, an ankle bracelet cutting into the flesh of her leg, her wedding ring buried in flesh, her elbows planted on the table, like all women at reception desks around the world. Her gaze glued to the screen, hoping that the onslaught of the sick would ebb. "Forgive me, I have a question."

She doesn't answer, though I know by the way her lips move that she has heard. Three times I spell out your name. You are unreal on my lips, like at the beginning when I mouthed your name in the dark, when I annexed your name to mine so I could get used to how they sounded together. "Family?" she asks with suspicion. I stop before I answer and in that second it becomes clear that I have no right to be at your bedside, we are something not yet legalized even though I feel you are my closest kin. "Sorry, we give that information out only to family members." "Please, just tell me whether she's here." "Sir, we can't allow anyone from off the street to charge into a patient's room. What are you thinking? This isn't a hostel." I retreat and my black forebodings rise, these feelings nudge me not to the door but up into the wards. After wandering around the floors, I come upon a dark and narrow corridor which opens up before me. On the door frame above the entrance are the words "Intensive Care Unit." It is empty and quiet, this doesn't look like you, you fill space differently. It's dead here. The doors to the rooms are ajar like windows into heaven or the underworld. One or two patients per room. They are lying flat, their heads on a level with their bodies so it's hard to see who they are from the doorway. I'll have to take a closer look. Beneath one sheet lies a corpulent body bristling with tubes; I can encircle your waist with one hand, so I breathe a sigh of relief. Short gray hairs poke out from the other bed. You are my Eddie Van Halen, that's how I tease you in the morning in bed, when you sit up after you wake and your thick blonde tousled hair still hasn't descended to your shoulders. I leave quickly and step into a different room. There is only one bed here. It's darker than the previous one. I move quietly toward the bed, under the sheet it's as if nobody's there, a slender body kept alive by machines. Just a little closer and then I hear the hurried pounding of clogs on the linoleum. A nurse's panicked, sharp voice: "What are you doing, who are you? No visitors allowed, get out or I'll call security." She is already turning toward the hallway and calling out, "Doctor, doctor!" I want to get just one step closer, but I feel the chaos coming and shoot a last look at the bed. The skin and that hand. Under the long white sleeves of the blouse. The slender wrists and the skin soft to the eyes, so clean it looks polished. That's why I always thought you must feel better than you do. Only someone wholly untroubled could have such skin. My skin cracked straight away, as soon as someone looked at me cross-eyed, as soon as they addressed me the wrong way or even if I was just feeling like they'd addressed me the wrong way, whenever I went home over the weekend I'd come back with cracked skin all over the middle of my forehead, eyelids and wrists, everything was visible on the outside, I could never keep anything in. But you walked around enveloped in your gleaming mantle, took care to see that I used sunscreen, sat for hours in the baking sun, came running out of the water as if this were nothing, frantically scratched mosquito bites and the red marks from your nails disappeared seconds later. Bare legs and arms, a bare back, the swimming of your bare body through our room, as if the world could do you no harm, I couldn't get my fill of looking. And that was why I thought you could. I didn't want to believe there was something unseen going on inside, at least not inside of you, when in my case—everything came down to that and only that.

# 25.

No way she'll call. Even if she has my number somewhere in her phone, I'm sure she won't. But I've got no one else to call, I don't have a single other number of a close friend of yours, let alone anyone from your family. When we became us, they all started falling away. I think you pushed some of them away yourself but I was reluctant to say so. You felt uncomfortable having to explain. I watched how you began closing up toward people so you wouldn't have to hear and see things that insulted you, insulted us. "What do you mean, he's always been a man? Well sure . . . I do believe you can fall in love with a person. This is so wild, come on tell me more. So what's it like for you in bed? Look, a person needs to try everything, maybe this is just a phase. Are you, like, a couple now?" Their eyes wide, they shake their heads affably, and below the surface they dig for dirt, the pathology, the childhood trauma that drew you to me. Then your cell rings, you don't answer because this isn't a good moment, then you forget to call back the next day, then you stare at your feet when we walk through town, you move away from me a little, then you begin cultivating contempt that spills over when the dam bursts and floods us all, the guilty and the innocent. I've been through all that. That is why the only person I have left to call now is your mother. I ought to punch in the number and ask: "Forgive me, but is your daughter at the hospital?" Maybe I could go see her, maybe I could wait for her when she leaves the building and follow her, maybe she'd lead me to you. My love, what have you done? Why didn't you tell me, why didn't you tell me everything, why didn't you tell me to go hell? There is so much I don't know. For instance about him. You seldom mentioned him. Only a few times. I always wondered whether he would respond the same way she does. Might I call him?

We stand there in the bathroom, I have disgusting sutures, now falling apart, but they're still dangling loosely from the places they stitched me up, I find looking at them turns my stomach, but you crouch down, come right up close and, with movements I can't feel, you tap the gel for healing the wounds into my mutilated skin. I make sounds and I ask you, "Love, how can it be that this doesn't make you sick?" You smile patiently and say, "Come on, why would it make me sick? This is a breeze, oh boy, what I've seen." "What do you mean, what you've seen? Folks sliced in half who look like Frankenstein's groom or bride, depending?" I wink. "Cool image." That's all you say. "I mean really, where have you seen worse?" "Well, when my father was wounded, at the spa, I was often there with him, sometimes for practically my whole summer vacation. There were plenty of kids there, wounded, missing an arm or a leg." "You never told me that, darling. All summer?" "Well, it was my life before, I mean during the war." You hold back from saying anything more, you prefer to take time to see to it that the bandage is perfectly aligned on my chest. "Might you tell me a little bit more?" I ask, anxious. "What might interest you?" you answer with a question as if we're discussing a job.

"Well everything interests me, what was it like for you there? How did you feel? What was your dad like? How did this even happen?" The questions tumble out because I feel there may not be many opportunities for us to have this conversation. You sit on the edge of the tub and twist the bandage you just removed. You sigh the way people do when they're getting ready to begin a long story about their life, and you say: "I was ashamed." The end. "Ashamed?" I ask, puzzled. "Yup." "I don't get it, what was there to be ashamed of?" "Well, you of all people should be able to understand, darling. I was ashamed that I have arms and legs, I was ashamed that sometimes I'm not good at hiding my joy, I am ashamed to this day that he killed himself, and I'm especially ashamed for feeling ashamed because I was right there the whole time, and yet he still killed himself." That is how you talk about your life. Layers of shame and guilt that you began collecting for yourself while you were playing nurse for the wounded children and your shattered father. How can I explore this more? What happened later? Where was everybody else, their families? I wonder all this to myself as I slide closer to you along the edge of the tub. "And I'm ashamed of the way she made this her own tragedy, and even more ashamed of my brother who embraced it and made it into his excuse for bullying. I'm ashamed I didn't have a normal life…" In short it turns out that you are more ashamed than I am, and I can't quite believe this mirror image which I'm approaching as cautiously as I know how. "Let's cut the pity party!" you push me away half-seriously, my little moppet who, after everything that happened, found me and redid my dressing. I want to pull you to me and protect you, but I realize I have to wait a little longer, till you stop feeling ashamed.

Your joints were white from clutching the bandages, just like mine are from clutching my cell phone. Still, I punch in the number. It rings a long time, she won't pick up. "Hello?" says a hoarse voice, I'd already moved the phone away from my ear. "Hello, hello!" I yell, loudly, so she doesn't hang up. "Dorian here, sorry, please, I apologize for the intrusion, all I need to know is whether you know where she is . . ." She sobs. At least she picked up. What is worse? That she hung up then or what her hanging up might mean. I think I'll lose my mind, it comes over me again, my fists clench of their own accord and I don't know where to take myself. My phone rings, I have trouble relaxing my hand enough to respond. "Hey, Doks, Olja here, just to ask, have you taken those scans to the printer?" "I don't know," I say dully, "no clue." "Doks, are you okay?" "Dunno, no, I'm not, I think Lucija has been in an accident." "What accident? What happened?" "I don't know, I'm not allowed in to see her. I think it's really bad." I start crying. Out in front of the hospital where other people usually cry, I didn't. I hadn't cried for ages, not since we began. I stop crying. I sit on the edge of the stone planters and no longer feel my legs. Everything would be different, if only she'd never met me. Everything. I did this. It is choking me. They were right. Every last one of them. With the posters, the balloons, with the children in strollers when they marched through town and demanded that I be erased. I bring nobody anything good. I am fucking sick, disease, disaster. And whoever's life I enter, I ruin everything. I don't give a fuck about anything, I ruined you. I don't know how much time passed, the phone rang a hundred times, I didn't pick up. Again and again. "Hello?" Olja: "Doks, come on tell me where you are, I'm coming to get you."

# 26.

All three are sitting across from me at the table, watching me with alarm. "When did the two of you last talk?" asks Dijana, she brings order to everything. My days have gotten all mixed up, a whole lifetime has passed since we last talked. "I don't know, maybe it's been three or four days." "Okay, so did you fight?" asks Olja gently. "Not exactly, maybe a little, we were downtown, I was going on about something stupid, and then this guy walked by and she thought the man was Tomislav, so then she went all pale and snapped, she said she'd had it and that she was going home. I let her go, you know what she's like, she always needs time alone, and then everything's fine. And I didn't call right away, really, I wanted to leave her alone, so she could call when she was ready. And then she didn't call any more. She never called." Dijana asks the question: "Okay, Doks, but why are you thinking she was in an accident?" I can't say it, I swallow back the words, I don't want these sentences to take shape in my mouth, in my throat, in my soul. "Because I saw a car on the internet, on the news, just like hers, a Twingo . . . the last letters on the license plate—the same." It is becoming real, I can hear the screech of the brakes and the train's siren as it tries to stop. First the screech, then the siren, alternating. I feel the creeping skin under your blouse and the tense muscles on your back, thighs, your body so tense that you can no longer feel yourself. And your pupils, large from the dark, narrow in the locomotive's lights, shrinking into black, terrified spots. And the blue metal of the car's body that has wrapped itself around you, melting like butter, not from the blow of the train and the devastating heat, but from your desire to leave everything behind. I start hurting all over at the thought of your crushed legs, your soft belly in collision with the sharp metal, your arms so incredibly light that they are able to fly through the air of their own accord, of your head that I most loved to kiss, the smell of you was there in that tangle of live hair, of your face embraced by my hands, I see those cheeks, I nibble them, you are my big Lupko. Did your face bleed? I drop my head to my hands, again I can't stop, I look down and through the water I see how Dijana is scrolling through the Accident Reports under the table and reading what she can find about the woman whose condition is still unchanged after four days. Olja's mother shakes her head, she gets up from the table, rests her hands on Olja's shoulders, protects her from our fate, knows her daughter was nearly lost to her, looks over at me with sympathy, and says, "This is not easy for you, child." Then she comes over to me and strokes my head. "Everything will work out," then she goes quietly off to her room. Olja puts coffee on the table, drops her hands onto my shoulders which are heaving and leaves them there, so I don't fly off into the air. I know the two of them are exchanging looks, I feel a wire tightening over my head, but words die out along it and drop it into the chasm of cliché, "Did anyone confirm for you that she is there, when you were there?" asks Dijana. "They didn't want to tell me anything, but I think I saw her, I was up on

160

the ward. I think it was her, hooked up to machines, I saw her arm." So what should the two of them do now? What can anyone do? "Come on, look, I'll dig up the number of the ward and try to learn what I can. Please, lie down here on the sofa, take ten minutes to calm down and then we'll come up with a plan." Dijana is one of those people who comes up with ways to rescue people from prison camps during a war when nobody else can. I have no choice but to lie down on the sofa, I have no plan and I have no right, no right to anything. Not even to information. I am not family, especially not family, nor will I ever be family to anyone except those from whom I came into the world, who have been trying this whole time to understand where to lay the blame. The error in the family that bore me. I sink into the sofa and want it to cover me over on all sides. I remember floating on it before.

When I came back after the operation you brought me here first, I couldn't stay at your place right away, too much of a risk, I was so weak, I wouldn't have been able to crouch down behind the mattress if someone came to the door. The first few days the two of them looked after me, I slept a lot, Olja washed my hair over the bathtub, they brought me soup and fed me while it was still hard for me to move my arms, and in the evening the three of us lay here like sardines and watched movies. You'd come over after work and bring cakes, I waited for you eagerly each day, I caught sight of my reflection in the bathroom mirror when I dragged myself to the toilet and lit up with joy, it was me, as I've always been. I waited for you to come so I could show you. I kept imagining. There'd be nothing standing in our way now, I thought, you'll be able to hold me proudly by the hand, we'll be like in my dream under the tree, sipping Coca-Cola. But during those days you came to their apartment a little timidly, I noticed it right away, your voice was soft when you said, hi, you'd sit next to me and only now and then you'd rest your hand on my back, as if you felt like an interloper. Then the two of them would slip away, they always had to pop out just then to the store or see to something for a minute, and we'd be left alone. "Need anything? What can I bring you?" you'd ask me as if seeking a way out of the awkwardness. "Nope, I've got everything I need, I'm good." "Enough clean clothes?" you'd ask, without looking me in the eye. "I have, darling, don't worry, they are terrific, they're spoiling me. Come closer," I'd invite you from my half-mobile position so you could curl up and lean on my shoulder. Then you started to cry. "What's wrong?" I couldn't imagine for the life of me what was making you cry, what was going through your mind; you didn't want me any more like this, you'd realized this isn't what it was supposed to be, I broke out in a cold sweat. "Nothing," you answered. Always nothing. "Please, tell me." I didn't mind pleading. "Nothing, it's just that I'm feeling sorry that I'm not here with you. Instead of them. What good am I? I think about you all the time, every morning and evening, every night, I wonder whether you're comfortable and whether it hurts when you lie down. I wonder whether you were scared when the lights went out, how it was for you when you woke up after the operation, how you mustered all the courage, how you dared do what you did, how you came to love a coward like me, how you must see me when you had to go through all this so we'd look normal and be happy, when until now all was normal, except that it isn't normal to hide, and that's why I

didn't bring you home to my place, there, that's all, nothing."
I felt a stab of pain shoot under my armpit, but I straightened
up and hugged you around the waist, I still couldn't hug your
shoulders. "How can you say that, why are you tormenting
yourself with such nonsense, everything is finally ahead of us,
my love. We just have to get through this now and everything will start to change, and then nothing will stand in our
way. You're with me all the time, as much as you can be."
Then we glued our wet faces together; we found a position
in which nothing hurt anyone and fell asleep close, soft, in
each other's arms. They came back, then tiptoed into their
room. They didn't turn on the light, they didn't talk loudly.
Until your cell phone rang around midnight. You jumped up
and answered. Your eyes shone darkly in the gloom, you were
upright and rigid, I was pulsing under my armpits, through
the dark and silence came the voice on the phone. "What's
going on, you're out again tonight? Don't you ever plan to
come home?" "Sorry, Mama, of course I'll come home, I'm
on my way now." "Oh sure you are—you're on your way
straight downhill." You pulled together all your things in one
fell swoop, bent over me and said: "I'll come tomorrow, I'm
with you, always." "Always," I say—our word.

"Doks, they called me from the ward," Dijana came over,
her lips pursed. "She's there, she isn't conscious but her condition has stabilized." "How? What did they say? Is it definitely
her?" I jump around the table. Dijana soothes with her voice
and says only what I can bear. "I said I was a sister who doesn't
live nearby so I was calling to hear how she's doing. She was
brought in four days ago, she has quite serious injuries, apparently also to her brain, but it's early days for predictions, they're

still running tests. They gave me the name of her doctor, visits are allowed every day but only for next of kin. We'll come up with something." She hugs me. We'll come up with something. Our words too.

# 27.

Duje is bare-chested. He's wearing cut-off Bermuda jean shorts, has hairy legs, a big bulge in the crotch, trim, his well-tanned body shows only barely visible signs of aging. His face, less so, what with the drinking, smoking, carousing, and partying. The wrinkles incised around his mouth, crowsfeet of laughter around his eyes. Vivacious black eyes and a tousled mane over bushy eyebrows. When he comes out onto the terrace, everyone looks over at him, here's someone older and tougher than you. He gestures with his long arms and is carrying cans of beer and charcoal for the grill. Before Duje makes his entrance a dismembering of animals always takes place. Hey motherfuckers. What're ya'll drinking? What'll we throw on the grill? Took me three damn days to sober up, I put two air-conditioners up in the bedroom, holy mother o' God, remember how we were like so totally wasted—this is the trajectory along which he paces up and down, shouting out lines that stop you cold. He doesn't spot me yet, I'm sitting in a corner, I'm not naked and sweaty, I'm not taking up any more space than I need, I'm just watching and learning. Still, when he sees me, an instantaneous bond forms. There's nothing of substance to the bond, but he offers me a hand firmly, resolutely, with full recognition and respect. When he meets you for the first time, my love, he studies you as if you're a lovely, precious box, interesting because he finds it pretty, but no clue as to what he'll find inside. That is how Duje is with all women. He cannot deal with what's inside. He doesn't function without the "hey" and the "motherfuckers" and the "took me three damn days to sober up" and so then he launches into complaints about his wife—"There she goes again, mother o' God, beefing about 'it's high time you take the kid to the doctor when you pick him up at day care, where's the groceries, were y'thinkin' we'd wait the whole damn day for you to get outta goddamn bed,' and me with my head pounding." He sees right away that my head is pounding, too—I'm hanging on his every word—and as soon as he starts in about his wife he winks conspiratorially, and asks me: "So whatcha drinking, man?" "Rakija," I say, "What have you got?" "We've got it all, my friend, all of it! And here I was worrying I'd end up with those bamboo cocktail things, heaven help me!" and then he turns to you and your friend we visited on the coast who is also his childhood friend. Their friendship dates back to discovering the world, before they'd taken on their life roles, and that's a special kind of friendship, the kind we have with people we'd never hang out with if we'd met them as grownups, because grown-up friendships are often friendships about roles. "God help us, Duje," she rolls her eyes, then you smile, and I accept him. I understand him pretty well, I despise him, I'm sickened by his simple world and the space he takes up, I ogle him with admiration, I want to be him, or if not him, his best friend. You look at me with surprise, I feel it. We start chugging rakijas, Duje is getting louder, I'm getting louder, too, you two are getting quiet, so it goes. That's how this works. Duje plays music on his cell phone, he plays Springsteen, Depeche Mode, some

Roma musicians who rip his heart out, he's curious but only within limits, certain he'll never be fully aware. That is his safety, his degree of ignorance, his lack of a grasp on the fears of the world, the height of the sky and depths of the seas, the fact that we are all of us afloat in an unhearing universe. He runs the show, he leads the way, capturing the audience with his boisterous behavior, interrupting others when they speak, spinning countless tales that include life on the edge, a great mindlessness and brashness fueled by booze, and when we succumb to the performance he's putting on for us, when we give up taking an equal part in the conversation, then comes the commentary. The commentary begins at about two o'clock in the morning. Duje's life wisdom has an answer for all dilemmas, the women from the terrace wander off to bed, but you stay with me to shield me with your fear, even though you're not comfortable you don't want to abandon me, but I'd like to confide in him, I'd like you to go. I have this crazy yen to pull off my shirt and turn his sense of security to ash, I want to explain myself to him. On the other hand I still cannot get used to the magic of my new beginning, that Duje from Podstrana is seeing me as an equal, I want you to disappear for a spell so Duje and I can have our little man-to-man, you have no idea how I've dreamed of this. Instead, the evening goes on as follows. Duje gives his blessing: "Ah, you're a good guy, you are . . . so like my buddy Željko, skinny as a rail but that man can put away drink like an animal." Duje admires me, my special human qualities that keep me on my feet longer than any bull his size. Duje has no idea that I've been drinking since seventh grade and learned a long time ago how to always be more, push to the limits, so nobody would ever see me as less. I drink then I go to the park,

I look for the guys with shaved heads before they come looking for me. When I go over to their bench, first they're confused, then they laugh at me, then they can't figure out where I fit so I smash a bottle on the concrete, I howl, I cackle, I have to be even crazier, only then will they leave me alone, a crazy man who has nothing to lose is a threat to no one. As part of the commentary, when the three of us are left on the terrace, Duje starts getting curious. "So hey, are the two of you shacking up?" "No, we're not living together." You answer tersely and nervously, while I keep track of what's happening inside the huge skull, I have a good view of the translation playing out in his head. "So, hey, whatcha waitin' for?" Duje keeps it simple while he uncorks the second bottle of rakija and pours us generous glassfuls. His gaze moves indecisively from you to me and then he addresses me as if you're not there. How many conversations at this very moment are underway around the world in the presence of a woman as if she's not there. "Look, bud, listen here, if this is it, and I'll bet it is, and what a looker she is, too, no point to thinking twice. Off you two to bed, dip your spoon, why dontcha, into that honeypot and give it a stir, God's gift. I ran away for a long time, y'know, thinking no one'll get their claws into me, and then I got Renata in the family way, and when the little devil was born, d'ya know what a fricking joy that was?! When he climbs into bed at six a.m., and starts stomping around on my head with those little feet, God help us, I'm a happy man. And she's happy enough, though she does grumble, whine and smash things over some crap or other, but you know women, that's what they do, she wouldn't want to be without me. I was a beast of a man, nobody stopping me, they knew me up and down town, three hundred people at the wedding, not to say I've stopped going out, no, but anything more—forget it. And when I've got me a free weekend, and the three of us go to Kaufland, buy us a mess of ćevaps, all this meat, she cooks up a storm, I throw myself into the grilling, we sit out on the terrace, the kid kicks a ball around the yard, 'Daddy, lookee lookee,' ain't nothin' can top that. So, I'm telling you, bud," and he winks once more, "put your spoon in that honeypot and stir it up, no regrets." And then, just to be polite, he turns to you, "Am I right or am I right?" You shake your head absently, and he says, "Hey, Duje ain't no fool, I know what I know." As you get up from the table, as the tin leg of your chair scrapes angrily on the concrete, you glare at me in rage and disbelief, or, as Duje would put it, ah, women, gotta love 'em. "I'm off to bed, goodnight." You turn and go, and I glance back once more, longingly. Is this a scene from the underworld? Who'll be turning to dust, you or me? I'm right behind you. "Another minute or two," winks Duje and stays behind, alone.

We sleep on a mattress in a little room, you have already put out the light and turned your back, I grab you around the waist, something else is sweeping me along, I pull you to me, you go all stiff. "Come over here and let me give that honeypot a stir with my spoon," I whisper in your ear, and you answer, "God, what a dumbass." I hear him guzzling the stuff down his gullet, not ten feet away from us, pouring glass after glass of rakija into his bottomless pit, and though at first glance the world is tailored to his measure, something seems not quite right. This is hard for him to think about so he pours himself another, then whatever is chafing and scratching at him goes dull, he pours because otherwise he can't stomach this life, the Kaufland and the ćevaps, the sobbing and the hysterics, the chasm of misunderstanding between his sense of who he is and the life he's living. Duje ain't no fool, once he'd cared to understand, once he seemed to, but that was so long ago, back when they were kids, the brief time when we were still at least partly undamaged and could be whatever we were. That's why he sighs, why he goes out, why he howls and drinks, why he doesn't feel much, he needs those two A/C units, aside from the little feet stomping on his head, because the secret lies in the fact that they haven't yet stepped into their role. My buddy Duje, how can I say he is endlessly dear to me, how can I convey all this to you, I'm more than what I keep to myself, and you are more than being angry.

# 28.

The most thrilling moment is when we come to the front desk and I pull out my ID card that I changed three times over the last year. Shiny and smooth. Bullet-proof. The first time when I decided to go ahead and change my name, I was so fed up with waiting for the National Health Board—that meets for epidemics and other threats to the nation's health and welfares—to issue its decision allowing me to change the letter designating gender on the ID card. The council only meets a few times a year and in the same round they'll pass both a report on the upsurge in measles and swine flu and my request for self-realization backed by psychiatric expertise. When the petition is submitted, you have to wait for the response, some for a few months, others for over a year. There's nothing to be gained by being impatient and petty like me. So that is why when the answer wasn't forthcoming the first time, I changed my name at the local police station, the only thing I could do, and lived for a few months in the limbo of the confusion aggravated by the ambiguity. More than ever I did my best to stay under the radar of the official institutions of the state—the traffic cops, the public transportation inspectors, the lottery, in short, anyone who would be likely to say: "May I please see your ID." The second time, the National Health Board shifted its attention to me from the epidemics and other threats to the nation's health and welfare and sent me their decision with a positive response that they were allowing me to be myself. "Hello, I have come to change the gender designation on my ID card." "Pardon?" "I said, I have come to change the gender designation on my ID card, here, have a look, all the documentation is here." "What do you mean, you're changing the gender designation? Who is this for?" "Me." "Sir, what I am asking you to tell me is: whose documents are these, and why didn't she come here in person? Requests are submitted in person, you can't just come in for someone else to request a change of ID." "But I am the person submitting the request, this is my ID card and these are my personal documents, and, if you insist, I am that woman." Anđela, the clerk, falls silent and the longer she doesn't speak, the more awkward her silence. This woman has a man's hair cut, a deep voice, and a beard. What is she thinking about, perhaps the man standing here is unhinged, maybe all of this is a tasteless joke, maybe it's candid camera, and then when she can't think about it any more, she picks up the phone and calls a supervisor. "A moment please, take a seat over there, I'll call you." The apparatus of approval. For an organism such as myself to become an individual, I must receive the institutional stamp, the only thing a person can count on in the dark of a park or when traversing this planet's fictitious borders. The state, in light of its ideology, issues every newborn a number at birth. It states birthplace, residency and gender designation. But what if the person, in order to become an individual, needs to step outside these designations? Will such a person be allowed to reject the framework imposed upon them if it turns out to be so confining that they don't fit into it? No, they may not. At best the apparatus must offer other designations in place of the initial ones. Though she was part of the approval apparatus, Anđela encountered this—unprepared. When I appeared for the third time at the small police station of the town where I was born, she jumped to her feet as soon as she saw me and hurried to fetch her more experienced colleague, unaware that this time I had come only to register a change of adddress. This was after I'd rented a new apartment. By then I had the little piece of plastic with which I could cross borders while driving, I could exceed the speed limit without fear that a police officer would give me a hard time about anything more than my speeding. Once I sped just to test this. My name corresponds to my picture, my picture meets your expectations, your expectations are a guarantee that I exist.

I tap the polished wood of the front desk with the rim of the plastic ID card, nonchalantly summoning the desk clerk, you press up against my other arm, we have fled to the seaside to spend the weekend, two days at the hotel were part of a package deal in a city where nobody knows us and where the air has the smell of salt, even if this isn't high season, and aside from us, most of the guests are Austrian retirees and a few other couples in exile. We don't need much, but it always turns out that we'd like just a little more. First, all we wanted was for nobody to see us, then, that they see us but leave us alone, then, that they leave us alone but acknowledge us as a couple, then, that we get through my operation, that we hold hands while we walk around town, that nobody mentions the past, and that maybe some day we'll want our past to be acknowledged, that is something I don't dare hope for now, but some day. When we enter the package-deal hotel, we are overcome by freedom fever, hand-in-hand we stride down corridors illuminated in milky light, swinging our arms wide, a child skips through between us, this is our own March for Life. We watch movies, we hardly leave the room and our king-sized bed, we interview one another holding our cell phones close to our faces, our heads on the pillow, Mr. and Mrs. Smith. I take a picture of your silhouette while you stand by the door to the balcony, your bouyant hair, slightly stiff shoulders and the metallic gray sea that fills the space between your arms and waist; between October and April the beaches are deserted and a little forlorn, but this time you brought your bathing suit because we have a pool, a sauna and a wellness center. Maybe tomorrow, we'll see.

The hotel restaurant was packed, throngs of people collided with steaming plates, greedily loading up on food as if this were their last meal. While they stood in line before the metal troughs where the food steamed, each was sure they'd grabbed the finest, the juiciest, the freshest portion. I had sea bream, smoked pork neck, potatoes with chard, potato puffs and a mountain of salads, with beans, cabbage, corn, and grated carrot. I always wanted everything. You brought a plate with one slice of cheese pastry and a green salad, you could always have everything but didn't want it. Here and there you cadged a bite from my plate, but held firm in your conviction. What happened once you'd tried everything? Which taste lingered in your mouth? The couple sitting near us organized things differently. She was always on her feet, bringing salads, waiting in line for the ćevaps, the fried smelts, jumping up each time something new was served and bringing it to the table. She was petite and plump, her face exuded a sixties cuteness, she tugged her brown vest down over her bottom with her free hand and kept peering around; while she stood behind a pillar, out of her companion's sight, she popped one of the potato puffs or gnocchi still on her plate into her little mouth. He chewed stiffly with his large, sinewy jaw, grinding up whatever was put before him. He sat up straight and like a machine he shoveled into himself meat, fish, greens, he tore at the bread with his teeth, looked up only to see what was coming next to the table A mother and daughter, both of them adults yet both little girls, both wearing large crucifixes around their necks, looked in our direction from a celestial height, the air began to seethe, crackle with suspicions, Mr. and Mrs. Smith, likely story. Still, by now we were seasoned when it came to dealing with looks, we no longer drowned quite so quickly, I had changed on the outside, you on the inside, especially when three hundred kilometers away from home. Over the screen of my cell phone lying on the table amid the crumbs and slivers of cabbage slid the weather forecast: an image of raindrops. I love it when it rains in the evening, there would be rain the next day, too, our room was plenty spacious for the whole day.

"Later we can go to the pool and sauna, they work till ten tonight," you say while you look at me through the tines of your fork on the tip of which is impaled the last tousled shred of lettuce. "Gee, I don't know, hon, all that's a bit, well you know, the pool, the sauna, people . . ." I give a squeamish wince, you already know what we think about people. Most of them. You roll your eyes, you are still smiling when you go off to bring back dessert. Now this is where you go overboard, you have to try all the confections, the pastries, the puddings, the cake, and then fruit at the end. "This is what I live for," you declare as you set your sugar bomb down on the table. I reach for a cookie, and you look at me solemnly and say: "Go get your own." I'd thought it was for both of us. We're feeling a little overstuffed as we lie down on the bed and choose which show to watch. It's still early, we're not up for a walk, the rain is pouring down in buckets. Now would be the best time for a swim. You won't relent. I sigh. "I don't get what the problem is now," you tell the ceiling, "you don't have to strip naked." "Fine," I, too, tell the ceiling, "what will that look like in the sauna?" I try to be conciliatory. I will not be setting foot in the sauna.

As soon as the heavy door of milky glass opens, we are hit by an invisible gust of warm, close air laced with the smell of chlorine. The lighting is subdued, bodies lounge on chaise longues encircling the round pool. Whenever you strip down to a two-piece you suck in your belly. You are obsessed with that little bulge that lends your slender, lithe figure a touch of softness, makes it more approachable, curvaceous, cheerier. You walk with your arms crossed or hold a towel in front of you. When you sit, you wrap it around or sit ramrod straight, to look more like snapshots of the nondescript bodies all around us. Both jacuzzis are occupied so we stand on the edge of the world of the sauna and wait for a spot to free up. We wait to wade into the cloudy, tepid water where we'll squeeze in among the other bodies obsessed with their bulges and hollows, with unfamiliar pigments, watch each other out of the corner of our eyes, uncomfortably close, so later we can say: "Wow, that was so wonderful!" While we stand there and keep an eye out for two places in the sloshing water, you explain to me the types and models of saunas. Where people are usually naked, the damp and dark ones, and where they are mostly wrapped in towels, the dry kind, Turkish or Finnish, either way, the skin under my tee shirt dissolves, and it's not about me but about everyone else, you'll check them out, they'll check you out. Finally, we secure a spot. The steamy water bubbles up out of jets in the ceramic tiles around us, hot droplets spray us in the face, under the surface a foot which isn't yours keeps touching me, and I can't determine whether it's the big toe of the bald guy across from me or his big wife's. I don't take off my top, I'm wearing a close-fitting sports shirt that highlights my muscular build, the black mesh isn't see-through, others probably assume I have a skin disease or am making a fashion statement. If they think otherwise, I can always pull out my ID card. The water is hot to the point of being oppressive, but I'm feeling cold. "How do you like it," you ask me sweetly. I shrug and make a inde-terminate grimace that has a precisely determined meaning: not well, threatened, plus, horrified by the closeness of all these bare bodies, and also, the filthy water might inflame my der-matitis, and then I'll be scratching myself all night and won't sleep a wink. Still, I am determined to stay here and sit so it will be indisputably clear that I am doing all this for your sake and, at the same time, I'm watching you eye that taut male butt in the Speedo briefs. Our intimacy is what makes it possible for us to understand each other so well with a shrug of the shoulders, an intimacy that leads to exposure, exposure that will sooner or later lead to mortal wounds. "Look, you don't have to be here, go back to the room, I'll stay a little while longer." A clear and simple sentence that would seem to leave room for my freedom of movement, but since I'm close to you, I know how to hear what you're really saying to my shoulder shrug: Don't go playing the victim, no need to force yourself to sit here, I really don't get what this is about, we're here together, and why would anyone be a threat to you when you have me and I have you, I won't repeat the same stuff over and over, no point, you ought to just go to the room and we'll catch up in a bit, okay? Fine. You get up, the level in the water-filled hole rises then drops: "I'll try the sauna, see you upstairs." You won. Let's go in peace, relax our hands. A half hour later you come up to the room. Differently than what I was expecting. I was bracing myself for: I'm so done, I met Mr. Speedo Briefs down there and now I know what I really want. But you're giving off something entirely different, the hot air has softened you. You throw off the terry cloth robe, you're radiating warmth in every sense, you tease out all the cold currents when you press up against me. Layers peel away, we're plugged-in, your eyes are murky. "Let's not be apart any more," you say, even when we're sleeping, oh so close.

# 29.

You fumble to open the door to leave my apartment, it's two a.m., tears and snot are fusing into a big shiny glob swinging from your chin. With the edge of my hand I push the door shut and ask you to come deeper into the hallway while we argue. You have worked yourself into a convulsion, in your coat and boots. Your backpack slides off your shoulder while you shout: "Let me go! I don't want to be here any more!" and then the belt snaps from the tension and the bag hits the floor with a thud. A moment of surprise in a well-rehearsed drama. For a second our attention breaks, and then on we go as before. These aren't frequent. These abrupt nocturnal departures of yours. They always happen when we are at my place, an area of great insecurity, far from Mama, far from home. I start shouting, then you shout, but first we wrangle in the dark while we're still lying in bed. We start out lying there stiffly on our backs, holding hands, and then we assume more and more explicit and distanced postures, our fingers pull apart so we can gesticulate, still lying down, to explain our views better. The room fills with voices that clamor more and more nervously, I don't see myself, I see you. You see me. You leap up and switch on the light, we briefly ignore whatever the reason was for the quarrel and both of us howl to outshout the other about who was the first to start shouting. You throw up your hands first. I fire off the first volley. When I look in through the window at us on that rumpled bed it's almost funny. Full of purpose, you are already on your feet, while I haven't quite pulled myself together yet. I'm gesturing argumentatively while sitting on the bed, the sheet twisted around my leg, I can't wriggle free, I look clumsy and hapless, so I crank up the volume even more. When I get louder, in two moves you strip off the pajama top and bottom I bought you so you'd have something to wear when you were at my place, you fling them onto the bed and furiously pull on your clothes that were folded on the chair. We'd been out, so you pull on your narrow leather pants and see-through blouse, and stuff your bracelet and earrings into the pockets, no point fucking around with them now. "I'm so out of here, I can't take this any more! You're revoltingly selfish, all you see is yourself!" What? My surprise serves as a punctuation mark for each of your machine-gun outbursts. "And why are you shouting at me? You don't even know how to talk like a normal human being, I can't deal with you!" I won't give way, not yet. Maybe my voice is raised, but for the hundredth time, I try to explain that I am not railing at you, I'm shouting because I'm angry at everything, and then I can't stop, and besides—you are on their side. "What?!" you start to laugh. I hate it when you burst out laughing mid-fight, I hate it when you mock and ironize, I hate it when I can't talk with you. Our fights are not like disagreements between me and Filip. You have so many more words that come from so much more freedom and you don't know where to go with it. "I am on their side? I cannot believe you can say that after everything. So what about those friends of yours—the ones you're not screaming at? Whose side are they on?" You stop. That hurt, your voice dwindles and now you're only sniffling. I know full well what it is that you haven't forgiven yourself for, I know what you're ashamed of and what's hurting you, and though I myself got over it a long time ago, sometimes I stick you to a piece plywood with a thin pin. Pain hurts less when you share it. You increase the amount of pain in the world when you do, but individually, you lessen it—this is the ultimate goal of every relationship. I still won't let you leave, and you no longer feel like arguing. You know I'll unlock the door sooner or later, so you slowly take off your clothes, like an automaton you put them back on the chair, pick up the flung pajamas, go to the farthest corner of the bed, huddle against the wall, and sob. For you I no longer exist. You'll come back to me tomorrow. For the sake of this evening. And for the sake of before.

Two incidents fused into one. The first, the reason why you wanted to walk out that night, had come up a few hours earlier. There were five of us around a table at the theater café after a show. With us was a woman you work with, a man, now a journalist, who had studied with you, and a friend of the journalist's who was the head of a security company and likes the theater. They started going at it after two and a half beers. The sleazy security guy went on and on about the gay cabal within the German police force and about lesbians in the security business, these topics were surgically dissected in great detail. The journalist and his friend were quizzical, a little bemused, not malicious per se, just stupid down to the last cells of their bone marrow. Their stupidity allowed them to hold forth on everything, especially things they knew nothing about, even second-hand. You and the woman you work with rolled your laughing eyes, nothing alarmed you, you just found the men a little irksome, but my gorge began to rise, first through my gut, then up my spine. When it reached my throat I stopped talking. I watched the gorilla across the table and felt a laugh coming on when the phrase: "Thick as a brick" popped into my head and I found myself thinking: "Thick as a prick." "So, time to go?" I asked coldly, already rising to my feet, leaving you no room to maneuver at all and decide for yourself; thick as a prick, I pulled on my jacket, you looked up at me in surprise, and then, though disappointed, nevertheless on my side, you stood up, said your goodbyes, the security guy kissed your hand, you walked with me out of the café. Our Uber was waiting outside and in silence I honed my poison darts. First I sharpened them, then I licked them, and then glued onto them, layer by layer, all the sediment that had settled inside me since I first started feeling and thinking. I ran them ever so gently along your skin, slipping the shiny tip along the taut surface, calculating where to plunge them in. "You are on their side," looked like the most delicate spot, dangerous, yet not deadly. Enough to push you to the far side of the bed beyond my reach. But before you went down, you had your comeback. You brought up my friends. This was in reference to something that had come before.

Once, you broke up with me for a month and I knocked around the Zagreb dives from Savska Road to Remiza. Helena was celebrating her birthday. She listened to me like a female witch doctor while I swelled and shrank, she nodded persuasively while smoke emanated from her skin. She behaved like she understood, she behaved like a friend, and you know how important friends are to me. As important as foes. I have never been able to explain this to you, how the world is split into two camps. Perhaps there is a third camp for free people. I can't speak to that, perhaps there are also people they're indifferent to, but I must always be on alert. Friend or foe. The latter are much more numerous, so the friends, the ones who are able to embrace me without question, are the greatest. Even if they aren't the real thing, even if they are the real thing for just one night. That night when I could no longer live with myself without you, Helena grew to be big and important. I sat at her feet while, wrapped in a shawl and fogged by the smoke of weed, she swayed like a prophetess and listened to me for a long time. "Bitch," she said, "you're so terrific." I protested loudly inside, and more softly outside, split myself into continents of loyalty to you and my desire to grind you down to dust. Bangles rattled on her arms as she brought to her lips a cup, dripping with superficial solidarity, that dragged me that night, out of the mire of pain. I felt less alone in the strange apartment full of ravaged hangers-on, it felt good when we shared the complicated stories of our failed relationships. "Tell her to go fuck herself, honey," she said. The night was moving toward morning, and she was confident in meaninglessness. There was something alluring about the hands massaging my neck, in this six-hour friendship where we give far too much and only when dawn breaks are we scandalized by our sketchy decision. I thought she was on my side, I needed to trust the shallow intimacy soaked in alcohol, my desire to escape myself. You know what happened one of the next evenings, though I haven't ever told you all of it. I let her lead me, and we ended up in a dive in the outskirts. She trailed me along behind her, I believe she was most of all nourished by my trust, the pain I'd given to her, with no ironic distance, pure and gleaming like a diamond. My adrenaline-fueled incursion into her intimate world was what led us to hold hands while we went looking for the man she'd been fucking over the last months, her unhappy love, someone who attracted and repelled, to whom she'd entrusted all she had, he was the drug she'd become addicted to, for whom she was capable of leaving everything she had acquired in her life until then, me included. We found him drinking at a bar. His eyes flashed when he saw us at the door, he was tall, bloated, and disdainful. Instead of hands he had bear paws, and in his eye sockets were the milky marbles of a rat. He did not say hello, he just slowly shifted his gaze to a friend, a squat man who was rearing up next to him, reminding me of a billy goat. Inside there was an animal smell, redolent of no restraint, of impulse, of pre-evolutionary anger that had taken the lives of the thinner-skinned species. Without a greeting, he hugged her with his paw and whispered something in her ear, and then I could just tell that both of them would look over at me. I knew he knew, I knew she had kept nothing to herself. I'd been through this so many times before that I thought this time I could stay on my feet. I kept it up for a long time, I was cheerful, called him buddy, I sought simple analogies to explain my place in the animal kingdom. I wasn't on the floor yet, even when, two hours later, they asked to see my cunt. I told them, fine, who will be the first to go to the restroom with me. They exchanged wild glances. They always exchange wild glances. Even this didn't knock me down, though I felt I'd been lying for hours on the sticky tiles as they kicked me, my innards came apart at the seams, while they watched and dared each other to see who'd be the first to pull out his wrinkled cock and pee on me. Helena knocked me flat. Her silence, her helpless expression while with bloodshot eyes she apologized haplessly, trying to cast the whole thing as a joke that had gone just a little too far. A deception I'd bought into yet again, and her word, bitch, aimed at you. Dozens of messages that arrived the next day, dozens of apologies, my politeness that drove you mad, and an agreement to meet again. "They are on your side?" you asked, fully in the right, pushing me away with a fat wad of coldness till just before dawn. Then with our eyes closed we found each other. Then we were home again, for the last time.

# 30.

I couldn't break through to you until they moved you to this forest. The state bureaucracy that dictates our relationships, that regulates who has the right to inquire about your condition, that knows exactly who should be holding your motionless hand while you lie there, punctured by tubes, has determined unambiguously that this cannot be me. The only people allowed to see you are your mother and brother. Dijana was quickly exposed as an imposter sister, and I—whose very existence had stymied the debate among the political parties just when they were about to adopt the Convention on Preventing and Combating Violence against Women and Domestic Violence, when someone introduced the dreaded ideology of gender and then the whole mess spun out of control—I must not come near. In the café, two men at a table: "Hey, have you heard? I mean, what the fuck, they've made it law now that men can get pregnant." "Fuck them all, them and fuck Europe, they're out to rip us to pieces." So that's why I snuck, unnoticed, through the green corridors of the hospital but didn't dare come any closer for fear my presence would bring even greater harm upon you. Your life belonged to the category of the most vulnerable, of the good vulnerable, the immobile and mute, the ones the state has deemed worth protecting. Then early one morning, because I was trying at various times of day to break through to you along the corridors of the healthcare system, I heard from a young nurse that you'd been transferred. Shyly, the same way I'd melted into the corridor walls, she asked me whom I was looking for. She must have been new and still willing to help. "But she's not here anymore," she said, softly, spreading her hands. "What do you mean? Where is she?" At first this news clanged in my temples and I was terrified to pursue it further. "Marof." She whispered. With pity. This was slightly better than my first thought had been. The air drained from my lungs and like an empty sack I sank back onto the wall. Then I went out into the autumn day.

They're dressing you, at least they're dressing you. They're packing up your handful of belongings. They're moving you gingerly from the bed to a gurney. You are light, even lighter than before. After weeks of staring at a single point, now you're seeing images dance before your eyes. You're taken on an elevator and nobody, but you, notices it bouncing. People don't notice much. You used to tell me: "We are riding in an elevator. Do you realize how far down and up the shaft goes, do you understand, dearest, how our life is hanging here by nothing but the cables installed by people at some point, and if they didn't do their job properly, we might drop at any moment into the abyss? And the electric circuit on whose uninterrupted current our safe ascent or descent depends doesn't take much to shut down, and then we'd be left in the dark, stranded in such a close space, and a long, long time might pass before anyone discovered where we were. There we'd sit, airless, consumed by panic. See, love?" and then you'd shoot me a wry glance, though I know you were being dead serious and these are all comprehensible things that worry you, but you hide behind your arched eyebrows and the corner of your lip that twists ever so slightly, "Everything depends on everything else, we rely so much on one another and people are so sure that their life is all about their choice, but one loose screw and everything goes to hell." I'd hold you close in the elevator and say: "Don't be such a worry wart," wishing I could go from screw to screw with one of those tool belts slung around my hips. I'd tighten them all. I've always dreamed of being a construction worker. I confess this only to you. They wheel your gurney out and the sky blinds you. When I first went outside, having spent five days convalescing in the hospital after the operation, I almost fainted from the lucidity, the perspective of space and freshness, the clouds and smog, the variety. Once a year people should all be shut for five days in a room with no windows, and then brought out into the sunlight. They wouldn't keep wasting time on inanities. Never you, though. Your gurney with its little wheels is loaded onto a large-wheeled van and off you roll toward another hospital where there are many more people like you. To reach you I have to take trains, first one to Varaždin, and then a second from there to Marof, and then walk for a spell before I catch sight of a tall ornate gateway enclosing lush nature. When we began spending time together, you always used to say, as long as there is good jazz playing, I'd rather sit at a bar, my natural habitat, than under a tree. Ticks and thorns, then mud, wet feet, allergies, let nature take its course, the rhythm method, abstinence, really? Thanks but no thanks. I laughed because you clearly thought of nature differently than I did, and soon we came to see that under the shade of a tree was where we were safest, under a treetop that shelters all equally we could most be ourselves. In nature nothing is unnatural, otherwise it wouldn't be in nature. So the building's surroundings brightened my mood a little, though only a little, because I didn't dare think what lay ahead, indoors. At the entrance to the hospital grounds there was a sense that this place was going to be a little different. The staff here also wore white and blue lab coats, the rubber wheels on wheelchairs carved shallow ruts in the linoleum, here, too, convulsed skeletons with gaping jaws sat in the wheelchairs, drooling saliva, and here, too, I noticed the smell of disinfectant cleaning supplies mingling with the smell of shit, but nobody here seemed to be in a rush. It was as if time were drip-drip-dripping at the threshold to the waiting room of the next-to-last station, the one right before the end of the line. Everyone was walking slowly, like in a slow-motion movie, nobody was in a big rush to get where they were going. A dense, unbearable drabness dripped from the ceiling and poured down all the room's surfaces. Society's apparatus for dealing with those so close to death was more flexible here. At the portal to this quiet building they didn't ask for a certified document from me stating that we'd shared a bed or eaten at the same table. Here they favored a more holistic approach, an approach which had been lacking in society my whole life, so when one drew the winning card in the lottery and was given a month in Marof, the maximum time allotted for this last stop, the bureaucracy loosened up a little and people made an effort to lighten up. The crush of visitors wasn't so overwhelming here, because what could they say to someone who was melting away? What to say to a person when you could see their demise in their eyes? There were no signs of death in the corridors and at the reception desks, they were bathed with the fragrance of fresh paint and the optimism of expanding the wards with the same European funding that would compel men to give birth.

They actually direct me to you. It still doesn't feel real. All of it, this paralysis, the sweat coating my palms, that I am really looking for you here. I approach the half-open door to the ward cautiously, at the end of a long corridor leading to your room, number 17, there is a big window looking out over the garden. In the counter-light I can just discern a small figure that is growing. A figure I can't recognize in the shadow, whereas I am fully lit and transparent. This gives her a certain advantage. Before I realize who she is, sound is faster than any image, the sound of the fretful voice over the door buzzer and cell phone, the voice planted deep down in your pelvis that kept you from orgasming, barks at me: "What are you doing here?" She is even more gaunt, even more petite than before, much smaller than even small me, embittered and shrunken by the horror in which she finds herself, her life. "I've come for a visit," I say calmly, my voice hoarse. Before I can brace myself, her clenched fists fly at my face, poke me as if we're playing a children's game, I could stop her by merely raising my arm. But I stand there like that and let the body of your flesh and blood pummel me. "How dare you come here after everything! Leave us in peace once and for all!" Two nurses come out of an office on the side, they aren't sure whether to interrupt this family drama, I'm not sure whether I should turn around and go before you have to hear from the corridor that we still aren't leaving you in peace. When your mother, her eyes welling with tears, her voice crackling, says, "I know full well who you are!" I take a step back and fall away into a chasm. Her words keep ringing in my ears, only I don't know whether I was hearing her right when she said that she knows. Who I am or what I am? Because I am sometimes a what, and not only a who. We all know full well what you are! I turn and leave because I don't want this to happen now, not like this, because I assume what it is that she'll say. She'll say "woman." She'll spit it out as if it is a dirty word. Woman. I could never bear the word. I hated it that I was linked to it in a way that was never me. I wanted to erase the existence of that woman. But even if I'd succeded, as I realized much later, erasing myself would have erased everything that had gone before. For a long, long time, I could not accept that nature had given me the gift of being a person who has experienced what it means to be a woman in this world. And much too much of my experience in childhood and youth was feminine. Sometimes only because the world saw me as a woman, sometimes because of my brother who didn't experience the world that way, because of the family where Dora must help her grandmother sweep out the yard, where she mustn't muss her shorts when she plays soccer, who would horrify everyone by refusing to wear a bra. That is how nature treated me, how it kept me down and shaped me. And how I fled. And now I am still fleeing at times—from your mother, a woman, who addresses me with scorn, speaks to the part of me that is so like her, we could be so close, bonded by a profound and total understanding of a world that has kept both of us down since our first cry. Because today, when that same world looks at me and no longer sees what is implied by the notion of "woman," I know better. I know how the attitude of the world toward me has changed over a short time; the breasts, ovaries, or chin I had didn't make me what I am. It is enough to raise my hand, show up, clear my throat, warn, to be taken seriously, to be paid more, to not be mocked, not exploited, not taunted, not slapped, not downplayed. But I still can't stand before her. I'll step aside and let her pass, and then I will make my way to you, to all that's left.

# Part Three

# 31.

I could have lived my life without the two of them. I could have traveled. I could have seen the world. I could have gone to school. If only someone had showed me how. I wasn't stupid. I could have given birth, like Zdenka, at thirty, I'd have had plenty of time. I could have left him a hundred times, I could've, but I didn't because of the two of them. And I could have lived my life without them. Now everything's too late, and even if it weren't, I still don't know how, I can no longer remember myself, I don't know who I was before, before all of them, I don't know what I like, I don't know what I'm good at, I don't know what brings me joy, so I make do with what I have become.

I scrub the inside of the radiator with a long brush, I vacuum daily, I polish the ceiling lamp inside and out, after that I sit on the floor so as not to spoil the sofa cover and check to see if there's even a speck of dust left anywhere. Dust always finds a place to settle in, like along the decoration on the side of the lamp. I'm expecting them any minute. Let them think this is who I really am, that will be easier for them. They know nothing of what brought me to this state. I am nineteen. I give birth to a son. His skin smells of the forest and honey, but when I look at him, he looks more like an earthworm. He's all red and wrinkly, skinny and gangly, and I can't believe this came out of me and I'm not sure what to do with it. They let me see him briefly, I don't even know how to hold him, and afterward they take him to the nursery. They forget me. They leave me to lie in the hospital corridor, it is badly over-crowded, many women are having babies, they've finished and forgotten me. I lie there, legs splayed, covered only by a thin sheet, good Lord, I gave birth to a child, laughter comes over me, I gave birth, and maybe I'd laugh if I weren't feeling the ache down there, first a sharp and then a dull pain. I am embarrassed to call out for help. Nurses hurry down the cor-ridor, nobody notices me, the doctor is nowhere to be seen. If I call them, I'm afraid they'll yell at me . . . It feels as if hours have already passed, the blood on the sheet is crusting darker, my thighs are taut with dried blood. I muster the courage and call down the corridor: "Excuse me, excuse me!" I prop myself up on my elbows, and a fresh stream of blood gushes from my birth canal. The nurse turns at the last minute before dis-appearing around another corner, and it's as if she's suddenly remembered: "Oh, that's you, why didn't you give us a shout! Oh no, we haven't stitched you up and now you're cooling off!" She hurries over, calls her colleague and they roll me back into the operating theater. The doctor comes quickly, with a hand he lifts the sheet, has a look, frowns, and, as if to himself, says: "Why'd we wait so long?" Nobody explains a thing to me, not that they'd made an incision, cut into my birth canal so they'd have an easier time delivering the baby— they used to say it was to keep the woman from tearing—and nothing is said about how they've stitched me up hours later, after the wound has gone cold, and they've done it with no anesthetic. Cut and stitch. As if this were a piece of cloth. Nobody asks me. My eyes are bulging, my teeth clenched, I count each needle prick, there have already been six, when the doctor slaps me on the thigh and says: "Good as new, I even tightened her up a bit, her husband owes me a bottle of cognac!"

I'm lying in a room with six other women, I've forgotten all about the earthworm, I can see my husband across the street, waving. In one hand he's holding a bouquet of flowers, in the other, a cigarette. He strokes my face while we sit in his brother's car. He tenderly dips his other hand down between my legs, so tenderly it makes my head spin, and whispers in my ear, "You're mine, I want you more than anybody, just say yes. We'll stay for a little while at my folks' place, and then on we'll go wherever we choose, we can leave here, we can go to Germany." They didn't let him into the hospital, so outside he circles the ward, hoping to call to me through the window. I can see he was out carousing last night, I see he's happy and tired, he's a father, nobody cut him without anesthetic, they didn't yank out his placenta, he's twenty-two, he knows even less about life than I do. I already know something isn't right. Every cell of my being is warning me about this, the warning was always there, but now there's no going back. I stagger around like a drafting compass, after three days I still can't bear to sit on the toilet seat, when I push I think my gut will come tumbling out. The bleeding won't stop. He is feeling his newfound fatherhood; he shuts himself in with the newspaper, plants himself on the toilet seat for a full ten minutes, groans aloud, has a fine time, while I don't dare bend over. Nobody ever told me anything, except vague warnings, like, you'll see when you give birth.

We live with his parents. His mother wants me to call her

Mother. I can't bear to say it. Now I, too, am a mother. It doesn't feel real yet. I'd rather crawl back inside my own mother, but I push this thought away before the tears well in my eyes. So be it, how else can it be. After seven days I manage a bowel movement. I sob in the outhouse toilet, I'm sick from the thought of someone hearing me, even just the seat creaking, all of them make me feel ashamed, especially his father, the Old Man. He paces in the yard back and forth with his arms crossed behind his back, curses, now and then he whistles through the gap in his front teeth. He shoots me sideways looks. In the evening, the Old Woman brings a wash basin into the room we share, she kneels in front of the Old Man, his ankles are a sickly white and swollen, shot through with burst capillaries and pimples from ingrown hairs. The water in the wash basin gives off steam. The Old Man hisses that it's too hot, and then he says to me: "Hey, kid, come over here, damn it." I'm not sure what he wants, I set the baby down in the cradle. The Old Woman is banging around the kitchen with pots and my young husband has gone out. "What do you need?" I say softly, and he sneers: "Old granddad can't bend over anymore, lend me a hand, would you?" He wants me to wash his feet. I never even did that for my own father. I stand there, mid-stride in the dank dining room, mid-stride between kneeling at the Old Man's feet, scrubbing his calloused soles as thick as a horse's hooves, and the cradle where the little lump of life that came out of me is groaning, mid-stride between who I really was and the role I'd been steered toward my whole life. My soul dries up and I feel like vomiting as I come over to the cracked wash basin, I'm not sure why I'm here, I can't remember the caresses that brought me here, and then one minute before I dip my hands into the hot water where the old man's feet are soaking, my young husband opens the door. Cold air gusts into the room with his bewilderment. I look at his face and feel humiliated, and though my humiliation comes from his father, I always take the shame upon myself. "What are you doing?" he asks sternly, though a little sadly, as if this were all my idea. He is not without feelings, he's just weak, first he's a son, and only then a husband, father, or lover. They didn't raise him right, so he doesn't know whether to yank my hands out of the hot water I've just plunged them into, these red fingers of mine that only a year before held a cigarette to lips smeared with lipstick the color of raw meat, and the cover to the Stones album he'd given me—his way of promising that we'd see the world. "Come over here, I need you for something." He barely says the words. His feeble urgency carries at least modicum of weight. These are words spoken by a husband. I stand up obediently, choosing whom I'll serve. Granddad doesn't say anything, he's scowling because he has been left without the touch of nineteen-year-old hands on his wrinkled hooves. In a raspy voice he shouts, irritated: "Old Woman, come over here, damn it!" My young husband pulls me out into the narrow hallway and instead of an explanation for the place he's brought me to, instead of an apology and us packing our suitcases that very night, even if we have to go right out into the fucking night, we'll take the earthworm if we have to, he plants a moist kiss on my mouth. My young husband, stupid boy. He shuts me up and kisses me, touches my breasts from which droplets are starting to drip, black stains spreading on the brown blouse. Just then the earthworm cries and disappointment sears my belly. I take the child, he vanishes, and what remains is a night interrupted by the baby's cries, the old man's groans from behind the plywood partition and my nodding off into fitful sleep. Day still hasn't broken and I'm rinsing diapers in icy water from a frozen faucet and then boiling them on the stove in a big pot. Before that I rinsed the rag rug from the kitchen and left it on the line to drip. The Old Woman gets up after me, clatters around in the yard in her wooden clogs and farts loudly. I never heard my mother do that. She splashes her face at the faucet and then blows her nose with two fingers and flicks the snot into the garden. With the same fingers she checks the rag rug on the line and when she sees it hasn't drained enough yet, she pulls it down and heaves it at my wash basin with the sterilized diapers. They all tip over onto the concrete. "Have you no hands?" She walks around behind me while I clean the house, licks her fingers and nabs the dust balls. Little Miss Dirty No Hands.

Every day, no matter what, I take the ladder and climb up to the ceiling light, I wrap a soft microfiber cloth around my finger and with it I wipe away the stripe of dust, pain sears through my knee, my back, I'm almost fifty, little is left, Little Miss Dirty No Hands. And the two of them think I enjoy cleaning.

# 32.

"Sir, can you give me some?" I ask my father, whom I'd never addressed without the "Sir," while I stand there, head bowed. "Some what?" is his answer. "Pocket money?" I say softly, ashamed that I'm even asking. As if I didn't know better. I don't look at his greasy forehead across which he combs his thinning hair to the right, my gaze is fixed on his vast plaid stomach. "Whatever do you need money for, God help you?" He never answered anything in simple terms, never. Whatever I asked for, he'd taunt me about. "We thought we'd go out for sweets," I say, ashamed. Actually, we thought to take the bus to the swimming pool, there was live music there. Too far for us to get there on foot and home in time. I was allowed to be out from seven to ten. It was school vacation, there was daylight until 9:30 p.m., and I was fifteen. "There's jam in the pantry if you're after something sweet." He sprawls in a green plush armchair, when he's home he always sits there. In one freckled hand he holds a brown bottle of beer, in the other his transistor radio. Mother stands in the doorway to the bedroom, I see her from the hallway and without a sound, she gestures to me to come. I turn to Dad, I see he has closed his eyes, so I go with her into the freezing cold bedroom, and softly close the door. He thinks we're always up to something against him. *"Miert zavarja őt?"* he scolds me in Hungarian, why am I bothering him. I'm not bothering him, it's just that I know she's not the one who has the money, she doesn't earn anything, he's the one with a job, he pounds train tracks with steel rods to redirect trains. Without him there'd be nothing, he repeats this at least once a day, especially when she gets ready to go out to the store. Mother briefly held a job, she did the cleaning at a tavern, and then they told him that when she finished work she had a glass of cider. Then he broke her arm and after that she didn't work anymore. For a few minutes she stands there, shoes on, in the kitchen, she has already done up her kerchief, under it her hair, still black, protrudes. Her coat is buttoned up, and she beckons to him. He reaches into his back pocket, without looking at her, puts a coin into her hand, and, disappointed, she asks: "Do you have any idea how much kajmak cheese costs?" "No, I don't," he says, "my mother always made her own."

The bedroom is always dark, the blinds are more than halfway lowered during the day because the window looks out onto the street. A porcelain doll the size of a five-year-old child sits on the bed covered in a silken bedspread that falls in tassels on all sides. At night the doll sits on a special little chair that came from Budapest, a second-hand gift from people whose children she'd babysat for a long time ago. Mother took off the doll's clothing twice a year, washed and ironed it, there were even two changes of clothes for it, one light-blue lady's dress, and the other red and multicolored, something like a Hungarian folk costume. When Mother stripped them off, she'd wipe it down with a moist gauze pad like she used to wash me when I was little. "Let's scrub that little disgrace!" she'd shout cheerfully, pushing a hot gauze pad between my legs, only just plucked from water in a kettle standing on the stove. She scrubbed the doll before Christmas and in late spring. I'd see her unusually focused and happy while she cleaned the big baby, arranged the kerchief over the black plastic hair, she combed it carefully and coiled the ends of the hair around her fingers, tied a silken bow around the pony tail, smoothed the hem on the dress, slipped on the hard little shoes, holding it tenderly by its immobile joints, all this while the doll was sitting, she never laid it down so the ritual could be easier.

Mother opens the big three-door wardrobe with the smell of mothballs wafting from it, and on the inside of one of the doors with a ballpoint pen are written the birthdays of family members. The name "Arpad" is scribbled out, but the letters are still legible, I'd seen a little casket under a heap of gladiolas in black-and-white photographs. She leans over into the depths of the wardrobe and digs around for something. In the dappled light coming from the street, with her bony fingers, she holds a wooden box purchased at a village fair. She flips open the lid and from it takes out rustling paper money, presses the smallest bill into my hand: "*Vesz egy tortát.*" Why don't I go buy a slice of cake. It bothers me when she speaks Hungarian, my main association with the language is a claustrophobic kitchen crowded with old ladies, aunts, women who always smelled of lard and poultry, wearing brown aprons, missing half their teeth, chattering on endlessly and never listening to each other until the men show up. Then they fall silent and stare at the floor. "Where did you get the money?" I ask Mother. "*A fekete napokra.*" For the black days. I take the bill and stuff it into my back pocket. We run for the bus. That is who I am. The two of them don't know me at all. They think I'd never run for a bus to go to hear music, they think that before they came along there was nothing in my life, they think they first heard the sound of an electric guitar in the blue twilight, they think the early '70s could never have been someone's now. The next summer I work at a gas station, I find my own job, I spend every penny I earn on clothes. When he catches on, he threatens to pour gasoline over my big pile of clothes and baubles but he's too drunk to remember where to find the matches. He sleeps for a day and a half and when he wakes up he has forgotten all about it. For that day and a half, I don't sleep, I imagine myself wearing the short skirt (I hid it from Mother), in the brown platform shoes, in dark-blue velvet jeans, in an A-line skirt I had made up from a pattern. I'll take it all to Zdenka's so he doesn't set it on fire. "You had to go and spend it all, just you wait, you'll see, you're thinking you won't need it, you could have set some aside," she grumbles, kneading bread for hours while he snores on his armchair. She leaves it to rise and then kneads it again. Rises, kneads. Rises. That was the last time I was able to spend all I earned on myself.

I come back from the factory. My belly bounces under the light dress, the Old Woman is waiting for me at the gate. The yard beyond the gate is a construction site and a septic pit. We live in a little house while the big house is being built. The closer I come, the slower I walk, I think about how I'll buy a bedside lamp at the Nama department store for my nightstand and maybe a new blanket for our bed. All four of us sleep in one big room, but divided by a sheet of plywood, so I thought I'd spruce up our half a little. "Were you there today?" she asks. "Was I where?" I don't understand what she's after. "Were you paid your wages?" She has never worked, so she is thrilled that there is money coming her way. "I was," I say. "You'll give it to me for housekeeping." I don't catch on fast enough, and every month they take all my wages. You have enough to eat, to drink, no need to go spending outside the house, a house that is under construction. Whatever you need will be bought for you. I quarrel at a whisper with him. "God damn, I have to ask for money from your mother for sanitary napkins? Is that normal?" He shushes me, says this won't last, the Old Man just needs to pay off his debts, soon. He says, tell me what you need. I have to ask for everything from the others, but I'm hard at work all day long to meet the production quotas. In the morning I go out to wash up in the yard, she slinks around behind me like a shadow, she is always skulking around the house. I lean over to scoop up water when she growls behind my back: "What are you going on about, what could you use sanitary napkins for, look how big your belly is!" she hisses by my ear. Tears fill my eyes. "No, you'd like to go out and waste your money, time to start saving for the black days, they're right here around the corner."

# 33.

There were three of us. Zdenka, Višnja and me. I didn't have my own bike, but they had theirs. Even if I'd had a bike, my folks would never have let me go far. "Where are you forever wandering off to?" Mother would grumble. He would do nothing but lash me with his eyes, once I'd stopped being invisible. But the previous night he'd gotten drunk, vowing he'd leave the house, go back to the station, and throw himself under a train. His shirt was wet to the neck, he foamed at the mouth, we first held onto him to stop him from going out, she around his belly, me clinging to his leg. The three of us crammed into the door frame and he could barely stand on his feet without toppling over. Then she let him go. "Damn it, yer better off dead!" He swayed above me, then staggered back to the couch. To the station? Hardly. He couldn't get to the bathroom. When he began to snore, I undid his heavy black shoes. The next day he'd be sleeping at least till early evening, and then she'd make him sausages with sauerkraut for supper. He'd lap it up until he burst. So, in the morning, while Mother was digging in the garden, I took his bicycle, he'd never know.

I cycled along behind them. They were on their bikes all the time, so they spun the pedals fast and evaded the potholes. I did what I could to catch up, but I could barely reach the pedals, and the handlebars kept getting away from me. His bicycle was huge, made of iron, which is probably why I was having trouble maneuvering it.

We leave our street, cycling along even when the path disappears, we reach the river, I see children swimming. There's a hill a little farther on, and Zdenka, who gets there first, brakes at the foot of the slope and dismounts. I've never been here before, it's an excursion spot. My family doesn't take Sunday excursions, we cook soup all morning, an early dinner, we're silent on Sundays. The three of us sit in the shade of a willow on warm ground. Zdenka takes out an apple turnover wrapped in paper from her bag, Višnja produces a glass bottle filled with lemonade, I don't have a basket on my bike, I am empty-handed, only with the flimsy dress I'm wearing. I could live like this, with friends. With nobody telling us what to do, boxing us in the head or tweaking us by those thin hairs that grow over the ear. Zdenka's family has money, her mother works at our town hall and knows German, her father is the director of the factory, and they don't hit her. She goes to the seaside for vacation every summer. Višnja has only her mother, she has always only had her mother who works in shifts at the store or sews in the kitchen. She has really nice blouses and dresses. "Is that Lacika?" Višnja hoots in surprise, and we turn in to see what she's hooting about. When there, in knickerbockers, bare to the waist, his chest bat-like, stands Lacika. He's our math teacher, without his glasses, without the ruler he usually uses to rap our knuckles, his legs white and his gut sagging, he leans on his fat wife's shoulder. "Mrs. Dumpling!" cries Zdenka, pointing to the butterball in a white bathing suit with big black polka dots. We double over laughing and soon we're rolling around on the ground. The world turned upside down. Everything looks different, our streets have vanished, now it's our river and even math class is changed, and Lacika and his wife, nothing is serious any more, or scary, only pee-in-your-pants hilarious. Like gasoline poured on a fire, that's how hard we laugh, burning and fizzling, blazing to the point of smothering. Everything hurts, we're ravaged by laughter, as if someone twisted the cork off a bottle of soda. Later we prick our fingers with a safety pin from Višnja's bag. We smear the droplets of blood on one another's' finger until we've all been bloodied. Zdenka takes out her lipstick. First we sniff it, then we tap our lips, look at our blurred reflections in the metal of the bell on the bicycle. We push our bikes to the top of the hill so we can ride down. We've seen boys going down like that, and when they get to the bottom they slam their foot on the brake and stir up a cloud of dust all the way to their necks. Zdenka goes down first, she's the boldest, she is never afraid or ever ashamed. She goes speedily down to the foot of the hill, almost loses her balance, and then at the last minute drops her feet to the ground, stirs up the dust with her sandals and scrapes to a stop after a few meters. Višnja comes down right after her, she has two brakes, so she doesn't go as fast downhill, down she rolls elegantly, almost like the boys, and turns sharply. From the top, through the cloud of dust, I see her teeth when she laughs. I am left for last. I'll go down, even if I end up on my head. It's not about the ride. It's the three of us. Girlfriends. I push off with one foot, I can't reach with both and in a second I'm hurtling down. I lose control, I can't steer the bike properly, suddenly on my back I feel heat tearing at my skin, the heavy metal frame is crushing my ear, I don't let go of the handlebars so yet again, along with the metal monster, I flip over, tumble, and end up flat on the ground. I can't exhale. The two of them dash over, one pulls the bike away, the other reaches to help me up. I'm all battered, there's blood, and worst of all is when I realize that it's dripping down my neck onto the collar of my dress. They brush me off and comfort me. This isn't the worst that could happen. Only then do I see what is the worst, something isn't right with the bicycle, once we get it up it doesn't go straight when I push it, the handlebars are all crooked and no matter how hard we try to twist them back we can't straighten them by as much as a millimeter. I haul the front wheel by hoisting it up in the air and roll the bike along on the back wheel, because as soon as I set the front wheel down, the bicycle starts going crooked again, my arms are feeling a little limp so my friends push it along some, too. By the time we get to my house it's getting dark, from a distance I can see Mother standing out on the street, looking left, right, and when she sees me, she starts wagging her finger, now you're going to get it. If she was the only one who spanked my heart would leap for joy. Then she slips back behind the gate, I move slower and slower, and then I see him. He strides out onto the street, blows his nose and glares at me with red eyes. Something warm is dripping down my leg. I'm peeing. He never even opens his mouth. She stretches out her neck, turkey-like, behind him and holds him by the arm. With my last ounce of strength I lift the bicycle a centimeter up off the ground so he won't notice how crooked it is. I stare down while I walk past him, as soon as I pass I feel the dull blow of a shoe on my rear end. I let the bicycle drop and start to run. I can hear him unbuckling his belt.

While I lie there, an almost agreeable pain courses through

me. There is a compress on my forehead, gauze over my ear, and rakija-soaked sheets on my ribs and bottom. He almost killed me. Now I feel so nice. She sits on the edge of the couch, watching me, worried, shaking her head and every so often she sighs into her handkerchief. Then she plumps the pillow under my head, and stirs chamomile tea on the table, then lifts the compress from the ribs to cool it and puts it back, then taps the wound on the knee. Then she pats me on the face, along the side that isn't bruised. "What were you thinking, child?" I don't feel I need to answer, I'm just happy. "You know what he's like, what good did that do you? Did they talk you into stealing his bicycle?" "No, they didn't," I whisper, "They're my girlfriends." "Girlfriends? Them? Your girlfriends! No such thing. You have only one girlfriend, and that's me, and don't ever forget it."

# 34.

The back room was where they kept the cakes, there it was the coldest. *Salenjak* puff pastries filled with jam, walnut bars, chocolate *madaricas*, cookies shaped like peaches, butter cookies, vanilla slices, cream puffs, and *Dobos* torte. You stepped inside and were hit by the darkness of the vanilla, rum, cinnamon, and apricot jam and then, darker yet, of the plums. My mother baked them all herself. "No buying!" she protested "Mother, I want you to be free that day, like everyone else, not having to serve and carry out the cakes." She was almost offended, here she was marrying off her daughter and some other woman would be making the cakes? Who knows what all they'd use, old eggs, margarine instead of butter, rancid walnuts, licking the spoon and then putting it back into the filling, please. I can't. My way or not at all. She wasn't stubborn except in this, in the kitchen, hers, she knew what she was doing. Midnight had only just passed, and her cakes were grabbed up like wildfire. Satisfied, her gaze moved from mouth to mouth, fingers stuffing in piece after piece, guests peeking into the trays across the table. On her black formal blouse, around the stomach and sleeves, gleamed white stripes of confectionary sugar, she went back for more and brought them out and the Old Man and Old Woman gobbled down whatever was put in front of them.

I was accustomed to good food, my mother knew how to cook, whatever she prepared was delicious, even potato dough. But when I moved there, God help us. The Old Woman threw into the pot whatever she found in the cellar or garden, she gave no thought to recipes, she'd stir potatoes and tomatoes into soup, all of it unsalted, bland, enough to turn your stomach. At least she didn't cook rocks. "Hey, girl, go make those *puvani* cakes of yours," the Old Man would call from the couch because the only cakes Old Woman knew how to make were doughnuts and spinach pie, and those aren't really cakes. What he meant by "*puvani*" was custard cream. So, I took up cooking, I hadn't had to while I lived at home, but now, what with everything, the child on the way, cleaning the house, doing the laundry by hand, and now this. Fine, cooking here we come.

I go out into the yard in the morning, I already threw up once, as soon as I sat up in bed the spit came up into my mouth, he goes off to work, and the Old Woman is standing by a battered, steaming pot. "What's the water for?" I ask, it can't be for boiling linens, we don't use a pot like that for the laundry. "We're butchering," says the Old Woman. I think I must have heard wrong, my folk never raised anything but horses and that was years ago when we lived in a village, so I'd completely forgotten about the cages and chicken coop out back. Well, it's not that I'd forgotten, exactly, only that I assumed they had nothing to do with me. What adorable little bunnies, I thought. What did I, at nineteen, know. "You butcher, I'll pluck," says the Old Woman while she turns up the propane gas burner. "I've never butchered, I don't know how, I couldn't . . ." she interrupts my protests: "But you can eat? If you don't object to gnawing on a drumstick, you can butcher. You'll get the hang of it, everybody does. Bring it here." She nods toward the back of the house, and off I go, crestfallen, to the chicken coop. I don't know what sort of chicken to bring, big, little, medium-sized, I can barely tell the rooster from the rest. I lift the metal clasp on the door and in I step. They flap up around me, hop up into the air, spread their warmth and fear. I grab one by the wing, but the silken feathers slip from my grasp, the sharp beak leaves a bloody gash on my ankle. The chicken coop is small, but too big for me to catch a single one. From the adjacent cage, black marble bunny-eyes observe me from furballs, pressed up against the opposite wall, pretending they don't exist. They wriggle their moist little noses and catch the panicked clucking in their long silken ears. I thought, one day I'll work in a stationery store or a book shop, I'd arrange books on shelves, carefully cut carbon paper to size, tap my fingers with my mother-of-pearl polished nails on the keys of my cash register. With my lipsticked lips, I'll say: "Good morning, may I help you?" I will not pluck chicken wings. One of them squats all the way in the corner. I lurch forward and grab it by the neck. So, with it in my clutches I dash out as fast as I can while it flaps on the chest where my heart beats and over my bulging belly where another heart beats, hoping it doesn't get away from me before I reach the Old Woman. I carry it, squeezing it around the neck and she yells: "Don't you go strangling it now, you still have to drain its blood, damn it, incompetent fool!" She shoves a big knife into one of my hands, grabs the hand that has the chicken by the neck and slaps it down on the stump that serves as a cutting block. "Chop!" she shouts. I start sawing at its neck as if I'm slicing bread, but she mashes my hand down and the knife catches the cartilage and together we press, saw, grind while blood gushes on all sides. The tiny head is finally separated from the neck, the fattened body slips off the stump onto the concrete pavement. For a minute it hops up onto its feet and trots around the yard. I press my hand to my mouth; I feel acid mounting in my throat and the Old Woman laughs. "See, like a chicken with its head cut off! Just like they say!" Then she scowls as she looks out over the yard: "You made an awful mess, you can't even butcher a puny little chicken, looks like we slaughtered three hogs here. Hose it down while I get on with the plucking." I go over to the shed to fetch the hose, my dress is smeared with blood, I didn't want to butcher the chicken, I wanted to go out in the evening like we did that once. He took me to a restaurant, held my coat, pulled back the chair. The tablecloth and napkins were white, the plates gleamed, everybody looked at us, we were a proper couple. I dig around in the corners of the shed, when I find the hose. I straighten up by the door and by chance catch my reflection in the rusty little mirror hanging on a cord. I almost scream. My mouth is covered in gore, my chin too, and I have red splotches all over my face. My hair is tousled, my eyes swollen, an old woman at nineteen, good for nothing but plucking chickens. "God damn you!" I hear her yelling. I peek out of the shed and see all the chickens on the run. They're skittering around the yard, flapping their wings, all over the place, animals, frightened, alive, fled the cage, the knife, and we care about only one thing, eating them. I have my supper around six, so eating is over and done with for the evening. I take a little oatmeal and mash a banana into it.

# 35.

There's no way to imagine what that must have been like. He was the first born, long-awaited. I came along two years later. His temperature shot up. My aunt told me about it, Mother never. For two nights she wrapped him in alcohol-soaked sheets, and he burned with a fever and coughed, his skin flushed and his tongue white; with it he pushed away the sugar cube she'd wrapped in gauze. He hadn't yet taken his first step. She massaged his chest with lard cooked with marigold blossoms, always the lard, you couldn't wash it off for days afterward. Heavy snow fell that winter. There were stories of people digging tunnels between houses, it was so deep, they had no other way of getting from place to place. She pleaded with Father to fetch a doctor, if only he walked to the main road he'd be able to make his way a little more easily, others were doing it. There was no doctor nearby, the only way to get around was by sled or cart and then who knew whether Father would even find the doctor at the clinic. "If his fever doesn't drop tonight, I'll go tomorrow." Twice he said that. Poor man, he barely slept a wink, pacing up and down around the room, he didn't change into his pajamas, kept fiddling with the wooden rattle he'd made the baby boy. He'd already carved all manner of things as soon as the boy was born, a little flute and a fishing rod and a bird rattle, but the baby still didn't even know yet how to coo. Father wasn't always so contrary. The second night they dropped off to sleep before dawn on the settee, sitting, fully dressed, with the baby in the cradle next to them. When they woke the sun was high in the sky, the little one was very quiet, he'd stopped coughing, and Mother, finally a little rested, leaned over the cradle to see whether his fever had dropped. He was all cold, his little fingers were blue. She sat there, shattered, and wailed. She drew him to her as his smell was leaving him. When the doctor left that evening, the men brought in a casket and took the baby away, two men weren't needed, it fit under one arm. She didn't go to the grave, never spoke of him. When she felt the butterflies flutter for the second time in her belly that was me, it is just like butterflies, she carried the cradle out into the yard and burned it.

I don't remember rattles, or flutes, or fishing rods, only that I wished I had a big brother. But I remember seeing my own son in a cradle, and that the sight reminded me of the story about the pyre in the yard. I look at his ruddy face, all radiant, I'd just bathed and changed him. His big dark eyes shone on his little face. You can see people aging by their eyes, as if there's someone smothering the shine and dimming them. He'd stuffed his whole fist into his mouth, sucked it then pulled it out, that is how he amused himself, laughing with a full throat, and I wished I could tuck him back into my belly.

At my back stands my husband, we are proud, I don't know what we're proud of, just that we can't take our eyes off this most precious thing in the world. Imagine, it was given to us. My husband steps around me and leans over our son, tenderly slips his hands under the bunting wrapped around the baby, and I feel as if he is cupping my heart in his hands. Fearful and awkward, he pulls him close while the baby's head wobbles, but his shining eyes are calm and widen even more. "Come to Daddy, little boy," he whispers, excited, and then the Old Man thunders from the sofa. "You're handling that kid like a woman! What an old biddy!" he snorts scornfully, and our son's eyes begin to go dim, shrinking and clouding over at once as he is carried back to the cradle. As soon as he touches the mattress the little one starts to wail, to howl bitterly, to protest. "There, you see, you made him cry!" jeers the Old Man and turns the volume up on the television set. My husband leaves the room like a ghost, I hear the hallway door, I hear the front gate, I hear departure. I think, these men, how can they carry dead babies, yet not hold living ones. Afterward it's all the same, anyway. "Come on, shut up that whiner, I can hardly hear a thing!" snarls the Old Man. I pick up the bundle and go as far away as I can, the farthest being the other end of the room, all the way to the armchair. This armchair is the only thing we take with us when we move into our own apartment. It takes eight years, an entire lifetime and a whole coming of age for me to convince him that he'd be able to live without his mother and father, my husband-son.

So now there was a little girl lying in that armchair in the new apartment, a daughter. We'd only just moved in, boxes everywhere, furniture to be assembled, we still didn't have a crib for her, but I felt so eager to get out of there that I'd have been happy sleeping on the carpet, just so his parents' faces wouldn't be the first thing I saw every morning. Our first night we'd spent alone since we married, the first after eight years, you could call it our wedding night. Our son fell asleep on the sofa bed, he'd already grown long, and he spread out in the middle. She whimpered from the armchair. "Our princess of the armchair," he said softly and glanced around as if someone might box his ears. He ran his thumb over her silken, chubby hand and added: "She needs lots of cuddling now, she's a girl, she'll have plenty to suffer with later." I stared at him, amazed, and wasn't sure I'd heard right. "So, what about me?" the words erupted from me. "Haven't I suffered?" I took care not to bite him too hard, though sometimes I did want to rip out his Adam's apple with my teeth, and he started and looked over at me and these children, our children. If only he'd stop being so snot-nosed and blind. Like the time when the Old Woman cracked her grandson's scalp open, when she smashed our boy on the head with a wooden spoon, and all he did was curse at her under his breath. Or like the time when the Old Man boxed our son's ears so hard the little one couldn't hear for two days, all because he'd scampered over newly poured cement in the back yard, and my husband didn't say a word that time. He often bit his tongue as our child watched the Old Man shouting at the Old Woman, shaking his fist, sneering. And the time a few months earlier when I brought her home from the hospital and the Old Woman wouldn't even look at her, when she told me she herself would never stoop to birthing a girl. They were our children already then, and already suffering. A little boy and a little girl, like what we'd been long ago. A young man and a young woman, now a grown man and a grown woman, yet all four of us together worth less than Masculinity. What this all comes down to is nothing more than that slimy stretch of skin between the legs.

# 36.

I was only six, so I don't remember what happened, I know
only we were still living in the village, our last year there. My
aunt said she'd seen my mother sitting up in a tree, staring
down. Most of what I've ever learned has been from this aunt,
she kept all the stories about everyone in her head, and she
knew how to tell them so the people came alive. When she
was already elderly, sometimes she'd walk over to my place. She
walked slowly, she used a cane with a gilt handle like a man. I
never had much time what with work, the kids, the ironing,
but whenever she came by, I'd always open the door. I was glad
to see her, she was different from all the women I remembered
from the kitchen. She'd sit in the dining room, I'd make her
Turkish coffee with three sugar cubes, she'd untie the kerchief
knotted under her chin, smooth the braid over her shoulders,
and start talking.

She was walking early one morning by the Berava, driving
before her a small gaggle of geese to pasture, it was summer,
but as the hour was early, there was nobody else about; the kids
who pranced around in the shallows of the stream, spraying
each other, hadn't shown up yet, the day was quiet, everything
was just beginning to stir. Just before she heard a sound from
the treetops, a rustling sound, there in the wet grass near a big

oak she spied a pair of women's black shoes. Up she looked and partway up the tree she saw my mother, her arms tightly hugging the trunk, half-sitting, half-dangling. Her face was contorted in terror, her feet slipping, her eyes darting in dread around her, she didn't dare turn her head. "Hey, what are you doing up there?" cried my aunt, appalled. Mother said not a word, she just scraped a branch with her shoeless foot. "Stop, don't move, I'll come give you a hand!" and she hurried through her soft flock of geese to the tree, looking around for whatever she could pass to Mother to help her down. "Don't, I'll jump!" shouted Mother, her voice cracking from above. "What are you saying, it's too high! You'll hurt yourself!" said Auntie, leaning on the tree trunk and peering up, Mother had climbed up high, her white underwear showed and so did her garters, squeezing her twisting legs. Auntie spotted a large branch on the ground so she dragged it out from the leaves and straightened it so she could hand it to Mother and help her down. "Step back, I'll jump!" shouted Mother while she shivered up in the tree. "Don't jump!" pleaded Auntie. This went on for some time until Mother began inching down along the trunk, the stitches on her stockings tore, her skirt hitched upward, and Auntie reached up and grabbed for her feet, her thighs, leaned her head on her belly to support her, and finally let go so both of them, toppling over, ended up in the wet grass. "Are you crazy?" Auntie sat up while Mother flipped over onto her stomach and buried her head in her hands. "I'm not crazy, but I wanted to be rid of it, I can't bear this any more, I don't want to go through this again." Only then did Auntie understand, this was a tree other women had jumped from, if they didn't have bitters or juniper to drink, or if horseback riding hadn't helped, or a long sit in a tub of scalding water. Auntie didn't ask her anything. Though Mother was married to her brother, she took her to see Marta, a self-taught midwife serving the three nearby villages. She took Mother there while everyone was out in the fields, and stood by her when Marta opened her dowry chest. There were brides who were given a glass or metal catheter as part of their dowry, and there were women in the village who would organize and collect money and then buy one at a pharmacy in the city. Often it would travel, wrapped in a dish towel, from one woman to another, as needed. "This is nothing to be afraid of, don't you worry now, there isn't a woman here who hasn't been through this. It would be much more awful if you were to chain yet another ball to your foot, if you can't do it, you can't. We should have the right to say what we want, it has to be up to us, too." Women in the village didn't talk that way, like Marta, at least not aloud. And neither did I. Mother never knew. Only three years had passed since we'd married, and everything was only getting worse.

I went back to work and stood on the factory floor for eight hours at a stretch. My hands went numb from the heavy flat iron, we didn't dare sit except for the twenty minutes of our break. We didn't even have time to talk. I'd get up at four in the morning because my shift began at six, took the foul-smelling bus in the winter or rode my rickety bike in the summer. Eight hours at the stifling factory plus the time to get there and back, and then they were waiting for me at home. The three of them: grandmother, grandfather, little son. He was working or was already out somewhere. Then cook, clean, sweep the yard, iron the clothes, wash the dishes, and on and on, while the little boy clung to my skirts, tugging them down. Quiet and convulsed

221

in tears. He pressed his little face against mine or pounded me with his fists, in the morning he whimpered in bed, if he happened to wake up when I was on my way out, I could hear him all the way to the bus. As soon as I left the room, if he didn't see me, he'd start to wail, and then they yelled at me, the Old Woman and Old Man, all they did was yell. In the evening the three of us watched the news, and my son with his little hammer pounded at a nail sticking out of a board his grandfather had given it to him to play with. I worried he'd hurt himself. He could have given the child drawing paper and colors, I cautioned the boy to be careful, but because of his constant pounding with the hammer and the clatter he was making, his grandmother suddenly, without a word, grabbed the hammer from him. "Mothewfuckew!" shouted my three-year old son. "Bad boy, watch that mouth!" I said to him, seriously, but with a belly laugh the Old Man replied, "Ah, c'mon, why scold hm, I taught him, he's a boy, ain't he, needs to know how to talk back! He's no pussy boy!" So that is how I knew I could not do this, not again, not then. I would have gone crazy, nobody ever asked me anything as it was, anyway.

Once you get kids, you're blackmailed for the rest of your life. There is nothing you won't do for them. People who have no children don't know that it's not what it looks like, it all looks more appealing when it's only in your imagination. And in the end, when they grow up, you're left alone, even more alone than when you didn't have them to begin with. That day I stayed at home to lie in bed. When the Old Woman came, surprised, to ask me whether I was planning to get up or would I be staying like that, lazing around till noon, that was probably the first time I told her off: "Nope, I'm sick, no work for me today." Confused, she closed the door and went out. When I'd washed myself and had coffee, I went to the hospital and had it done. I wasn't sorry, because of that, ever. I was only sorry about my boy. And for her. I wanted her, by then we'd already agreed we'd move out.

# 37.

We streamed out of the factory like ants. My dress stuck to me, sweat dripped down my legs, they were all hurrying to the bus stop, elbowing to grab a spot by a window. There was no air-conditioning back then, we were packed in like sardines, and some people even smoking and held their cigarettes up high so the ashes floated above our heads. I, too, hurried to the stop, but someone across the road honked and honked and I thought maybe I'd heard my name. I looked a little closer through the swirl of dust, and there, leaning on a red Škoda, a foot in the car and a hand on the wheel, stood my husband. With his other hand he was waving, calling to me, and laughing. I broke through the mob of sweaty women and ran across the road. "Whose car?" I asked, amazed. "Ours," he declared proudly and slapped the red chassis. "Ours, the devil it's ours!" I saw he was up to his mischief, he did that some-times, still, after all that had happened, he still had the habit of surprising me. He'd once said he would have to work for New Year's but just as I was about to change into my nightgown and get the children ready for bed he appeared at the door with a plan all ready to go. "Pack up the little ones, they're going to sleep with the old folks, and you and I are off to a party at the hotel, Father Christmas has come for you!" From a plastic bag he took out a new white box, and from it—silver party shoes, my size, he bought them in Germany from a business partner. I didn't like surprises like this, I grumbled, I was not in high spirits, but he grabbed me by the hand, waltzed me through the living room while the little ones giggled and crowed. I wouldn't admit it, but later I was pleased.

"Come on, I'm serious, where did you get this rattletrap?" I shoot him a reproachful glare and his face falls. "What's wrong with it? It isn't brand new, but it is in working condition, we're off to the seashore!" He opens the door for me like in the movies, gestures gallantly and invites me to take a seat. He'd really bought a car. How, I don't know. From whom and with what money, I have no clue. This was a time when state companies were prospering; he started out as a salesman and advanced to sales rep. Though reticent, he knew how to be a gentleman, smooth, he had a way with people. "Buckle up, ma'am!" he winked and gunned the motor. "Aha, watch out we don't lift off!" I teased and ran my hand along the inside of the door, over the heated plastic, the gray upholstery. It was clean inside, though it rumbled something terrible, and looked a little like a credenza on wheels. Apparently, we really had a car. I turned the handle to lower the window, wind filled the sweltering box, we drove through town and a little more beyond, just the two of us. "Where would you like to go, ma'am?" "Are we going to the seashore for real?" I asked, shouting over the motor, with the noise that came in through the open windows. "For real, we're going for seven days, the kids aren't so small anymore, and the old folks will manage that long without us."

We traveled by night, she poured a whole juice box of juice all over the seat in back, and he finally fell asleep after throwing up twice into a bag. The cassette player in the car didn't work anymore, and then somewhere, I don't even know where we could have been, probably Bosnia, the Škoda overheated. It rolled to a stop, shuddered, and started to give off smoke. "Fuck the sea, and the car, and travel, and throwing up, we should've stayed home, why can't we swim at the local pool? Does everything in my life have to turn out backwards and upside down, can't we do anything right!" I fumed while he fiddled under the hood, he had no idea what he was doing, and for the hundredth time she called from the car, Mama, Mama, Mama. "Cover yourself with the blanket and go to sleep!" I snapped at her. I remembered my own mother when she stood by the gate last week after lunch, her hands crossed over her stomach, and every so often brushed away a tear when we told her we were going on a trip. I knew full well that Mother was crying out of fear. "Get into the car," he said to me grimly. "Not there, move over onto my seat!" he ordered. "How do I know what to do? I haven't got a license." "Sit there and do what I tell you, if you want us to get moving." I pushed the pedals, left, right, turned the key: "Don't hold it for so long!" he shouted from the dark, and then the car finally started. I didn't know how to drive, but suddenly I felt I'd like to get a move on. Press the gas, grab the wheel with both hands and move the car, take them wherever I felt like, to the seashore, the mountains, far from here, farthest from the shadow I was dragging along with me.

I dozed all day at the beach on the sand, and they splashed around in the shallows, romping, I was scared something might happen, though I couldn't figure out when anxiety had taken root so deeply in my bones. Or even whether it did. The children weren't going out far, my son stood waist-deep in the water, doing cartwheels and handstands, "Look, look!" he kept calling as if he were still a little boy, though he was already twelve. She didn't go any deeper than the shallows, spent all morning building sandcastles with the little pail and obeyed each time I told her to splash her head to cool off. The two of us were on a big towel, a new one, it still hadn't been washed, and he took me by the hand. He slipped his fingers through mine, our palms were coarser, the skin darker, but the feeling was like it used to be, before. We looked each other in the eyes, we're still here. That was the one moment. In the afternoon she developed a sudden fever so we didn't go out for a walk. I went to the post office instead to call my folks. "Hello?" Mother said when she picked up in a subdued, emotional voice. "What happened?" I asked right away, I knew it was something. "What else? Last night Joza from down the street brought him home, he's still lying there, so drunk he shat his pants, God willing he'll drop dead." The moment passed. I went back to the room, she was whimpering in the bed, the two of them were getting ready to go into town. I stayed behind with her, with the shadow.

# 38.

At night I'd lie under the quince bush, listening intently to sounds from their room and imagining how it might happen. Waves of pleasure rolled through me at the very thought. Someone rings the doorbell, Mother opens up, Joza or Marija, one of the two, is there looking serious, takes a step in and sighs. Then Mother covers her mouth with her hand and cries a little. He fell off his bicycle, a car hit him, the ambulance came and took him, but there was nothing more they could do. There'd be tears and whatever, at first, and then the two of us would be free and live happily ever after. That's not what happened. He'd been going downhill for years. First his knife-edge dulled, he shouted less, he flung his slippers less at the window, he stopped saying he was going down to the station to throw himself under a train, he lingered longer in bed, and after he retired he wouldn't even get up sometimes for a day or two at a time. When he was awake, he was darker and more bitter than ever. He'd retreat to the shed behind the house, close himself up in the little room with the one lightbulb that hung from the low ceiling and poke around among his tools, rearrange the wrenches, pliers, screwdrivers, little tins of Nivea hand cream where he kept his screws, arranged by size. He'd sharpen the saw and clean the plane, sometimes he wouldn't come out of there all day except to eat. Once when I stopped by, Mother sent me to fetch him to lunch; the door to the shed was ajar and when I pushed it open a little more, sunlight poured in and lit him with a broad band of light across his hands and bald head. He sat there, hunched on a three-legged stool and started as if he'd been dozing. Before he had the time to turn away, I saw he was holding something, an object he was trying to hide. He muttered, "I'm coming," bent over toward the curtain that was drawn under his work bench and stowed whatever it was away behind it. When he fell asleep a few days later, after he staggered home from the tavern before morning and threw up all over the bathroom, and Mother shouted: "Drop dead, why don't you!" and I'd made sure he wouldn't be getting up until afternoon, I went out to the shed. I slipped in quietly, drew open the metal latch and groped in the dark for the pull string. Yellow light spilled over the junk-filled shed, the discarded, useless things, the coarse cloth of the little curtain. When I drew it aside, I couldn't see anything under the table that looked special, nothing mysterious. I thought at least I'd find a bottle of rakija. Sometimes Mother would come and pour out whatever she could find. Instead, under a heap of sandpaper, I saw a pretty box made of wood, the size of a shoe box. It was smooth, planed and varnished. When I opened it and brought it out into the light in the middle of the shed under the lightbulb, in it I saw the wooden rattle, flute and bird rattle, polished, as if he'd made them only yesterday.

Water began building up in his lungs and went to his head. This is how our neighbor Marija's daughter, who was a nurse, explained his condition. He had less and less air in his head and that was why he'd forget where he was going, what day it

229

was, and sometimes, whom he was talking with. They'd keep him at the hospital for a week or two and then he'd be another week or two at home. He hadn't put shoes on for a long time, his swollen feet only fit into slippers, he looked as if he were all full of air. On his way to the bathroom, he had to hold on to something with each step, and then she, when she saw he was moving, would drop whatever else she was doing and run over to help him. I had already left. I mean I'd moved out, I never actually left. Every spare moment I'd rush off to Mother's to help her, see her, be there for my parents. While I lay at night in that house with the old folks and couldn't fall asleep, I often thought about how I'd left her, how she was alone with him, how she had nobody to lend a hand, and he was out cold. I wept into my pillow, I cried for every year she spent with him, I pitied her more than I did myself. "Pity your mother," was a sentence I grew up with, one that hung over the door of the kitchen full of women.

When it happened, it was a Sunday. I washed the dishes from lunch, went over to see them, I had at least a half-hour walk to their house. I saw her at the gate, purse in hand, her kerchief over her hair, in her small-heeled shoes. I began walking faster and she came toward me. "What happened, Mother? Where were you going?" She grimaced, but she was full of passion and concern: "They've taken him to the hospital, they told me to come. And I was waiting for you so we could take the bus, couldn't you have come a little sooner?" By the time we reached the hospital it was all over. The water had come on so strong he couldn't breathe any more, his color changed, and he was done for. The doctor was waiting at the front desk, he held Mother's hand in his and conveyed his sincere condolences while she sobbed uncontrollably. "I'll be so miserable without him!" she said, sobbing. "How could you leave me, we could have lived a little longer!"

I asked myself, as I stood to the side and grieved for her, when was it that they'd lived, and what sort of life had it been that I never saw it. After forty years of being locked-in, I said to myself, this must be what freedom looks like.

# 39.

He was one of the first. They didn't have to summon him. While the others all went over to the other side of the street whenever they saw the postman coming, he went straight down to the town hall to sign up. His parents egged him on, maybe that was a lot of why he did it. The Old Woman began coming by our place though she never had before. She'd drop in on Sundays after mass, take a seat at the table, her fingers linked. She'd search for any sign of dust on the shelves, and then she'd start in. "Son, there's none of us who have ever shirked our duties, except for that uncle of mine, but he did it because of Belgrade. It would be a disgrace for them to come after you and march you off to jail. This is your country." He just looked at her, fingered his cigarette lighter, and said nothing. "Cut it out, what are you saying, where should he be going? This will simmer down." I tried to shut her up, I tried to be reasonable and calm, I couldn't understand how a mother could encourage her son to take up arms.

During the other war, as she used to say, when they were living on raw eggs and rakija, when the children were raised on fried flour and water, she lost two of her elder brothers, they never came home. Before that she'd broken one brother's tooth when he scooped up too much corn mush; her turn came and she saw the dish was empty, she tried to wrest the spoon from him and as they struggled, she let go of it and he knocked half his tooth off when he whacked himself. A young girl—the middle child between her two older brothers and two younger sisters—she always used to say, "Once the boys left, I had to put the pants on, there was nobody else." Her father died young, shriveled right up, and her mother fed them as best she could. They sent one sister to Dalmatia when she was old enough to work as a maid, it's not easy getting rid of girl children, and the youngest, Katarina, stayed with her, their mother and grandfather. She smuggled tobacco across the border. This was a time when the state had introduced a monopoly, they didn't allow you to plant as much tobacco as you wanted, the Old Woman repeated bitterly, and all of it went to Belgrade, so they lived more from the smuggling than from sales. They'd hide part of their harvest and then sneak it over the border. This was dangerous, she had to evade both the financial inspectors and the gendarmes, she'd be sent to prison if they found out, because nobody had the one thousand dinars to pay the fine. Her uncle was jailed in Mostar for one hundred and thirty-four days because they found twenty kilos of broad-cut tobacco on him, and nine men from Čapljina drowned in the Neretva River while fleeing from the gendarmes. So she borrowed clothes from her brother, dressed up like a slip of a boy, took Katarina by the hand, and off they went on foot across the rocky terrain. Before she put on Katarina's clothes and cinched them with a leather belt, she stripped her down to the bare skin and lined her little body with the tobacco leaves. Five-year-old Katarina giggled and shrieked, and this sister-brother quieted her, explaining she had to stand still, that they were doing something really important, something to save them from starving. So it was that they set out one morning, without their mother, at the break of dawn. First they counted, then they sang, then they learned the birds and the trees, and then they walked a long, long way. Katarina slogged along slower and slower, holding her sister's hand in a sweaty grip, moving the whole time in the direction their grandfather had told them to go. The sun had risen high in the sky, exhaustion took hold, but nowhere ahead could they see the dirt road she remembered when she'd gone so many times with her mother and grandfather. When they finally arrived at the canyon, there along the rim where the trees began, she could see men in uniform. She was scared to keep going, to show herself to them, so she took cover behind a stone wall and drew her little sister to her. This was August and the heat was still fierce. She put the little girl under a stunted fig tree, gave her what little water there was left, but then she felt Katarina going cold. Amid all the heat, like a little icicle, she was going stiff, icy, her eyes glazing over. She coughed every so often until she threw up all over her sister's pants. Katarina just needed to catch her breath, she thought, she's small and this is rough going. Green tobacco sickness, that's what it was called. The leaves of the tobacco, damp from her sweat, released their poison into her tiny frame. She died in her sister's lap. Then the older sister had to step out from where they'd hidden to call the gendarmes to help her, she couldn't carry Katarina herself. When they brought them back to her mother the next day, one dressed in a boy's clothing and the other wrapped in a burlap sack, in a casket, with the threat that they'd give them prison time, a fine, that they'd take away her daughter, if they planted so much as one more tobacco plant, she swore she'd never have a girl child. "Let them go to war, it will be no worse for them than it is for us."

She wore pants until the day she married. When the Old Man proposed to her, she paced up and down the room and counted her steps: I will, I won't, I will, I won't; the room was small, five paces and "I will" came at the end. And so, she and the Old Man married and came here. With two little boys, one who went off to live in another country and the other who stayed behind to defend this one. One of the first, a volunteer.

# 40.

The war didn't touch the two of them much, luckily. The boy was too young for the army, barely more than a child, only on the verge of puberty, and the little girl was full of games and play. They watched it all on television, and sure, they went to the spa over summer vacation while their father was in treatment there, but being there wasn't so bad. Fresh air and swimming pools, and there were other kids. The countryside was so beautiful. I took care of everything, nobody knows how I managed. Mother called every day to say she wasn't feeling well, was having trouble walking, there was flashing before her eyes, nobody would know if she keeled over. That she was only glad he hadn't lived to see all this, what animals people had become, it would have killed him. Better that, I thought, than the bottle, but I didn't say so. What else could I have done than bring her to stay with me, she'd take the small room, nobody'd even know she was here, she'd come out to eat with us and the rest of the time she'd shut herself away and wouldn't trouble a soul, that's what she said. And that is how it was at first. He was away in combat, I kept waiting for the phone to ring, sat in the dining room on pins and needles and watched on television all the danger zones in the country marked in red. She propped herself up right next to me, leaning on the arm of the chair and she'd start to sigh, cluck her tongue, and wag her head, like I needed that. We didn't have to go down to the cellar to shelter as we were living in a basement apartment. Our life went on uninterrupted despite the air raid sirens. He came home every two weeks, brought his dirty uniforms, thrumming with adrenaline, yet, with each arrival, more withdrawn. He hadn't been long in combat when they walked into an ambush. He barely survived, and then the blood transfusion, God help us, what it did to them. When I saw him in the hospital, I thought he was done for and I had to be strong for them, bring them to say goodbye to Daddy. Imagine. And then he pulled through somehow, nobody could believe it, he came back to life, started rehab, and we all thought this was better, it would go well.

Mother was getting worse and worse, she was always arguing with me, she traipsed around behind me and carped, pitied herself. She stopped closing the door to her room. She'd crank up Radio Marija and listen all day to rosaries and those funeral dirges. I yelled to her from the kitchen: "Hey, turn down the radio a little, it's turning my brain to mush! The same thing over and over." No way, she wouldn't answer, let alone turn it down. I tossed the dishtowel into the sink and thought, now I'm going to tell her a thing or two. I brought her here, she doesn't have to lift a finger, she gets cooked meals and clean clothes, she can lie around all day long or go for a walk, whatever she likes, but all she does is snipe and carp. So this is my thanks, is it? I marched angrily into her room and before I could say a word, I saw something seemed wrong. She was sitting on the chair as usual, holding her rosary in one hand, the other hanging limply over the arm of the chair. Like the hanging arm, whole side of her face sagged, all oddly skewed, as if someone had drawn a straight line right down the middle of her face and body and on one side her face was still normal, while on the other it had melted. "Mother, Mother! What's wrong?!" I shouted and shook her by the shoulder, but she just mumbled. This was her first stroke, later she had three more. With each one she sank deeper into bed. She walked by holding my hand. She withdrew into herself, but she did not give up. She was always asking for me, she wanted me by her side. When I went into town or had to leave her for a few hours, first I'd take her to the toilet, then I'd put a clean diaper on her, just in case, so she wouldn't have to stand up if she felt the need to go. When I came back, I'd find her either on the floor in the bathroom or on the edge of the bed, sobbing and showing bruises from where she'd fallen. She wouldn't do what I told her, she refused to pee in the diaper, and every time I went away, she'd get up and fall, just so I wouldn't be able to go anywhere, day or night. I thought I'd lose my mind, him at the spa, her barely able to walk. I'd go to see him and bring him lotions, elastic bandages, painkillers, and I'd come home with a packet of diapers, teas for digestive health, stomach tablets, like a nurse, except no wages. At the spa, he was sullen, taciturn, and did nothing but sudoku, the only thing that interested him, he wouldn't say a word to me. We sat in the café at the spa, smoking and saying nothing. At home she pouted, again I'd left her, again she could break her neck and breathe her last on the bathroom tiles. And then there were the two of them I was toting along through life. They were always squabbling about something, he'd tease her, like he was six and not sixteen, and that would set her whining, they couldn't seem to grow up enough to cut it out. His schoolwork suffered and they found a knife and brass knuckles in his school bag.

I wanted to pick up and get out of there. Once I went to a café in the neighborhood, just like that, I'd gone crazy in the apartment, I picked up my purse and walked out of the building. I had no idea where I was going. Then I noticed the bar, went inside and sat in a booth, ordered a shot of pelinkovac bitters. I'm not going back, fuck them all. I've had it, I sat there for a long time, downed two shots, until the waitress came over and asked if I was doing okay. She threw me off. "I've seen you around the neighborhood, you live here, don't you?" she added. I had never seen her. She was younger than me, tall, slender, short blond hair, in a plaid shirt and faded jeans, looking like a pretty boy. She reminded me of my Zdenka from my past life. "Yes, I live here, in the building." I was ashamed to be sitting there, drinking, but I couldn't lie, what if I ran into her again. A few days later, I started going back, I didn't order the bitters, just a macchiato. If she wasn't busy, she'd sit with me and we'd smoke together and sometimes we'd talk a little. I didn't burden her with my troubles, that didn't occur to me, nor did she burden me, but sometimes, in passing, you let something slip about yourself. Once I asked her where she lived, was she from around here. First she said nothing, and then she said she had rented a studio apartment after her parents threw her out, she was living with her girlfriend, then she looked down at the floor. Only later did it hit me. My mother would have said fairies, that's what they called them in the village, fine, that was for men, there didn't seem to be a word for the women, but they made fun of them. So, I stopped coming, I don't know why, and I was ashamed of myself for it.

# 41.

He'd left long before they found him there at the playground under the basketball hoop. I understand. He took his time leaving, from the moment he opened his eyes for the first time to that night, when he pulled the thick rope out of a cardboard box in the garage, coiled it around his hand and elbow, noiselessly lowered the metal garage door, not quite all the way, and set off for the playground. He wasn't himself anymore, just a painful little knot, all that was left of him, he had been dissipating, on his way toward the metal hoop with its tattered net ever since the earliest days of his childhood. He took his first steps toward that night many years before, when he walked into the stuffy kitchen where they all lived, thinking how strangely quiet it was and that something odd and electric was in the air. Before coming in he'd been sitting with his older brother on the old walnut tree at the back of their yard, smoking for the first time. He was nine years old and felt he'd finally done something like a man, something right, and he was determined to walk into the house with the smell of tobacco on his face and fingers so his mother would slap him lightly across the mouth, and then he'd announce, gaily, that he could no longer live without cigarettes, he was hooked, and like all the men in the household, now he was a smoker. There was a little pantry off the kitchen, and he thought he heard noise in there. When he cracked open the door, he saw a bizarre sight that stopped him in his tracks, at first, with its lack of logic. His mother's legs in brown, plaid slippers hanging some ten centimeters off the floor, twitching slightly and his father's big hand, his red-white fist that was squeezing her around the neck and pressing her up against the wall. His mother was gasping, his father growling, his mother's eyes huge, and his father's pressed in a thin line of mindless rage. This lasted a second and then, like a panther, he threw himself on his father's back, howling and tearing at his vest. The Old Man sloughed him off with a single movement and tossed him forcefully in among the sacks of onions and potatoes. When he launched himself at his father, his mother slumped to the floor and the Old Man turned to go. When, a few days after this, the Old Man went to the hospital for stitches because something sharp had lodged under his ribs and he'd almost bled to death, the boy told no one that while hiding his pack of Kents under the mattress on his mother's side of the bed he happened to see a small pen knife that he recognized as the jangling bulge in her apron. Supposedly his father had been injured at his con- struction site on a sharp blade-like wire protruding from a slab of poured concrete, this happens, everybody knew that. The only thing that was a little odd was that he came lurching into the hospital before dawn, at the darkest part of the night. His second step toward the playground happened when he saw my hands plunging into the wash basin. I know that. Not because of the scene, not because of the sickening sight that likely pro- voked disgust, maybe even disgust for me, no, he took the step because he did not fling the filthy water at the Old Man's face, because he did not grab me by the hand and pull me up from where I was kneeling, because he didn't pack us up and curse his parents, because he didn't take us away to another, lighter darkness. Instead he waded even deeper into defeat. He sank in a little deeper yet that early morning when he returned from the night shift. I was sitting on the edge of our bed and his little son had spread himself across the whole mattress, his head bandaged, breathing loudly in deep, painful sleep, the way children sleep after a fierce, humiliating thrashing. At first he thought the boy had fallen off his bike, that he'd tumbled off the scaffolding he was always climbing around on, he circled around me, alarmed, and with his eye on the child slumbering under the covers he whispered, what happened, what happened? Your mother. That's all I said, and he sank, taking more steps on his path toward the playground. I was calm, unfeeling, decisive in offering him a choice for the last time: us or them. After a lot of silence and another few years he seemed to have chosen us, but by then we were already much less ourselves. He came even closer to the playground and the basketball hoop when she was born, when he began, for the first time in his life, to sense what it is to be a little girl. When he thought, though only with a corner of his mind, how there would be someone coming after her, someone who teased her, someone who grabbed her by the tits and ass like they always do, someone who shamed her, someone who shat all over her, someone who locked her up forever, someone who lifted her ten centimeters up off the ground, by the neck. Maybe he realized then that I, too, had been a little girl.

He came very close to the square on the plywood that held the basketball hoop at the moment when his father and mother said they would always be ashamed of him if he didn't volunteer to fight in the war. He never actually chose us. He took the gun and came yet another step closer to the shadow of the metal hoop. Here he stood for a time, and he saw the mutilated bodies, the torched houses, the madness, he saw himself with his own hands pressing someone's bluish intestines back into the warm hole of their gut, it was unreal, he wanted to go back, he wanted to choose us, but the choice was no longer there for him.

When he came out of the coma, out of the nether worlds, when he came home from the spa, one night I lay down next to him in bed. With a mixture of sorrow and excitement, I groped for him under the duvet, and when I mounted him with all my love, while my mother was lying in the next room with only half her body, while our children were growing up to become unfamiliar, alien people, I desired to save only us, but he had already gone numb. He didn't budge. He couldn't anymore, too much darkness had moved into every corner of his soul and body. Then he threw the rope over the hoop. Placed the noose around his neck, where his skin still pulsed but his heart no longer beat. He tightened the knot and bent his knees.

# 42.

Finding a pathologist took a long time. I traversed the labyrinth of hospital corridors that were down in the basement. I
thought, this really does make sense that they're located below,
underground, the passage will be easier. I thought, she's really
gone now. I thought, could she still be herself when half of
her body had given out? Or when she dropped to a mere thir-
ty-eight kilos? While the flickering neon light softly hummed
underground and cast light on those metal coffins where
human bodies were stiffening, I thought, now I no longer need
to feel guilt and disquiet at her puzzled gaze. I had to find the
pathologist. I had to get the document listing her data so I
could request her death certificate. "Ma'am," they told me at
the counter upstairs, "here are your instructions, everything is
set out clearly here for what you'll need to do." I held the long
slip of instructions the administrator had snipped crookedly
from the grayish print of a photocopy: "The report may be
submitted in writing or in person to the regional registrar for
the site where the death occurred or where the deceased was
found, within eight days from the day of death, accompanied
by a certificate of death issued by a pathologist or healthcare
institution. When an official, a coroner, certifies the death, the
documents required by the registrar's office are provided imme-

diately in certain cases, while in other cases they may be sent through official channels." That is how it went with him, too, they sent everything through official channels, the coroner, the police, the registrar, they steered him through the system without me feeling a thing. At the end of that path, all that was waiting for me was a box with his clothing and billfold. He'd left his cell phone at home. That is nearly always what happens. When someone who is close to you is on their way out the door and leaves their cell phone behind, you can rightly assume they will not be coming back, they've left for good.

"The registrar who receives the report of the fact of death," this is exactly what it said, "fills out the death certificate with special information about the deceased, the property, the heirs and submits it to the competent court for the purposes of probate proceedings or may deliver it to the individual at whose request they filled it out." Mother died. The fact of her death was that after her third stroke she had grown so weak that she could no longer get up out of bed. I couldn't even tell whether or not she was in pain. Her eyes were a cloudy yellow and she stared straight ahead, sometimes she moaned. Mother, does it hurt? She wouldn't even look at me. Every day I came, with lotion I'd rub her dry skin that had thinned to wax paper, through it you could see the wasteland of her burst veins. It seemed, if her skin were punctured with a needle, that there would be no blood but instead a dry, colorless, thirsty sand. Before she was hospitalized, between her second and third stroke, she was bedridden at home. I carried her to the bathtub and bathed her twice a week, Wednesdays and Sundays. I'd prop her up under the arms, my hands would sink into her loose skin, and only on her third or fourth try could she lift her spindly, scaly foot high enough up to step over the edge of the tub and plant it inside. First one foot, and then after clenching her jaw a little more, the other. Then I'd lay a thick towel across the bottom of the tub so she could sit on it while I washed her, there was no longer any flesh on her buttocks, just a layer of skin and underneath poked spiky bones. Sitting was painful for her, lying was painful for her, she couldn't walk. I'd adjust the warm water, then run it over my hand, then channel it to her wrinkled back covered in skin tags, then forward, under her neck, to her breasts sagging down to her waist, to the rest of her body without a single hair. She'd close her wrinkled eyelids with no lashes and let the thin streams of water enter her toothless mouth. What everything comes down to. All desires, hopes, fears, passions. I touched her all over her bare body, but never did she thank me. She had touched me all over my bare body, but I never thanked her. That wasn't the way we spoke to each other. When I rubbed her down with a soft towel and applied body milk to her skin, I'd sit her down on the chair to dry her hair and she'd look as if she were angry, insulted, humiliated. And then, pouting, she'd insult and humiliate me, disparage all the sacrifices I'd made, all the adapting I had done to meet her needs, all my focus on her. When all these rituals of unbearable closeness were happening, my son had already moved out. He was living with a girlfriend and rarely came by. When he did show up, he'd scarcely do more than glance into her room, say hi with no more than a nod, and tell me that the apartment was starting to smell of her. I should be doing something about it. He didn't want to hear about all I was doing. He wouldn't even take off his shoes. My daughter was still staying with us, but she was more like a shadow, floating between our silences, trying to say something, but what did she know, what did she know about anything, about my mother, about me, about my life? I'm sure she grieved inside for her selfish father more than she did for me, so I left her alone. I had Mother to look after, I had no time, for weeks, months, years. But not anymore.

"What do you need, ma'am?" a figure in green scrubs at the end of the corridor shouts to me: "Who sent you here, what are you looking for?" "I'm looking for my mother!" I yell back through the stale air.

# 43.

We rocked him between us at night. He'd start to cry and groan a little before midnight, my heart would clench for his sake and at the thought of the alarm clock that would be going off in four hours—this usually came over him when I was on the early morning shift. We'd press him firmly between our bodies and he'd wail, my stomach hurts, my stomach hurts. Sweat would begin soaking through the soft hairs on his temples, the sweet-smelling sweat of a child who hadn't yet reached puberty, he'd toss and turn first in my direction, then in his, nervously kicking off the covers. I rubbed his cheeks, his head, and he'd press my palm to his face, his lips, I thought, any minute now he'll bite me. Sometimes he'd wail for an hour, like an animal caught in a trap, mournfully, painfully, curling up around the knot in his stomach where he was carrying something, we never did find out what. Months of testing gave us no concrete results, your son is nervous, nervous stomach, in those days they didn't talk about other things, he was healthy, well fed, no bruises, a good pupil in school, a child with a mother and a father. And grandparents. Forever wailing. And with so much bitterness and violence. They called me once to school, he was in the first grade. He was sitting on a chair at the principal's office and his legs were swinging back and forth above the floor, that's how small he still was. He swung them without stopping as if he were kicking at and chasing away everything around him. When I came into the office, he didn't even look over at me, even then he was alone with himself. I was appalled that they were calling me to the principal's office, me, because of my son. I sat meekly across from the principal, his fat double chin trembled, pinched by his greasy tie, he looked like a turkey, exactly like that, like an old turkey, and first he pushed a piece of paper toward me over his desk stating the amount the school expected us to pay by the end of the week. "For what?" I asked. "The boy will tell you, this son of yours, this jackass, pardon my language." I was shocked by what he'd said but I gave no sign, I was bothered by him calling my boy that, but I didn't say anything. Those were different times, it's hard to understand now. Children could have their ears boxed by any grown-up, in fact doing so was a duty of sorts. That is how children were raised, how boundaries were set, and how boundaries were breached. The jackass sat there and said nothing. "Come now, you were so brave this morning, show off to your mother about what you did, you little hero." He went right on stubbornly pressing his lips together and clenched his round little jaw and tiny fists. The fat principal pulled his huge belly out from under the desk, as if taking it out of a drawer, stood up on his short legs and, like a grizzly badger, waddled over to the chair where Tomislav was sitting. With his meaty fingers he grasped the boy by the hair and the skin next to the ear, yanked and repeated, show off to your mother, son, but Tomislav said nothing, shutting down all access. I stared at the floor, there was no other way. Nobody dared. Now I'd have spat in that turkey's face and I'd never have agreed to pay for the glass door Tomislav had kicked that morning, shattering it into a thousand pieces, glass scattering across the school corridor. He was late, they wouldn't let him in, he hadn't slept well, the Old Man and Old Woman had spent the whole night caterwauling, he was late, his stomach hurt, I wasn't home that morning, he hadn't left on time, he was late, he kicked the glass with his foot, all he wanted was to get to his classroom. He continued on this path. When his father went off, so reluctantly, into the army, Tomislav became his father's opposite. He procured brass knuckles and a knife, a blue scarf with a bulldog around the neck, all the back issues of the *Croatian Soldier* magazine, and even a beret. But not from his father, from his father, no, his father never spoke about how he spent his days, doing what, he only sank more and more deeply into silence. Tomislav didn't even call him Daddy, he called him, "Hey! Hey, I'm going out, can I have your camouflage jacket?" Hey would answer. "Leave it there, stay away from those things." Tomislav would slam the door and leave without a goodbye. "Hey, were you really near the front line?" "Go help your mother bring the things in from the car." "Hey, did those guns arrive for you?" "Leave me alone." Then he joined forces with his grandparents, they egged each other on, counted and listed the dead, who was doing what to whom in which war, who should be avenged, whose church should be burned because of other burned churches, who should pay for the tobacco that was stolen, the land that was seized, the horses that were robbed years ago.

When all this ended, when we buried him, when he finally went where he'd been wanting to go, when I wanted—at a funeral I don't even remember—to lean on my tall son's arm, to have him hold me a little, to trade places with him just for a moment, above the dirt with its powerful, acrid smell, I remember that best, the smell of the earth that was waiting to digest him, without even looking at me, Tomislav hissed: "This is all your fault." And then, just like my father, and mother, and husband, he left me.

# 44.

I had no malicious intent. Good heavens, why would I want to stand in her way? All I cared about was her happiness.

"Leave me alone, leave me alone!" she screams, all red in the face, and I can see she isn't well. I don't want to lock her in, how can I, all I want is for her to tell me what is going on, what is happening. I'm her mother, for God's sake.

She was as red as an apple. "You're my pumpkin," I said, "My bumpkin," she'd say and giggle when I held her in my arms, while her blond, papery curls fluttered through the air.

Her hands are red and she's digging her nails into my wrists, my fists are clenched, the key is jabbing me in the hand.

I sat on the edge of her bed, she whimpered softly, her lips were pale, I stroked her hot brow, I waved the moist patches of gauze soaked in alcohol in the air to cool them, wrapped them around her neck, rubbed her palms, the soles of her feet, there behind her knees. "My little darling," I whispered to see whether she was sleeping and when I stood to go, all I heard was the soft, pleading, "Stay." I came back, sat down against next to her, picked up the plush toy at the head of her bed, had the brown reindeer prance around across her stomach and up to her head and pretended it was talking to her in a funny, growly voice, through the nose: "Sleeeeeeep . . ." She giggled and whispered, "I really love being sick." "Don't be silly, who loves being sick, how could you love that?" I asked. "It's the only time you play with me," she said.

"It's just that I'm concerned about you, Lucija!" Okay, true, I am yelling at her, but it's not that it hurts me that she's gouging my hands and trying to yank the key free, what hurts my heart is that she's gone. I see it when she walks with her head bowed, fish-like in her silence, this is not my little girl. And she doesn't say a word to me. I look out the window and see her before she comes upstairs, she drags her feet and right then, when she opens the door, I want to tell her, I miss you. But she is holding up a shield, she is pinioned by an iceberg, she has hardened bit by bit over time, and ever since she brought that young man into her life, she doesn't need me anymore. How can I bear this? So, when she listlessly opens the door, when I see her tightly pressed lips and constrained step toward the table where lunch is waiting for her, instead of "Darling girl," I find myself saying, "If I didn't have you over for lunch, you wouldn't even know I'm still alive." I already see she's rolling her eyes, I already see she's one foot out the door, I already see she can hardly wait to get away, so then I clutch at her in a panic. I use all the resources I can. "You don't care at all, if I were to die tomorrow, you'd be glad!" First and foremost I make use of her childhood love and guilt, the way I carried her in my arms, that she was born from my body, this indissoluble bond that gives rise to the eternal desire for affirmation, praise, I return to her first unconscious construction of herself, when she said, at the age of four, "Mama, look at me."

I take all this, I feel I have the right, along with the key, just to hold her close, now, forever, when everyone else has gone, after they've taken everything they needed and abandoned me like a dog. She was the only one who knew how to give back. That is why I didn't allow her to leave, why I locked her in, because I was left with nothing. I didn't know, I didn't understand it then, that only when I let her go would I get her back forever. I didn't want anything more than for her to stay. And when I felt she pulled back her hand, stung, after she'd broken my skin with her nails, I realized she would always stay here, but never again would I have her. Now all I have is what is left of her.

## in place of acknowledgments, an apology:

This novel was written as an apology to all those who are forced to live, invisible, in this society and this world, convinced since childhood that they do not deserve love, dignity, and, above all, freedom. This novel was written out of a desire for all of us to stop, while we still can, being hostages of our own kinds of locked-in syndrome. At the same time, this novel is the deepest possible apology to all those who were forced to live in Croatia during the adoption of the Istanbul Convention, and especially to those who have systematically suffered violence. This novel was written out of love.